Storm Wrack & Spindrift

Book 3 of *Remnants*

MARGARET PINARD

Taste Life Twice Publishing

Praise for Previous Works:

"*The Grasping Root* brings to life the family I secretly dream is my early North American-Scottish ancestry. Muirne, Neil, Sheena and Alisdair each do battle with their hopes and fears, big and small, guided if not protected by the quiet strength of their Mam. They weave a drama of exiled pioneers navigating the narrow ridge that would lead them to security, resolution and perhaps even happiness…" -K. McClain, Amazon [*The Grasping Root*]

"*The Keening* is a compelling story of a working class family's struggle to stay together and thrive through tumultuous times and increasingly challenging circumstances…Ms Pinard's knowledge of the subject matter and brisk movement through the story make it a fast paced read, but engrossing."-ct1156, Amazon [*The Keening*]

"Pinard has reached her stride! This book sings with the winds of Scotland to the chill of Nova Scotia. My husband and I, both retired English teachers, thoroughly enjoyed it and look forward to the second in this emerging series." GVWM, Amazon [*The Keening*]

"Dramatic, engrossing, and a must-read…Her vivid depictions of life and landscape on the Isle of Mull and in urbanizing and industrializing Scotland allow you to be swept away by her story." -Tonya Rawe, Amazon [*The Keening*]

"If you like Wilkie Collins' *Armadale* and *The Woman in White*, you would love this one." -Larry H., Amazon [*Memory's Hostage*]

Other Titles by Margaret Pinard

The Grasping Root (Book 2 of Remnants)

The Keening (Book 1 of Remnants)

Dulci's Legacy

Memory's Hostage

Storm Wrack
&
Spindrift

MARGARET PINARD

April 1833, The Ridge

Sheena stood in the early twilight with one hand on the rough seasoned wood of the cabin, sighing a soft breath before rejoining the lively gathering inside. The cabin, *Sealladh Cùil* to their family, held upward of thirty people stuffed inside: neighbors, former neighbors, mountain friends, town friends, her sister Muirne and her brood. Sheena felt a lightness in her head but a heaviness in her heart.

She and Gordon would be leaving them all for Scotland soon. Friends, those who had helped them survive early on in this Nova Scotia wilderness. And her family! This would be the first time she was separated from them all. No asking Mam about the right proportions to affix a sleeve, no laughing at Letty's forthright teasing of her brother Neil.

And no exchanging glances with Alisdair, communicating all her thoughts in an instant.

The chill was still in the air and the top of the stream frozen, as it was still April. She and Gordon would be taking a ship in late May, but they had wanted time to say goodbye to everyone together, with a proper cèilidh. Hence the loud voices, the fiddling and piping, and the ready whisky for everyone this night.

Sheena remembered her little plot of garden from when they first arrived. It was practically abandoned now, as she'd lived in town for the past year. But the idea of taking seeds from their home island and bringing them here had held her fast when as a young girl she'd felt unmoored from everything. Crouching down now, she ran her fingers across the ground covered in late spring forest litter: pine needles and dropped lichen and partially decomposed oak leaves. No, she wouldn't need to bring anything with her this time. She had Gordon.

When she straightened, she saw spots swimming in front of her eyes and put out her hand again.

"Ho, there. Someone's been at the sauce a bit much."

She felt Alisdair's hand at her back and smiled at the flicker of warmth his voice stirred. "Just a bit woozy, is all. Headed back in. But—" She cocked her head to narrow her eyes at her younger brother in the scant light. He'd composed his features to look innocent. Easy, with his blonde hair and soft skin that didn't need to be shaved yet.

"I am a woman expecting; I had to use the privy. What's your excuse for being out here?"

"Oh, looking after that fool sister of mine. Did you see where she's got to?"

Sheena felt a perk of confusion—was he searching out Muirne?—then realized he was referring to her. She sighed theatrically. "Oh, the funny mannie. Come on, let's go in."

Alisdair took up her arm and opened the flap of canvas to allow her entry. Immediately the noise trebled. Sheena stepped through to the tented area between the two cabins, Mam's and the one made for Neil and Letty's family. They'd had only the one child yet, but Letty was finally pregnant with another and hoping for a boy this June. *Just after we leave,*

Sheena thought. *But we must leave sometime. Gordon has already stayed here two years longer than he expected to.*

And maybe I will be away for two years before I see any of them again. She felt a little squirmy twist near her heart and sucked in a breath. Not wanting Alisdair to worry, she strode in to join the circle and started clapping her hands to the rhythm of the music.

April 1833, New Glasgow

Alisdair woke in the stillness of early morning. The party now a days-old memory, he lay in bed with his nephew Gil, in the room they shared in his sister's house in New Glasgow, where he'd spent the year studying with his tutor, Mr. Hoggs. He was coming on to seventeen this autumn and wanted the man's support in starting his studies at a university. Not that he was arrogant enough to think that Mr. Hoggs had no more to teach him, but Alisdair was beginning to see that in order to go further, he needed a different sort of guide.

Hoggs was all right for academic subjects: natural philosophy, geography, calculus, astronomy. But with those disciplines —what could he do? Teach them. Maybe. No, he wanted to be involved in the law, and justice. And one needed to know the right people for that sort of education. Which is why he needed to get into university.

Kings' College in Windsor was only four days' walk from New Glasgow, and that he could manage. As long as he got a scholarship. For, as much as he knew that Mam would support his schooling however she could, he also knew that every bit of money they'd made in nine long years had gone into farming improvements. If he wanted to use any of it, he'd have to confront his older brother Neil. Who hadn't got half the time in school he had. He hesitated in pulling that string of discord in his brother, even though Neil seemed happy enough now.

Into this swarm of worrisome thoughts, Alisdair heard Gil gasp, a small muted sound. Alisdair looked over at his six-year-old nephew and confirmed he was dreaming again. They lay on the same big pallet, Gil on his back with his hands under his chin, wringing the linens.

"Oi," Alisdair said softly. "Gil." No need to wake him, Alisdair just wanted to catch enough of his sleepy attention to pull him out of whatever fright he was having. *Although it is getting light out.* The second bedroom was at the front of the house, facing the street, with a generous window opening. The light coming in through the shutters turned yellower as he watched it.

"All right, time for me to be up, anyway," he groaned as he pushed himself up and out of bed. The slight shift in the pallet, the rustle of the stalks beneath them, were not enough to rouse Gil. But he had let go of the sheet and commenced snoring open-mouthed.

Alisdair wiped his crusty eyelids and crept out the hall to the front door. He opened it slightly, peering out to the right, up north along the road. Strong light, but no one about yet. A noise behind him caused him to shut the door.

"Saw that," sang Muirne's voice from the back of the house. "Keeping an eye out for your sweetheart, are ye?"

Alisdair rolled his eyes at the suggestion but couldn't see his sister. He sniffed appreciatively at the smell of sizzling fat as he passed their main room, knocking on the box bed containing Mollie as he went. A muffled, sleepy voice answered from within, and his face twitched in amusement. He could still play the scamp, even as an uncle, when he wanted.

"Good morning, Muirne. Ed still about?"

Muirne stood at the new stove, which sat in the lean-to room at the back of the house. Her small bump of pregnancy made her stand away from the griddle, but she'd had enough practice cooking like that to make it look easy. Rashers of bacon popped and steamed in the pan, while the potato mash fried alongside.

"No, he had an early call. The Ferrises, just up in Trenton. A sick baby, probably the croup."

She said it matter-of-factly, but Alisdair could tell she was worried. Even speaking of such a misfortune felt dangerous, like you were calling it into your own house. Muirne briskly wiped a hank of hair back with her wrist. The honey-blond hair that had been in a braid while Alisdair grew up was now almost always back in a bun. Today there was a ribbon around it as well. A sky-blue ribbon, to match her eyes. Well, perhaps Edward had brought her a wee present. He was a good husband to Muirne.

"Well," Alisdair harumphed. "Hope it's a mite warmer today. I've not got lessons, just dropping a letter off at the general store. Can I bring anything back for you?"

Muirne eyed him curiously. *What type of letter?* her almost-smile may as well have asked. "Ah, yes. Borwick's baking powder and tea. Low on tea. That's all, I think." Her light tone nettled him, as she was obviously feigning indifference to the letter in order to hear more about it. Well, he wouldn't give her the pleasure. At least not until he'd got an answer from university.

Mollie yawned a sleepy good morning at him as he passed her coming into the kitchen. The bright sunshine outside did little for the piercing cold of an April morning, and Alisdair pulled on his lined mitts quickly. When he arrived at the general store it must have been just after seven, for, looking through the glass part of the door, he could see Mr. Bracethwaite still setting up his counter. Alisdair knocked on the glass and pointed to the sign which still read closed. Mr. Bracethwaite squinted over at him then waved him in. The door was unlocked, at least.

"Sorry, there, Mr. MacLean. Still opening the place, as you see."

"Of course, take your time. I need to draft the note." He strode to the other side of the counter where the scales stood next to the proper paper and wax seals. He unscrewed the inkwell, dipped his own pen in, and commenced to write the note that had formed in his mind on the walk over.

Dear Sir,

If you could be so kind as to send me the materials to submit my application to the College, I would be much obliged. I am prepared to obtain a letter of reference and my record of performance from my tutor, but please inform me of any other supplemental materials deemed necessary for entry for Michaelmas Term, 1833. I am,

Cordially Yours,

Alisdair MacLean

He only used such language for writing now, but who knew? Perhaps when he met other young men at Kings' they would all speak thus. He gulped.

"Going far, is it?" Bracethwaite asked, at his elbow.

"Ah, no. Just to Windsor." He quickly folded the note in thirds from the top then in thirds from the side. He used the candle to drip wax onto where the edges met.

"Be tuppence for the post, a penny for the paper, ink, and wax, then."

"Oh, my sister also wanted…baking powder and some tea, please."

While the grocer was busy measuring out those items, Alisdair addressed the front of the envelope. No signet or stamp for him. Maybe someday.

April 1833, The Ridge

"A brither, a brither, who's lighter than a fither…"

Mairi sat outside in the sun of the afternoon, plucking a chicken while her mother skinned a rabbit.

"He don't feel as light as a feather anymore, darlin'!" laughed Mammy. She was bent over a makeshift table of two sawhorses and a wide plank, the knife handle mostly hidden by her long fingers. The large bump made it so she had to bend over almost horizontal. "But I do enjoy your songs. Go on, then."

She nodded at Mairi but kept her eyes on her work. Mairi bubbled on about brothers, meandering to the subject of the two she knew best, Daddy and Uncle Alisdair.

"And he 'ud do for him, and him would do for 'e, if they got in a tree or if they got in a——" She paused, trying to find a word to match him that was a place.

"Was on a limb?" Mammy suggested.

Mairi cackled.

"Keep plucking now. We want that old hen clean for tea tonight."

Mairi plucked and plucked, even though her fingers were sticky and the fluff from near the skin was getting everywhere. At least they were outside and there wouldn't be a fussy clean-up. She'd stopped singing to concentrate when she noticed her mother was silent too.

Mammy was braced against the plank, breathing slowly with her head hanging down.

"Mammy?"

"It's all right. This—rabbit just doesn't want to come apart. Just taking a breath." She glanced up and met Mairi's eyes over the folds in her sleeve. Mairi saw the space next to her eyes crinkle, and she relaxed a bit. Black hair like her own and eyes that were so much bluer. A sassiness that she wanted to imitate when she was older. For now, it only got her in trouble.

"There y'are," said her mother, but she was looking down to the ground. To her brother, maybe.

"'Ave ye got all the feathers off ye can?" she asked, after a moment.

"Yes, Mammy."

"Then take it over to yer Grannie to do the singeing. I don't think you're ready for that part yet. But you can watch 'er."

Mairi took the bird over to the bigger cabin, whose door stood open to let in the fresh air and sunshine for the few hours when it was strongest. She stood in the doorway to accustom her eyes to the dark within. "Gran?"

"Aye, Mairi," came the voice, off to her right. She walked carefully to the center of the open room, where the big pot hung over the cook fire.

"Mam says you need to do the singeing now."

"All right."

Grannie made her way over to the fire slowly from her bed, using a cane in her right hand.

"Mam?" came another voice—Auntie Sheena's—from outside the cabin. Her outline blocked the light from the front door. Mairi and Grannie both turned to watch as she came in.

"I can help with that," said Auntie Sheena.

"Where'd you come from?" Grannie asked, a question that Mairi had wanted to ask but was afraid would be impertinent. Her aunt was staying in the cabin with Grannie for a few weeks more, while Gordon had business in town to finish up.

"Oh, just down the way, delivering some presents to Mrs. MacGregor." The MacGregors were their closest neighbors, with a large cabin a mile off to the west. "Since we won't be taking our leathers with us," she added.

Mairi wondered why she hadn't left her leathers for them to use. They made the best shoes in winter, and the warmest rugs when you had to go out in the cold.

But her gran smiled and nodded. "Tha's good. They're good neighbors to have, for certain."

Auntie Sheena removed her shawl and hung it on a hook before taking the bird from her. She sat on a stool and picked one of the light twigs from the fire to start singeing off the down. The disgruntled smell quickly filled the space. Sheena wrinkled her nose.

"Whose pot is this for, then?"

Mairi looked to her gran. "Ours," she said. "But you're invited."

"Well, that's very nice of you," Sheena said.

"I saw Letty out in the courtyard, but where's Neil? He wasn't below in the field."

"Out wrestling with the early potatoes, I expect," Grannie replied. Mairi nodded.

"Just us women, then," Sheena mused, as one twig burned to her fingers and she waved it about to put it out. Picking up another and adjusting her hold on the bird, switching wings, she continued. "Is Muirne coming up for Letty's lying in?"

"Aye, come any signs, I'll dispatch Neil, or she'll be up the first of June."

"Good, good."

Mairi knew June was after Auntie Sheena's ship was due to leave. Standing, she looked directly into her aunt's eyes. "You won't be here for when my brother comes?"

"No, my dear. Gordon and I will be packed off to Scotland by then."

"So, just Grannie will be here in the cabin?"

"And Alisdair! Don't forget he's always back to help with the plantings and harvests." There was a twinge of something across Sheena's face as she said it. Mairi uneasily bit her lip. She looked to Gran.

She had a sad smile, but lifted her eyebrows to make it seem less so. "Yes, you're all mine for the winter. I'll have to make cake after cake to fatten you up!"

Mairi ducked her head. She crept around the fire to stand by Grannie and hugged her waist as they both stared into the fire.

April 1833, New Glasgow

Alisdair was spending his days mucking about the cow byre, raking over and shoveling under all the manure that had accumulated over the winter. When it got solid enough they could pour it over the fields and then repeat the process of raking and folding, to get a nice topsoil for the planting. Mam said they used to do it with seaweed, and had to carry it up from the rocky island shore. He didn't much remember that. Just the burning.

No burning seaweed here. He tried to remember the smell of it as his arms swung and dragged, poked and patted like clockwork. He couldn't recall it, not with his nose as full of shit as it was now, but he knew it had a specific smell. A memory of a scent lost, until he came near it again, perhaps.

It got onto late morning, and still he saw no sign of Neil. He took a loaded barrow down to the field, and the sun was high up, near to ten o'clock, before his brother finally appeared. Neil marched down the hill from the cabins, a couple long-handled tools in his grip.

"Oi," Alisdair called when he was within hearing. "What you been up to, then?"

He meant it as a tease, but as Neil drew closer Alisdair saw the bunched-up brow and the firm set of his mouth and realized Neil was upset about something.

"What's the matter? Letty all right?"

Neil jerked his head up quickly in a cursory nod. "Fine, fine. Startin' in on the sickness again, is all."

Alisdair shrugged. "Guess you'll be happy when Muirne comes up, won't you?"

Neil blew out a breath. "Can't come soon enough, I reckon."

Alisdair smiled. "Well. We'll need another barrow full of manure to finish this field. Your turn."

"All right. Brought the mattock for making furrows. I'll start with that on the west side when I come back."

Alisdair nodded. Been having a bit of a rough time, had Neil, lately. Mam still unable to do two-handed chores since the fit, Letty no longer able to do heavy lifting, Sheena about to abandon them all. He was glad to be helping this spring, but he hoped to be off to university after the harvest was in, when they could celebrate a full larder.

By then, Mairi'd be a bit more help. Letty'd be back on her feet. Things would calm.

Alisdair wondered about what Sheena's life would be like. She and Gordon were going back to Scotland, one of Sheena's cherished dreams, he knew, but what would it be like now? How would she take the differences? They weren't going back to Mull, but to Argyll. And his sister would be living in a proper stonebuilt house, not a blackhouse.

Better health. Better food. More security. Yes, but what about the neighbors? Would they resent them? What about the factor and tenants? Would they make trouble for the incomers? Sheena would be torn between the world she had grown up in and the one she now entered, Gordon's respectability and position as a professional man demanding something different of her. Alisdair hoped it would go smoothly for Sheena, but he worried. He was a realist. After seeing Neil's struggle with the conviction of Mr. Brown and his short sentence, he suspected that the breaking of a dream dearly held was a very difficult thing.

When Neil returned, he was at the opposite end of the half-acre, but Alisdair could hear his grunts of effort. It was a quiet morning, like so many others they'd spent out here together. He'd miss it——eventually.

Another half hour and Alisdair straightened, stretched, and exclaimed, "Neil! D'ye hear that?"

"What?" Neil stood still, listening.

"My belly! Time for breakfast, surely?"

"Oh, right. Go on, I'll be along in a little bit. The wind's picking up, so I want to finish out the barrow."

"All right. See you inside."

Alisdair left his rake and shovel near Neil's tools on the ground so he could put them away together and clambered up the hill, eager for the scent of frying ham. He was not disappointed for as he passed the byre and then the smoke shed, he saw Sheena coming out with a joint in a cloth.

"Hungry, then?" She grinned.

"Full well! Neil's only just out, so I been working on my own since first light. Famished!"

"Come on, then."

He followed his older sister, no longer his bigger sister, into Mam's cabin. He touched the stones above the entryway as always, to remind him to duck his head.

"I thought marriage was supposed to make a woman put on weight," he said. Three heads swiveled his direction. He laughed. "Morning, Mam, Letty. Only I meant for Sheena. Married a year now and still slim as a wand. And short."

Sheena shot him a look as she slammed down the joint of meat on the table.

"Easy now. Don't bruise the shoulder," tutted Mam.

"Sorry, Mam. But he *will* be an eedjit." Mam raised her eyes to the ceiling. Letty smiled at their family goings-on.

"You all right, Letty?" he asked, abandoning the teasing. "Neil said you had a rough wake-up."

"Aye, you could call it that." She rubbed her belly, the size of a rising two-pound loaf by now. "Yer mither's porridge is setting me right, though, and no mistake." Mam smiled.

"How are the fields coming, young one?" Mam asked him.

"Still pretty wet, but they'll come along." She nodded. There was a clatter behind him that was Neil, boots scuffling up the wood sill of the doorway. The floor was still pounded-dirt, something that Gordon had been surprised by, and Sheena momentarily embarrassed by, a year ago, but no one wanted it different, really.

"Aye," Neil agreed. "Rain's coming on. May as well chop up kindling to get it under cover before it starts."

"Sure, right after I make that whole joint disappear," Alisdair quipped. The sound of it sizzling in the pan in the lean-to room made Neil smile. Sheena came back in to sit with them as Mam went out to monitor the pan.

"Of course." He sighed as he sat down opposite Alisdair at the table. "Any word from Gordon?"

Sheena shook her head beside Alisdair. "Should be something soon, though. He was finishing up some deed or other for the Board of Trade, then seeing about purchasing one of those new steamer trunks for us." She beamed. "Also, some provisions. Even if the journey is half as long now, we still can't rely on the shipping company's supplies."

"Well," Alisdair said. It was the perfect introduction for him to say he hoped Sheena's dreams would stand up to being lived, but he couldn't figure out how to put it to her, with her face all amused and her eyes sparkling like that, looking up at him. "Oh, nothin'. Just don't want to see you go, is all."

"Oh no? Wee shortie taking to the seas?" Sheena looked like she wanted to stick out her tongue at him, but a married woman should be too good for such nonsense. "Well, I'm glad to hear it, brother. But we'll be seeing ye, I'm sure."

A rap at the door claimed everyone's attention. Neil went out and they heard him hail the postman, Morrissey. He popped his head in to look round and nod at the family members at table.

"Something for you today, Mr. Alisdair."

"Ah, of course. Been waiting for this," he said, and rose to take the letter from Morrissey.

"Tuck in, then," he called, and left. Mam came in with the

meat a-sizzle in the pan and placed it on a rag on the table. They prayed quickly and dove in.

Alisdair stuck the letter in the back of his trousers while he ate. If the others knew what he'd been waiting for, they were respectfully talking around it as they happily set into the food prepared.

"Be a good time to bring in another round of salt cod, Neil."

"Aye, Mam."

"Did ye hear young Thomas is walking?"

"Oh, aye, with three siblings, he'd be getting no mercy until he did."

"Maybe a horse this year, Neil. Fer Mam."

"And how would I get on the thing, I'd like to know?"

Finally his belly was full, the plates were empty, and a general sigh went round the table.

"Now, then. You ready to open that letter yet?" Neil flashed him a grin, quickly shared by Letty and Sheena and Mam.

"It's just the application for entry to university. I had to send away for it first," Alisdair said, trying to quell the expectation in the room as well as the flutters in his belly. He carefully edged his finger around the flap, prying off the seal.

"Entry into where?" asked Mam.

"King's College. In Windsor." A hush descended on the table.

Alisdair withdrew the single sheet of folded paper, a bit surprised it was so short.

"Dear Mr. MacLean…thank you for your interest…by your reference we may infer that you are a member of the Church of Scotland, and therefore inadmissible to our institution…"

There was another line or two, but Alisdair stopped reading out loud. A teeming silence now held the company at the table spellbound. Alisdair scanned the writing again. That was the only reason. Not even allowed to apply.

"We're not even Church of Scotland!" Frustration gave a sharp edge to his tongue.

Sheena, on his left, touched a hand to his shoulder. "I'm sorry, Alisdair. But surely there are others?"

"Not in this colony."

The silence changed from shock to disappointment and resignation. Alisdair felt the sigh and the shrug coming, cleared his throat against it.

"Will you go up inland, try Upper Canada?" Sheena asked him in a tentative voice. He knew why. He looked up at his mother, who sat with her hand pressed to her mouth. As soon as their eyes met, she thrust herself up, awkwardly swinging one leg and then the other over the bench, and hobbled to the back of the cabin.

"It would be too much like following in Father's footsteps, wouldn't it?" he murmured to his sister.

"Maybe——" she started, but a look from Alisdair stopped her from continuing.

"I'll have to think it over. See what's best to do for the family."

"Of course," she replied. She'd reddened a bit. Alisdair wondered why, what she had been about to suggest, but quickly dismissed it.

"Ready, Neil? I'll help with some chopping. Then there's the summer pasture to check on. I'll take that today."

Neil nodded. Alisdair went out first. His mind felt like a brick wall, but he knew sooner or later there would be an opening.

May 1833, The Ridge

Sheena stared at the clothes laid out on Mam's bed. Her best dress, the one she'd been married in, was still so precious that she stroked the starchy folds of cream silk carefully. She had worried about her wedding dress ever since she had seen Muirne in hers, for how could she ever make something half so beautiful as what their mother had started and Muirne had finished? But Gordon had taken her to a seamstress in New Glasgow, recommended by his employer's wife, and told her he would pay for her services. La! The delight in his smile when he saw her excitement! He was a man who would try to give her everything she wanted.

Sheena blinked away the cobwebs of memory and folded the dress in layers of clean cloth. Blue skirt, black skirt, brown skirt. Blue jacket, brown jacket, black overskirt and bodice. Stays, stays, stays, and shifts galore. Her hands shook out each one, checking for damage, before folding shoulder to shoulder, sleeve to sleeve and running her hands down to fold the middle. Her hands relished the soft smoothness. *A respite from the hard life*, she thought.

Poor Alisdair. Poor Mam. But it would come out right. Alisdair would go away for schooling, but Mam would still have Neil's family at hand and Muirne's a day's walk away—or ride, perhaps. Her eyes drifted to the cupboard where scraps and remnants were stored for other uses. She opened it, the darkness showing only shadowy humps of material. She pushed the door wider and stepped to one side to allow the candlelight in. Yellow boiled wool. Grey cotton flannel. And the shreds of petticoats too threadbare to be decent. Her hand passed over these as well.

Goodbye, scraps.

She turned and saw her mother leaning against the door-way to her room.

"Mam! I didn't hear you come in."

"Lost in thought, I shouldn't wonder, as I do make a bit of a clatter," she replied. Her eyes went to the bed, took in the neat stacks, then to the cupboard.

Sheena turned back to close the cupboard door slowly. "Everything all right?" she asked.

"Oh, aye. It's good to have everyone about, even if it is before ye all go away ag'in."

Sheena turned to face Mam, her eyes full. Her throat closed over words she wanted to say.

"I'm happy for ye, *mo nighean*. He's a good man, and he'll take you far." Mam's creased cheeks dimpled. "You know what I mean."

"Yes, Mam, I know. And there will be visits."

"Well, I don't know how many I'll be around for, but I'm happy to see—"

"Don't say it, Mam!" Sheena hugged her mother fiercely. "I couldn't leave if I thought I'd never see you again." Her words were muffled against Mam's shoulder, but she was sure her mother knew what she meant to say.

Mam's left hand soothed jerkily over Sheena's back, reminding her of her weakness. Sheena straightened, cleared her throat.

"I shall try to do lots of new and exciting things so I can write you about them. And of course we'll visit once this one is crawling about." She gestured to her belly.

Mam smiled a little wistfully. "Aye, well. You finished packing?"

"Just about, until Gordon arrives with our trunk."

"Not taking any of the tools?"

She meant the spindles and pins and needles and combs for transforming wool into serviceable material.

"No, Mam. I won't need them." They'd buy their woolens from now on.

"Then let's have a sit by the fire for a wee while. Gordon's due tomorrow, no?"

"Yes, he's on his way now."

"Our last night together, then."

They turned the two ladder back chairs, carved and joined by Neil some eight years before, toward the fire. Sheena stared into the flames while Mam worked a darning needle into one of Neil's socks. The crackle and breath in the snug cabin lulled Sheena almost to a sleep. But ten minutes into their vigil, the door swung open and little Mairi rushed in.

"Mairi! What are you—" Sheena began, but the fear in the

child's eyes gave a jolt to her insides. "Your mother?"

Mairi nodded. "Da says you need to go to the MacGregors, ask 'em to send for Uncle Eddie, then hurry back." The girl took a difficult swallow.

"I will do just that. Let me just get coat and boots on." She glanced at Mam, who was up out of the chair and beckoning to Mairi to help her over to the other cabin. She swooped out of the house, grabbing the crusie lamp to light her way to the MacGregors' farm a mile away.

Within the hour, one of the older MacGregor boys had been roused and sent down the mountain on their horse, and Sheena was making her way back with Mrs. MacGregor, who knew more about midwifery than any other nearby. By the time the two women reached the MacLeans' clearing, Mrs. MacGregor's hearty chatter had strengthened Sheena. Sure, she hadn't even seen Letty yet! It could be false labor—or something as easily righted—that Neil wouldn't know two cents' worth about.

It was just that Mairi had had such a frightful look about her. It could only have been communicated to her by Neil, and Neil was usually such a level-headed steady one, that she'd instantly given credence to the alarm. They made for Neil and Letty's cabin and hadn't yet reached the door when a wail broke the stillness of the night. They hurried in.

"I've brought Mrs. MacGregor," she called out as she struggled out of coat and gloves.

"And I've sent Lloyd to town for your doctor," Mrs. Mac-Gregor added. She was already looking at the source of the wail. Letty sat bolt upright against the wall, her arms pushing into the low bed. Sheena's panic returned as she saw her sister-in-law with her teeth gritted and lips pulled back, eyes squinched hard shut against another cry that was bound to come out anyway. Neil knelt by her, holding her hand, while Mairi fitted between them, her bottom half nestled against Neil while her top half leaned heavily on the pallet's edge.

"What do we need, Missus? Mam's already got me boiling water on the fire," he said, and gestured with his free hand toward the wall where the chimney was. Mam stood by it, watching the large iron pot.

Sheena could tell by a glance at Mrs. MacGregor's face with its wrinkled nose that this was no easily remedied false labor.

"Good. Blankets to keep her warm. Wood to keep up the fire. And keep her sipping some water. And tea—I've brought some herbs that'll do some good."

"Go on, Mairi, fetch the blankets from the press." Neil nudged the reluctant bundle in his lap.

"I'll fetch more wood from our pile," Sheena said.

"Good, good. And Sheila, good to see you getting about." Mrs. MacGregor gave Mam a warm smile. "We'll hold the fort til your young doctor gets here, don't you worry."

'Worry' was the last word Sheena heard before stepping out into the cold, sharp night.

May 1833, The Ridge

Auntie Sheena fled into the night, her dark skirts' swish cut off by the bang of the door. Mairi pulled out the two biggest blankets from the press, leaving the whole drawer empty, before shutting it with a bang to match. She dragged them across to Da, who held them up high to shake them out a bit before laying them at the foot of their bed.

Mrs. MacGregor spoke softly to Grannie, and she saw Grannie's lips move and her head shake. She watched but couldn't tell what they were saying because she was once again by her mother's side, the groans and keenings right in her ear. She put her hand on top of Mam's and Da's hands, then looked to her mother's face. Nothing. She was gushing breath through her teeth now, creating bubbles of spit at her lips. Mairi leaned away, then crawled out of the space between her da and the bed.

"It's all right, Mairi. She'll be all right. Don't you—"

Mam blew out a full breath, gasped, and tried to catch her breath once again. Mairi walked behind her da so she could see Mam's face again. Her eyes were open, with tears pouring out the sides. Tears leapt to Mairi's eyes as she saw. Mam looked at her, her eyes sad and pained and reaching. Mairi burst into sobs, going forward to claw at the blankets and find a piece of her mother to touch.

"Mairi, come now, it's going to be a hard one, just like you were. Don't take on so," Grannie limped over with her cane and tugged at her arm. "Come on over with me. We'll let them in peace for a bit, see if your Mam can rest."

Mairi let Grannie lead her away but turned to watch her mother as she went. Her vision was blurred through tears, but she watched as the expression on Mam's face went from gasping to clenching again.

The door opened. They were outside. The cold air stung her wet cheeks and chin. Grannie couldn't hurry, so they walked over to the old cabin carefully.

"We'll light the torch to put out, eh? So it's easier for us to walk across the yard, eh?"

"Is the baby going to come tonight?"

"I very much doubt it. Maybe tomorrow though. You took two days, missy."

"I did? That's…awful."

"Well. There's some as have it easier than others. Muirne's one of them, God-be-praised. But yer mother, now, her body's just made different. It's harder for the baby to come out. Takes a lot of patience. And pain."

Mairi whimpered. She didn't want her mam to be in so much pain. And for two days? Was a brother worth all this?

"Will Uncle help?"

"Aye, Dr. Turner and Mrs. MacGregor will both do all they can. Dr. Turner can bring medicines to ease the pain, and make sure that baby's ready. And Flora can make potions for the body to not try to resist so much. It is painful, but it is Nature's way. God's way."

Mairi still felt bleak inside.

"Ye'll sleep with me the night," said Grannie. "She's in good hands, don't you worry."

Her grandmother smoored the fire and put out the candles, after lighting the promised torch so the family could cross the yard easily. Mairi had been woken clean out of a sleep by her mother's first cry and felt that she would never be able to go back to bed. But the cabin was quiet, the air under the blankets with her gran was warm, and an arm snaked over to hug her close. The words of a cradle song came out haltingly, as if Gran hadn't sung it for a long time. Mairi listened long enough to hear,

Bheir mi ò hu ò hò
Bheir mi ò hu ò hì
Bheir mi ò hu ò hò
'S mi fo bhròn 's tu gam dhìth…

When she woke the arm was no longer over her shoulder. She rolled slowly backward and met no resistance. Mairi turned her head left: the wall. Oh, Grannie's wee room. Was it day? Why was her Grannie up without her? She remembered the night before and breathed in such a breath that it choked her. She scurried from the bed, coughing and sputtering, into the main space of the cabin.

It was still mostly dark, but a slight grey light drifted in from the window. The fire was still smoored. She could hear the cows lowing in the byre. It was chore-time. Where was Gran? Where was everyone?

Mairi placed her hands on her knees and tried to draw breath evenly, but the choking took on a rhythm of its own and forced her to gasp and cough again and again. She was red in the face with tears streaming down when the door opened and Da stepped in.

"Mairi!" She felt his broad hand on her back. He swept over to the back kitchen in the lean-to and returned with the bucket of water. He dipped the cup full and knelt by her, easing his hand on her back in circles until she drew a shuddering breath that caught but did not launch a new attack.

"Here, girl. Take a wee sip."

"I—k"

"Nay, dinna talk yet. Just drink, and nod, or shake. Were ye crying?"

Shake.

"Coughing?"

Shake.

"Did ye just wake up like this then?"

Nod.

"Well, I'll be. Didn't know that ran in the family."

She gave him a weak smile. A throaty vibration made her cautious about speaking, but she raised an eyebrow toward the door.

"Ye want to go out that door? Now why would that be?"

"Daddy…"

"I know. Ye want to see yer mam. But she's not up to visiting right now. Mrs. MacGregor's been to stay all the night, and she's holding on, but she needs to rest while she can." A pained sort of look came over Da's face, which caused Mairi to tense her face again. *Please tell me she'll be all right, Da.*

"She'll be fine, daughter. Just let her rest. And me, too."

"Here?" It came out garbled, but intelligible.

"Aye. Just be quiet the day, can ye now? I'll catch a short nap then be out in the fields again." He yawned and left Mairi with her ladle of water to seek and collapse into the other bed.

Mairi stood, undecided, until she heard Grannie's clomp across the sill minutes later. She set the ladle in the bucket and returned them to the lean-to. Grannie stood in the place she'd just left, gazing at the back of her son, sprawled out fully clothed on the mattress. Grannie sighed, and rubbed at her rear end.

"A night for waiting up, and not too easy even on the old ears," she mused. "Now why don't you go out for a while, Mairi. Check on the flowers coming up, hey? After we've slept it off, there'll be some breakfast for everyone. Go on, now."

Mairi coughed a little to make sure she could speak unobstructed. "But Mam! I want to see her—"

"She needs her rest, dear. Just a couple of hours now. Then we'll bring her over some nourishing porridge, all right?"

Gran made a fist then waggled her fingers, as if she'd been clutching something in her hands for a long time. Mairi worried her cheek with her teeth but didn't speak out again. She wore only her shift and one of her father's shirts for warmth. But she supposed if Grannie said to go off and explore, that would have to do.

She drew the wool shirt closer and set off to the byre to see to the cows first. They'd be glad to see her coming, she was sure. Blackie was louder, so she set the pail by her first. Warm, frothy milk pegged into the pail. No flies yet. Then Darien. Working her hands over the slick teats rhythmically. Emptying her mind as she emptied the cows of their milk. Lugging the large pail carefully toward the door to the byre, she looked back at the cabin. *Probably not time yet.* She took a folded length of cheesecloth from the top of the churn and lay it over the pail to keep anything from dropping in.

Maybe I'll go down to the creek. Past Auntie Sheena's flower patch.

Mairi wound her way down to where the cleared land started. Meadow cranesbill, marsh marigolds, and yellow irises grew along the wet edges of the field, where the water ran down the cliff and along the edge, before pouring down into the creek. Mairi looked down the few feet where it plashed and sparkled. It was chilly enough that there was no temptation to take a dip in the waters.

She gathered some of the drier leaves and made a hump to sit on, drawing in her knees and wrapping her arms around them. She watched the water, listening to its low voice, observing its unhurried swirl. Its shadowed depths.

May 1833, New Glasgow

The Turners were having an early breakfast together before Edward went out on his rounds. Alisdair sat hunched at their table, pushing his stewed veg this way and that. Thomas was running after Kitty in the enclosed space, while Mollie and Gil sat with their parents at the table. Muirne and Ed were paying his black mood no notice, but the older children kept glancing his way, wondering why he was so sour the past week. He'd told them he was rejected by King's, excluded from even applying. He'd felt a little awkward with Edward, who was Church of England and who had gone there himself. But most of all, he wanted to have an answer ready for when they asked what he would do next. Problem was, all he could think of was to try his fortune in Halifax, which might break his mother's heart just as sure as leaving for Upper Canada.

They all heard the hoofbeats at the same time. Alisdair looked to Muirne, who looked to her husband. The crisp, even thuds skidded to a stop, and Edward rose to get the door.

He kept the door closed behind him at first and Alisdair heard nothing of the words spoken, but soon Ed clomped inside, and the door was shut to. Alisdair was surprised to see Lloyd MacGregor, standing there with a dripping nose and red cheeks.

"Lloyd! Is your family all right?" he blurted out.

"Aye. I'm sorry, Alisdair. We went astray a bit in the forest in the night. I've been out since eleven. Just made it in. Doctor's wanted for your brother's wife. Early labor."

The ragged words came out in spurts, and Alisdair took a moment to understand that it was his family in need, not the MacGregors.

"I'll just get a few additional supplies and be on my way," said Edward, who had already put on his coat and changed his walking shoes for riding boots. His matter-of-fact voice, his peck on his wife's cheek: so normal. *Well. Perhaps it is normal.*

"How early?" he asked Edward.

"I'd say a good three weeks," he said, the calculating in his brain producing a frown and a thrust-out lip.

Alisdair saw Muirne's hands loop over her belly protectively. *Maybe not so normal.*

"Should I come?"

"Oh, no. No need. Unless you want to. Lloyd says his mother's been with Letty, as well as Sheila and Sheena."

And who's taking care of wee Mairi?

"I'll come," he said, providing no other reason. He felt rather than saw his sister exchange looks with Edward. "I'll come up later, with Lloyd, once he's rested and eaten summat."

The young man did look worn out. He gave Alisdair a grateful nod.

"Very well. See you in a bit." He dashed out with bag in hand, intent upon the horse in the paddock. The shed attached to the small sheltered paddock functioned as a sort of apothecary's closet. Alisdair knew Edward would pick up his additional supplies there. Was there anything he could bring? But it was too late to call out after him. He looked at Lloyd, who was peeling off his clammy layers. Muirne rose to take them and hang them out to dry.

"Glad it's not raining no more, and that's the truth."

"Aye. Appreciate you coming in the night, must've been a miserable run."

"Oh, probably my fault for overruling Lolly—probably what got us lost up a blind creek for a while."

"Oh, the switchbacks coming down the mountain can be hard, and no mistake."

They pattered on politely until Alisdair saw that Muirne had maneuvered the children out of the house for a walk. Alisdair met her eyes under the brim of her hat before she closed the front door.

"I'll try to give ye an hour," she said.

Alisdair indicated the mattress he shared with Gil; Lloyd fell into it gratefully. Alisdair threw the scraps into the bucket for the neighbor's pig and quietly placed the dishes and forks in the washing sink. He stood by the mantle in the middle of the house, chewing on a hangnail, feeling the creeping, buzzing sensation he always hated when he had to be patient. He went out back. Found a stool in the tack shed and placed his head in his hands.

To put the worries of Letty's birthing out of his mind, he tried to think what he could do about his schooling, his plans for a career. He'd already pumped his tutor for any useful connections but the man was too complacent, hadn't done any hobnobbing to get him in with the dean of a college some- where. And more important, his tutor was a Presbyterian. What a big bother over signing a stupid pledge. *Bishops*, he sneered. *I'd like to meet one o' them and tell 'em what I think of the necessity of their whole profession.*

He sighed. No, that was not quite right. Tarred with the same brush, and all that. He relented. *But then that's exactly what they're doing on the other side, painting me out to be unworthy of their knowledge. Pah!*

He wondered briefly if he could appeal to the Reverend Balwhidder, who had greeted them upon their arrival so long ago. He was Church of England, but would he recommend him? And would his name carry water?

He had very few patrons to appeal to, and he squirmed at the thought of doing it. Neil had always taught him to stand up for himself and let his work show his worth. But that wasn't working. *What I need to do is insert myself in a situation where they assume I'm one of them*, he thought. *Then questioning my right to study would be awkward. And I know they dinna like that.*

A foolhardy adventure, probably, he admitted. *But what else am I to do to get where I will?*

It didn't seem long, but the air was warming with the weak sun when Gil ran back to find him.

"We're back, and Mr. MacGregor is up!" he shouted. All the ignorance and optimism of his six years. The same age as when Alisdar had emigrated. He shook himself, clapped a hand on the young one's shoulder, and followed him back.

The young men set out quickly with a piece each for their lunch on the way up the mountain. Lloyd, his spurt of news exhausted, relapsed into his calm, slow way of walking, his horse Lily following companionably behind. Alisdair somewhat regretted saying he would come, but couldn't very well say he'd prefer to stay and mope and wrack his brains for nonexistent possibilities, could he?

Muirne had given him his space when he returned from the ridge. He suspected she knew it was something to do with the school, though how she knew, he couldn't fathom. But in her manner the past few days had been a sharp expectation. He had to move on somehow. The last few sessions with his tutor had been painful, with the same sensation hammering at him. *Move on.*

Well, there was the whole planting season to think about it. Then a whole round of harvesting to be done. He hesitated to ask Neil about his thoughts, knowing that there would always be a slight resentment in his judgment, that what they had wasn't enough for Alisdair.

By dint of steady, silent climbing, the lads arrived at the ridge that evening and parted ways. Alisdair trudged on the half mile to the east. When the cabin came into view, he noted a stillness about the place that felt foreign. Not snug at home, not the satisfying sigh after a long day, but the drop of wind that signaled even the oceans had ceased to blow. He hurried to Mam's door.

Sheena and Mam turned to look at him mutely. Edward

sat off to the side, hunched over the tray of tools on his lap. Alisdair's entrance interrupted some reverie of his and he startled.

"Ah, Alisdair. We've…suffered a loss."

He continued to stare forward, not meeting Alisdair's gaze.

"The baby?"

Edward nodded.

"And Letty," Sheena half-said, half-whispered.

A small gasp and his mouth dropped open. The noise made Edward blink, and finally he turned toward Alisdair.

"Yes…I'm afraid a fever took her suddenly and she passed away a couple of hours ago. Neil and Mairi are with the body."

Alisdair struggled with the sudden change—referring to Letty as 'the body,' for God's sake.

"I'm sure you tried your best," he mumbled.

Edward blinked again. Moved a corner of his mouth to indicate his gratefulness for Alisdair's offer of comfort. "I'm sorry," he said. "I'll head back to town and—tell Muirne now." He turned to Mam, who sat with an elbow on the table and a handkerchief in her hand. "Is there anything I can order for the burial? Someone I can inform for the services?"

Mam looked so weary. Her drooping eyes met Alisdair's briefly before shaking her head. "Neil will do that," she said hoarsely.

"Or I can," Alisdair said softly. She nodded, accepting the help. "Shall I go over—I mean, shouldn't someone check on them?"

He saw Sheena draw herself up, push herself up with two hands, and turn to face him. "I'll go with you." Her eyes were red. Her hands bore all sorts of scratches and dried blotches of red clung to her wrists and nails. He gulped uncomfortably, then nodded.

Before he went out the door with her, he turned back to where his mother sat. She was bent over the table, hands in her lap.

"I'll stay here, Mam, as long as you and Neil have need of me."

Her watery eyes raised to his, she blinked, sending two new tears running down her cheeks.

Alisdair followed Sheena out of the cabin and ran a hand over his face. His stomach rumbled. He hoped his sister hadn't heard it. His nose ran. He sniffled.

They stepped onto the wooden planking of the stoop, then Sheena opened the door. It was no good to knock on the doors of the dead; it would scare away their spirit too soon. Alisdair took in the sickly odor, the pile of wrinkled, bloody linen in the middle of the usually spick-and-span interior. He saw his brother's back first.

Neil's pale skin, ringed with red at the neck and arms, almost lit up the dark room. He sat next to their bed, and Alisdair saw Letty's feet: the bottoms still shadowed and dirty from when she was walking around the place. The rest of her was covered by a sheet, or blocked by Neil, whose head bowed over hers. Sheena moved to the other side of the pallet and Alisdair followed, seeing Neil's shirt laid carefully over his wife's head.

Alisdair cleared his throat. Neil didn't look up.

"Where's Mairi?" Alisdair asked. Sheena looked about her.

"She was in here a little bit ago. Mairi?"

Sheena's voice was thready, delicate. As if she wanted the girl to give herself up without a fuss, because a fuss would just completely do her in.

He touched her back briefly. "I'll give it a look round," he said. Maybe when he came back he'd be able to approach Neil. He seemed carved in stone. Deaf as stone, too. Didn't he care where his daughter was?

Alisdair left the heady interior and felt the cool air outside. May already, and time for another growing season. Alisdair began his circuit of the cabin to his left. Corner, chimney, corner, kitchen shed; ah.

"Mairi."

The wee girl lay curled up in a ball next to the butter churn. She had at least four fingers in her mouth, hanging open as she slept. She'd got all muddy in Neil's shirt, but at least it wasn't so cold that she was shivering. He squatted down and smoothed the hair away from her eyes. Those liquid brown eyes popped open a second, then scrunched down again.

He didn't know what to say to her. She wasn't all right. He didn't want to lie. There wasn't anything he could do. He tried to think of what would have been good for him when his own father Gillan died. Nothing came.

He picked up the little girl, whose eyes stayed stubbornly shut.

"I'm here for you, Mairi. We'll take care of you."

Her eyes opened, terrified that he was confirming what she wanted to push away: her mam was gone. Then she put her face against his chest and wailed.

She cried it out, and he patted her back. He saw Sheena come to the door of the shed. Her chin trembled a bit as she watched them. Without meeting his gaze, she walked forward and leaned her head on his back. Cloaked in weeping women, he was.

Sheena sniffled and wiped her face then reached out for Mairi. He inclined his head inside, and she nodded, preceding him in. Mairi was quieting down, but must have realized they'd taken her inside. Alisdair let her down to stand in front of him. A furious scream poured out of her as they stood. Waited. Neil still didn't move.

Finally, a lurch. From his stool by the bed, Neil swung his body to the left. His upper body still drooped. Alisdair felt him take a shaky breath and straighten, his back jerking as several bones popped in protest. He reached out an arm to Mairi, who hesitated a moment before joining him.

Sheena stepped forward to whisper something in Neil's ear. He nodded. Tried to stand up, but dizziness made him swoon a bit, and he put a hand down to the mattress to steady himself. The shift in weight jostled one of Letty's feet. Neil stared at it for a long moment. Alisdair felt the urge to shout, to scream as Mairi had, at the unjustness of death. But he chewed his lip and turned away. He went out the front door, hearing someone follow.

"I told him to take a few minutes more and we'd be in to wash the body, Mam and me," Sheena said.

Alisdair nodded, feeling the blockage in his throat move too.

"Alisdair." He stopped, turned. They stood in the yard between the two cabins, under a twilit sky. "I'm scared."

He scrutinized Sheena's face. She was worn out, for certain. Worried. Why?

"What about?"

Her eyes got bigger as he spoke. A hand crept over her belly, protectively, just as Muirne's had. Of course. Sheena was worried that she'd have trouble with her baby. But she thrust the hand down and said, "Nothing. It's just, the leaving, now—with everything so—"

He sat down on one of the cut logs laying about and waved her to do the same.

"I know what you mean. I wanted to be away to Halifax myself, but talked myself into helping out Neil with the crops one more summer. Well, now…"

"Halifax…to go to work?"

"Aye. I've got to be able to find something. I'm not—I want to do different work. Like Gordon. Oh, is there—"

But he cut short that thought. Why hadn't he thought of asking Gordon for help with his application? Or finding a clerkship somewhere? He hadn't spent much time with him, sure, but the man had worked for some of the higher-ups in the Board of Trade for two years. There must be some avenue he could try. But not now. He slammed a hand to his face. He couldn't be thinking about this now.

The tremulous, forgiving smile on Sheena's face when he looked up again showed she guessed where his mind had been. She took the handkerchief from her belt and blotted her face with it. A whiff of camphor washed over him and he turned away his head. It looked like one of the ones Letty had made. His muscles bunched.

"You're set to sail next week, no?"

"Yes."

"You think Gordon will change the tickets for—well, we'll have the funeral by then, but ye may need more time to travel to port."

"Yes."

Sheena looked defeated. He didn't like it. "I'll be staying here, Sheena. I'll help look after Mam and Neil and Mairi. And Muirne will be visiting, too. Dinna worry about us."

Sheena nodded and walked slowly back to the old cabin. Alisdair stayed where he was. Aye, he'd stay the year, but what then? Time enough for stability and security to reestablish themselves. Then he'd strike out on his own.

May 1833, The Ridge

The minister came. Consecrated the ground for burial so that they'd have a family plot on their land instead of surrendering their dead to the town down below. Letty was laid in and everyone seemed to mourn her differently: Neil, as if the center of his life had caved in. Mam, as if she had no more energy to continue after the setback. Mairi, as if she would lash out at whoever had taken away her mother.

Sheena listened to the preacher's words, feeling numb except for a prickling sensation down her spine. Like she was sweating, but it was nothing near a warm day. The ground had only recently thawed enough to allow the digging of the grave. She shifted from foot to foot to try to allow some air between her layers of black calico, but the sensation wouldn't go away.

She looked to Gordon, who had finally joined her on the ridge. He'd brought the steam trunk. They were ready to leave the next morning. He was suitably somber, in his black felt hat and black wool suit. His profile, even drawn in sadness, lifted her heart. He had come into their family, promised to help, because of her. Because he loved her. Now if only the consequences of his love wouldn't lead to similar complications in birthing. Sheena gulped and looked away, ashamed of where her thoughts had gone. But the preacher had concluded. The family was throwing dirt on the wooden coffin, already bedecked with the fragrant mayflowers that Letty had loved to gather.

Sheena took her turn in the line, bending over to scoop a handful of earth. A searing pain in her lower back caused her to stagger. She put a hand to the ground. It was like lightning, and the impression of it echoed in her body, which trembled in case another should strike. Gordon helped her up.

"You all right, Sheena?" he whispered.

She shook her head.

"Let me take you inside then." He bent and swooped her up, and she felt another pain, this one lower down.

"Ghungggg," she groaned, trying not to scream. The next she knew was being jostled over the ground. A bed. Dr. Turner bending over her.

Rolling from side to side. Being bent forward.

A stillness.

A murky feeling in the back of her throat.

Shadows danced over her eyes, silly brown shapes of fantastical animals. They grew and shrunk like shadows thrown by firelight. She tried to put her hands through one, and it curled round her fingers like smoke. Something—the smoke? —seized her hand, then her throat. She screamed until her voice felt hoarse, but there was no one in the place but her.

When she finally woke, the pain made her realize the fantastical animals and hands of smoke had been a dream. The muddy feeling in her mouth—she guessed laudanum. The pain?

She glanced around her and saw sleeping bodies on pallets. She raised herself up a little on her arm, grunting a little at the unexpected pain in her nether parts. The pallet nearest her was empty. While she was raised on an elbow, the door opened. A pale pool of starlight shone on the head of dark brown hair that ducked under the entryway.

"Gordon," she whispered, even as his gaze found the change in her alertness.

He picked his way to sit by her side.

"Are you yourself, Sheena?"

"I feel like myself. I had a sort of dream before…"

"Yes. Turner had to give you laudanum and it seems you had a bad…nightmare. I'm sorry, my dear." He took her nearest hand in both of his, looking down at it.

Sheena observed his pained face; it was still agitated by something.

"I've been sleeping then…for how long?"

"Letty's funeral was only yesterday morning, not long. After you lost the babe——" His eyes flicked to both of hers, searching for confirmation. Yes, she could feel its absence, but was not thinking about that now. Trying to fit into their plans

——

"But you've got to get to Glasgow for your post! The ship is leaving——"

"I know, Sheena. I know." His brow wrinkled as he looked anxiously at her. She eased her head back to the pillow as he stroked her hair. The pain throbbed somewhere near her sex, the medicine giving it no precise location.

"I wanted to know that you were safe from—that you were out of danger. But I really do need to see the man from the estate. It's not a government appointment like this was; it's a private agreement, and he can break it easily if I don't abide by the terms, including the commencement date. I could write, but—"

"But you could get there faster than the letter," she finished, and smiled weakly. "When's the next clipper sailing?" She knew he'd have checked already.

"In another week." The agitation fell from his face, replaced by some misery of guilt. "I think I can still make the ship with our reservations, if I leave now. And you could stay here 'til you're recovered, follow me in a month. Yes, I think that would be best."

Still his face yearned for her to assent, for her to agree with him that separation was best. He was only a year older than she, but seemed so much younger sometimes. Less sure. Not like Gillan or Neil at all. She took care to let him grow up gently.

"If you think it's best, we shall do it. You'll have everything settled in Ardkinglas for when I arrive, and we'll...start again."

Sheena crossed an ocean in that statement. Gordon remained on firm ground.

"Yes. I shall see about a traveling companion while I am at port. And be sure you are fit for travel before you reserve a place, will you? Oh, my darling, this is not how I wanted us to arrive—"

"I shall be in good hands the while," Sheena said. "And mind you get a good accommodation for us, now."

"I shall do. And may Sheila's hands, and God's, cover you 'til we are together again." He kissed her clasped hand, then her forehead, then after a moment's hesitation, her lips. It was a tender kiss, full of care and fear and the wrench of parting. Sheena craned her neck upward to kiss him back, her intensity the wound she inflicted on him for leaving her so soon.

Gordon humped their trunk outside. Sheena listened to the noises in the dark, the rustle of the travois across the ground, the squeak of the leather thongs tied to the saddle. Then the slither of the burden being towed away, the muted clip of the hooves in the wet undergrowth of the forest.

As her family slept around her, Sheena stayed wide awake. She stared at the dark rafters. If this was God's doing, then let Him have the next one healthy. If this was not God's doing— but there her mind stopped. Did she dare ask Dr. Turner why the baby died? He might tell her her body was ill-suited to birthing, just as Letty's had been. She couldn't—could not— let that be her fate with Gordon.

Gordon had already left her behind. Chosen his career over her. She was to follow, blindly, in faith, no doubt. Meanwhile, her body had no strength, had rejected its own work as unworthy.

Sheena wept bitter tears that night, as the effects of the medicine dwindled.

June 1833, The Ridge

Auntie Sheena was on the mend, Grannie said. Not a serious illness, just a bitty shock. She'd recover and sail on to Scotland in another week or two.

Mairi sat on a log between the two cabins at midday. The heat of the day was coming, but not yet at its fiercest. Da and Uncle Alisdair had come in for breakfast and gone back out to the fields, where she heard their occasional yells to halt or meet. She sat in the shade, one leg scrunched up to rest her chin, the other dangling to the ground. She peered with one eye toward Gran's cabin, where her aunt and uncle stayed. No sound.

She peered at her own home, where she and her father slept. Definitely no sound there.

A bleat from one of the sheep in the pen called her attention and she rose to wander down that way, away from the cliff and the fields, toward the road and the creek. There were two lambs this spring, and they stayed with their mothers nearer the enclosure while the other half-dozen grazed farther afield on grass and the weedy undergrowth.

No bleats as she approached. One lamb stood facing her, its hindquarters up against its mother. The other one cropped a bit of grass that managed to grow among the mud by the entrance to the pen.

"Was it you?" she asked the one facing her. She'd named it Tooksweenoo in her head, a nonsense term that sounded like the Native name for the Bird Hunters in the night sky. She'd heard it once at the mercantile in town and latched onto the fantastic story. This lamb always seemed to have his black nose in the air, scenting the air. He didn't bleat again, but lifted his nose to the air. She smiled.

She snapped off one of the willow-herb growing by the road and walked down, whacking at the air in front of her. Before the road veered north all the way down to the valley, she stopped and stood. The view was spectacular: rolls of green hills racing each other to the sea. Or perhaps to a very grand river; she didn't know.

She turned back to the road. After a hundred yards, it met the creek, which she followed back eastward to their fields. It bubbled and trickled, a friendly noise to have at her side.

"Hup, ho, there," came Da's voice, a ways off. Talking to the horse under the plough. She dawdled a bit, not wanting the men to see her. Mairi looked across the creek to the forest. How cool and sheltering it looked. A bird swooped down from a nearby branch and vanished deeper into the distance of trunks. She stepped into the cold creek water. It felt so good! Seeping through her knitted socks, and oh! She didn't want to lose her clogs that way. She took them off and held them in her hands as she waded across. The water came just above her knees at this point, so her skirt and shift were also wetted through.

Perfect, she thought. So nice and cool.

The squelch-squelch of her socks as she stepped onto the opposite bank made her wrinkle her face up, however. Ugh. Mairi continued on along the far bank until she'd skirted around the field where the men worked. There she found the maple and black willow standing together, sheltering their family plot, with its one lonely stone. Mairi sat on her heels at first, but that made the damp water press through to her bum. She changed to sitting on the ground, her legs sticking out in front. That wouldn't do, either. She swung them around and lay on her belly, resting her chin on her folded hands and observing the dirt.

It had gone dry this past week and changed color, from the rich, dark brown to this reddish-brown that looked more like dust than real dirt. She watched the ants going about their business, the flies, a cricket, and a tiny green spider, hurrying along. Before she knew it, the warm air, the caressing breeze, and the solid, supportive earth beneath her had lulled her senses and she dozed.

Much later, she heard voices and jerked awake. The air was cool, and the chill of evening had spread a blanket of dew over the grass around her. She crawled her way backward to sit, noticing that her skirt was dry but her socks were not. She was putting on her clogs when her Da's voice called for her, quite close.

"Here, Da!" She wiped a hand across her face.

In a few seconds he was there, scooping her up, then holding her away from him.

"Aw, Mairi, what have ye been into? And why did ye wander off without telling a body? Ye gave us all a fright, there, when we all went in to supper!"

His voice shook her. Something in it that scolded.

"Sorry, Da. I fell asleep."

"Sprawled out on the ground. Smelling like pondwater. Oh, dearie. Ye canna just disappear!"

"I didn't know it was so late. I'll be more careful, I promise."

"Aye, ye will. And then there's that to remember it." He let her down to the ground and whipped a hand across her bottom, which stung. She coughed, knowing she shouldn't cry, and avoided looking at him, even though he squatted down to be at her level.

"All right, then?"

"Neil! Did ye find her?"

"Aye, Alisdair. She's at the gravesite."

Uncle Alisdair appeared, his brow going from creased to relaxed as soon as he saw her.

"Here again, Mairi? Ye know, if you take to sleeping here, someone's liable to take your bed at home! Least that's what would happen to me."

She looked from one to the other, not knowing whether she was allowed to smile after being scolded. She looked down.

"All right, then?" Da asked again, looking her in the eye.

"Yes," she said. He straightened and put his hand out, palm down. She took it, and they walked back together. Uncle

Alisdair made a few comments about the work for the next day, but her da was mostly quiet for the few minutes it took to reach the cabin.

Grannie had the door open, her arms crossed over her apron. Once she saw them come round the corner, she went inside. Mairi wondered if she was angry at her too, but when she came in she saw Auntie Sheena and Grannie were both smiling at her, so she must've told Auntie she was safe. She felt worse now that everyone had been worried, and told her Grannie so.

"No harm done," she replied briskly. "And supper's better for the extra crispiness of the tattie scones." She smiled at Mairi, then waved the men off to clean their shoes. The smells of the kitchen—sweet and roasty and spicy and nutty—banished any memory of pondwater, and Mairi joined her aunt and grandmother at the table where they were serving soup into bowls and scones onto the trencher. She remembered the compliments someone had said about her mother's gravy, and started looking for the bowl of it on the table before remembering that her mother was no longer part of this circle. Gone to Heaven, or gone to ground, depending on who was asked.

Mairi swallowed and served herself. The men came back in and sat. A hurried grace. The rattle of spoons on crockery. The hot slide of sweetness down her throat. Tomatoes, a new tartness in the mixture, bought from a trader. And a restrained sort of hush to the whole affair. It heartened Mairi, for it finally felt as if she could sense her mother here. If only in the silent spaces.

June 1833, The Ridge

They'd tended to all four fields and finally took a short rest. Alisdair reread his favorite novel, *The Fortunes of Nigel*, in the shade of the tall oak tree by the cabins. He was just to the part where Nigel's faithful servant Richie leaves for Scotland in protest, telling him that his corruptors are laughing at him, when Morrissey came by with his bag. The postman touched his forehead in a casual salute to Alisdair, who waved back.

No post for him.

He remained on the soft lawn as the man ground-tied his horse, walked into the cabin, and came back out. They exchanged another silent wave-salute and Alisdair waited for the bustle that must be brewing inside. It must be for Sheena from Gordon. There was no other news they waited for. Soon enough, his theory was confirmed.

His sister opened the door and blinked as she looked around for him. Spotted. Her smile bid him sit up and pay attention.

"What have you got there, Sheena?"

"It's from Gordon, at last. He's arrived in Glasgow and had his meeting. He was to set off for the coast on the fifteenth of June. He may be there already." She smiled to herself, and sat down by Alisdair. She sighed, which Alisdair judged to be one of relief, not sadness.

"That's all right, then. Should have the place all ready for you. Does he send a date when he'll meet you, which ship you're to take?"

"Yes, he has: if I am well when I receive this, I should depart on the *Jean Hastie*. I am to travel with a Mrs. Hambly, to put his mind at ease." She smirked a bit as she said it.

"It leaves the second of July, from Halifax." She bit her lip. "It does not leave much time, does it? But then—"

Alisdair saw what she meant to say: she was ready. Ready to leave here, strike out on her own, build her own family. She just didn't want him to think she was glad to leave him.

"I suppose ye are ready," he said. "We never choose the timing in our lives, do we?" He looked away as he said it, realizing it could also be said about childbirths. He did not think she was ready to face another one of those quite yet, not after Letty's death, and losing her own child so quickly afterward.

Alisdair reached for her hand, put his underneath, as they used to do when he was a small boy, and she the older sister. Now his hand dwarfed hers, and sitting, he was still a good four inches taller. But she'd know what he meant. Sheena always understood.

They sat a moment together in the quiet warmth of the day before Sheena squeezed his hand and stood. She brushed off the dirt and leaves that clung to her dark gown as she went back inside, and Alisdair catalogued the days they had left.

Second of July. That left only two days here. Then Alisdair

would be the one to escort her into town and then to port, where she would, as Gordon had arranged, be met by a paid traveling companion.

Well, that's nice work if ye can get it. Go from one paying job to another, and be paid to make your way there. Huh. He'd never known people to do the like. People traveling alone... well, it was usually men, he supposed, or women with their families. Odd situation, that, when women were traveling alone. But in Sheena's case, he believed she'd have been fully capable of getting from one port to another without incident. But what did he know of such proprieties. Hidebound, he was.

He blew out a violent breath and lay down with the open book on his chest. So Sheena would leave. And so would he, by good God damn, eventually. Eventually. He would make use of this trip with Sheena to Halifax to speak with a few tradesmen and clerks and to see if he could get an interview, based on his references. That would do very well.

And thank you Sheena, for that parting gift.

"It'll be just the three of you for a wee while," Alisdair told Mairi, who sat next to him at table, the night before Sheena's departure.

"Three?" Her small, round face registered alarm.

"Aye, can you count who?"

They all sat together, five around the table, with steaming mash and barley cakes and trout smothered in mushrooms.

Mairi looked around. "Da's staying. And Grannie's staying.

And me." She turned to Alisdair and lowered her brow. "And you're staying, too!"

"I've got to help Sheena with her bags and see she gets off safely. Then I'll be back." He mashed his fork into the barley cakes busily so he could not see whatever pitying looks his mother or sister were giving him. They felt for his missed opportunity with King's. Neil didn't seem to register Alisdair's situation. Well, of course not. He'd buried a wife. Alisdair tried to have some compassion for his brother but he was so distant. Seven weeks and not much change in his behavior. Some slight inattention, lack of focus, was in evidence when they were together, but never in the fields, where he always seemed driven by the devil's own whip. No, he was having a hard time figuring out how to comfort his brother.

"Who am I going to get to dig up my beets, now?" his mother said, in an effort to distract Mairi from her bitterness over their departure.

"I will," Mairi replied, a little sing-song note in her voice. The girl loved beets, and her mother and grandmother had both grown them for her. Alisdair looked to Neil quickly.

"How is your patch coming along, Neil?" he asked.

"What's that?" As expected.

"Your kailyard, your vegetables. Are they doing all right? I haven't seen any of that—"

"I—I—dunno." Neil looked perplexed, and Alisdair wasn't sure whether it was the thought of the vegetable garden still being there or it being his responsibility that perplexed him. His eyes slid over to Mam, who watched Neil a moment, then replied for him.

"I've kept an eye on it, son. Some of the plants died back, but the roots will still be good eating. It's got good sun there, you know…"

Sheena said nothing, merely munched through her barley cakes. Neil nodded and started shoveling food again.

"Ye might teach the young one how to tend it, with the few days ye have 'til the first wheat is ready to cut." Mam nodded at Mairi. "I'm sure she's a fast learner, aren't ye, girl?"

"All right," Neil agreed.

Mam always had a way to bring them back to themselves. He looked at his mother as she nodded and spoke to Mairi, explaining about the seeds and the bolting and then singing John Barleycorn. She got Sheena to join in on the first verse of the song, and they laughed and laughed.

July 1833, The Ridge

The dread had been building in her all evening, and by the time she went to bed, Sheena didn't know how she'd face them all in the morning. She slept in the old cabin, between Mam and Mairi, and had to will herself fiercely to stay still so she would not wake one or the other. Mostly it was Mam waking and quietly pitying her that she could not stand.

Lying between them two, she felt stifled, muffled, frozen over. It wasn't their presence—no, that was rather comforting. It was this in-between stage. She'd already said her farewells, months ago, and got all choked up about leaving Mam. Now, here she was again, but eager to get out and be alone for a bit—couldn't stand being around all these people who cared for her, when she could only let them down with her weakness.

Where was the farewell for her babe?

Sheena tried to keep her chin up as she went through the routines another final time. Every time she felt her lower lip curl into a sob, she turned her head to cough once, violently, and that usually removed the desire to give in to the hollowness inside.

Mam saw it; she knew. Even now, she was probably feigning sleep to ease Sheena's mind. God, her throat ached with the withheld tears. Like there was a rising river starting at her breastbone and sloshing up the windpipe. Mairi didn't seem to notice. Neil, either. Poor things, she didn't know how well they would get along without Letty. No, they were too wrapped up in their own grief to cling to her. But Alisdair.

Oh, her moody younger brother was nothing if not observant. And she would have a day and a half journeying alone with him, during which she would have to keep a firm hold of herself. Sheena was five years older, but marriage, and miscarriage, made her feel as if she could be his mother. *How will our leave-taking go? How will we, as close as Neil and Muirne ever were, separate our lives into two indefinitely?*

At last, her eyelids grew heavy and she lost track of each minute movement of the straw beneath them. Sheena dreamt of ships and water and books and an ever-growing vine that circled the world. It curled around people's legs and tried to draw them into the ground, but Sheena woke just as it grabbed for her.

Mam was up—just up. She sat on the edge of the mattress and readied herself for the big push. Sheena watched from behind, amazed to see this woman as a complete stranger might: hardy, determined, but old. Some way to feeble already.

Mam balanced on two feet and reached to her right for her cane. Sheena rolled to her side and reached out an arm. Mam stilled as she saw her hand. Took three tiny steps to turn and look at her. Mam's face was wet with tears, and creased by a smile.

"Away with ye, then," Mam said in a rough whisper.

Sheena couldn't remember ever seeing her mother cry like that, with a smile on her face, except when she'd been laughing. It gave her a queer turn, it did.

"Ye're all right, Mam?"

A quick bob of the head, and three steps in the other direction had her walking away.

Sheena stayed in a stupor of feeling for another few minutes, coming back to herself when she heard the shed door clack to, as someone came back from an early morning privy visit.

A flash of waters rising and a vine at her legs pulling her tight before she remembered: leaving day. The torrent of emotion lodged in her bladder; she hurried into her dressing gown and out to the privy herself. She was a bit shaky, but a good breakfast would settle her down.

As Sheena returned to the cabin, the gorgeous sun warmed her dark hair and she sighed a little at the first glimmer of hope being allowed back into her thoughts.

Mairi refused to eat, but clung to Sheena's leg in an attempt to keep her from leaving. Sheena let it go on for a minute, with Mam cajoling her to come to the bench, until Neil interrupted.

"Mairi, take yourself off. At once."

Her dark head popped up at that tone of voice. She slunk to the bench, head low and penitent.

Once they had finished the meal and packed the leftover portion, Neil stood and held out his arms to Sheena.

"I've got a few things to take care of in the kailyard. With Mairi. We'll be off and let you away."

She walked into his embrace, feeling none of the affection and little of the warmth she knew her brother had for her. She put it away in her mind. She looked him in the eye.

"Until we see each other again."

"Yes."

Then, Mairi.

"Will I be an old maid when you visit next, Auntie?"

"Old maid? I should hope not! But I expect you will be very much taller. I shall miss sewing pretty patterns for all the skirts you shall outgrow."

She grinned, a new plot hatched. "But I shall write and tell you all about what I am doing!"

Sheena laughed. "Yes, that is a wonderful idea, Mairi. Thank you for that promise. I will wait for your first letter with pleasure." She looked at Neil at that, but he looked away.

"Come, then, Mairi." He beckoned with a hand, and she followed under his wing, sending a glance back before going out the door.

"Mam."

"Aw, do it quick and short, like Neil. I can't bear a long farewell."

But when Mam hugged her it was long, and full of desperate love. She felt the strength her mother put in it to help her on the voyage, in her recovery, in her journey to start over.

Finally, they parted. Mam gave Alisdair a quick hug and kiss as well, and the two went through the door, each carrying two small bags, Alisdair with another slung across him. They headed for the road and didn't look back.

Sheena kept her eyes on the well-traveled terrain. Sunlight covered the road, and showed in dappled slivers on plants bordering the road. It was not hard to find her footing, but she focused on the ground. Her hands clenched until she could feel the sharp snags of her nails digging into her palm. She measured her breaths, picking her way forward, feeling the rigidity finally start to relax in her spine. She needed this time before she could turn to her brother and form any sort of sentence without betraying the oppression of her feelings.

When they reached the part of the road that was more traveled by mail coaches, Sheena cast a glance at Alisdair.

"Happy to be coming to Halifax, Alisdair?"

His shocked look! She almost laughed. She! Laugh! At this moment!

"I don't—I haven't—What do you mean?" he spluttered.

"Well, aren't you going to use the trip to your advantage in some way?"

"That's not why I came," he said quickly.

"Of course it's not. But since you are going—"

"I haven't—I don't have a plan yet, other than to see if I can speak to any of the senior men at Wicke's or at some of the shipping concerns—the ones with connections to the Council of Twelve, the ruling elite in Halifax. See if they might hire me on."

"Shipping and government," Sheena murmured. "You've given up on the idea of university, then?"

Alisdair shrugged. "I don't like the idea of going so far away from the ridge—from home."

A jolt to her bowels, that. Sheena knew Alisdair's circum-stances were entirely different from hers, but she felt another tearing pain at the thought of all the distance she was putting between herself and her family. *Nevermind it*, she thought. *Think of Gordon and Scotland and a more rooted life.*

"Yes, well," she hedged. "That's true. But Alisdair, I know you wish to. I know you've the aptitude. You could even be a teacher yourself in a few years."

The look of surprise on his face made her smile. He creased his brow at the new thought. "But I'd still need to have higher qualifications than I do now."

"That's as may be, but there may be opportunities. Think of those, instead of the limitations!"

Alisdair chewed on his lip. "Is that how you're bearing up?"

Sheena went slack-jawed, arrested in her tracks. She dropped the bundles in either hand and brought her hands to her face. Had she not hidden it well enough? Was it inhuman of her to want to ignore it until she was away from everyone? She felt the rigidity flood back into her spine and wept in jerky sobs. Alisdair put down his bags as well and put an arm around her.

The violent coughs she had used to cut off each burst of tears had worn her throat ragged, and now the sobs tearing out of her castigated her with the pain she'd inflicted on her-self. This brother, who had seen through her wall of strength —how would she do without him? Could Gordon fill that role? She knew he was learning but now…she'd outdistanced him in experience yet again.

The urge to retch by the roadside left her abruptly and she leant on Alisdair, panting. He pulled a handkerchief from his pocket for her.

"Since when," she growled out, "do you carry." Cough, spit. "A handkerchief?"

Alisdair smiled slightly. "Since when am I going to the capital with my sister?"

Sheena stared at him. *The little upstart. The conniving*—but she laughed. And laughed. And felt such a change in the tides of emotion in her that her whole being flushed with the warmth of her blood.

He still had to support her, now because she was laughing herself silly. She should really rein it in. Oh, but she felt so giddy with the relief. But what relief would there be later? She was leaving him, leaving them all. She sobered.

As she wiped at her face with the handkerchief, they could hear the rumble of the mail coach. Alisdair ran back up the hill to flag it down, and by the time it stopped it was only a little ways past Sheena. Her brother jogged back to pay the driver for them, and the porter loaded their bags on the top. Alisdair retained the bag slung over his shoulder, as Sheena kept her reticule, a new thing she'd had only since marriage. They got in, nodding to the other passenger in the coach, a blond woman with a very smart hat. Sheena touched the back of her hair, wound up in its coil.

After the outflowing of so much emotion, Sheena was sure she looked a wreck, but as they didn't know the lady, there was a certain dignified silence she could keep in the coach until they reached New Glasgow and changed for the coach to Halifax. She'd been there once before, with Gordon for their wedding-clothes. She remembered how bumpy it was. Alisdair had never been. She looked at him as he sat across from her. How much he had in front of him. *Of course, so do I*, she reminded herself.

The discomfort from the ride was moderate, for which Sheena gave thanks. They stopped long enough in New Glasgow to have a quick meal with Muirne and the children, whose farewells Sheena undertook more easily. Muirne was doing well.

"Do be good, and stay well on the voyage," Muirne was saying as they embraced hurriedly. Sheena didn't need reminding that her experience on the voyage over had been fraught with sickness.

"I'm sure it'll be better, or at the very least, quicker!" But Muirne's expression of anxiety didn't change at the joke.

"Take care, Sheena. All my love, and the best of luck." Muirne embraced her one last time, then it was Alisdair's turn for good measure. They walked quickly back to the square where the post horses were kept.

"Almost left without ye," the driver scolded. "Come up, then. We're away."

They clambered in and were immediately thrown to one side as the horses swung around to head south. They sat across from one another, as the two other passengers took up half of each bench.

"Beg pardon," said Alisdair to the older woman next to him.

Sheena repeated the phrase, as she'd been thrown onto the younger woman seated beside her, and took the first of many deep breaths for the journey. Sheena's seat mate looked like she wanted to introduce herself, but did not dare in front of the other, more stoic lady.

It was a newer coach, with better sprung wheels, and she wasn't quite as uncomfortable as on the previous journey. They changed horses after eight hours, stopping at a mountain hutch with a large stable, lonely in the middle of forest. The passengers had a chance to stretch their aching limbs and nibble on the provisions they had brought before they were rounded up again. They took off in darkness, the horses finding their way more by footing than the lamps at the front, which seemed to be more for the driver's nerves.

Sheena felt the veneer of dignified silence replaced by a dream-like haze. She couldn't lay her head without it being slammed violently, but she could hold her head erect with eyes closed and allow the calm of the last minutes to settle over her thoughts. She wished she could sit next to her brother and feel his comforting solidness jostling next to her, instead of this empty space surrounding her. He was too far across even to hold her hand.

After another eight hours, another stop, another change at midnight. Sheena had a vague impression of people moving and lamplight sifting in, but she stayed sitting and felt the swaying recommence, prompting strange dreams. She gave herself up to fretful unconsciousness until the next stop, where she got out to use the privy at the back of the stable. When she realized the relentless light of midsummer had returned, she roused herself. The carriage was greeted by smells of smoke and sounds of habitation. She blinked her eyes clear of sleep.

"Are we there?" she said abruptly. The lady to Alisdair's right glared, the younger one next to her waking. Alisdair merely smacked his lips in sleep.

"Alisdair, are we there?" She kicked his foot neatly. He jolted awake, looking again at the two strange women in confusion. He remembered where he was and collected himself. *Goodness*, Sheena thought. *If he can be the next politician then so could I.*

He peeked around the curtain. "I dunno. Looks like a small enough town to me."

Sheena tugged a corner from her side. The view down the hill showed small wooden buildings, much like those in New Glasgow. The smell of the sea. And masts, she saw, over the roofs.

"I believe we are close," she said, letting go of the curtain.

They shared the last of the bannock crumbs and the maple candy they had packed. A few hours later the driver yelled to a comrade, the staggering pace slowed, and Sheena's numb limbs and bum seemed to buzz with the absence of it. She alighted carefully with the aid of the driver and took several awkward steps before finding her land legs. *Land legs*, she thought. *Oh dear. Three weeks or more on the sea. I do hope the movement of the new clipper is better than the carriage ride.*

The coach was at the very beginning of the docks, the coach's schedule managed so as to deliver the passengers just before departures. Some of the matelots were already coming to load the baggage onto the boat, which looked frighteningly small to carry any number of people across the vast ocean. Sheena turned to Alisdair to grasp his forearm. Sheena was vaguely aware of the ladies milling around beside her, and another lady approaching. Sheena hugged her brother ferociously, knowing the moment was come.

"I don't know why I'm being such a ninny now," she said. "I'm sure I'll see you soon. Braw lad." She sniffed and looked up at him.

"Aw, Sheena. You will. And I'll look after them. I promise."

The moment was interrupted by a presence at her elbow.

"Mrs. Lamont?"

Sheena drew back a half-step, releasing Alisdair. "Yes."

"I am Mrs. Hambly, your companion to Glasgow. How d'ye do."

"How d'ye do, Mrs. Hambly. This is my brother, Alisdair MacLean."

"How d'ye do, Mr. MacLean." She smiled coolly and dismissed him with a nod. Perhaps she was eager to be underway.

"Is there anything you need before we walk aboard, ma'am? Last privy on land? Last prayer to say?" There was a coy wit about the older woman which Sheena was not sure she liked. She shook her head.

One more clasp of Alisdair's hand before her boots hit the wood of the jetty.

July 1833, The Ridge

"But when?" Mairi demanded again.

"I don't know when, pet. By my calculation, he should be back tomorrow, but perhaps there are additional tasks for him to perform while he's in Halifax. It's a long journey to make, and he'll not get another chance soon," Grannie said, prodding Mairi's conscience with a raised eyebrow.

"I see." And she did see. Uncle Alisdair had More Important Affairs than helping her father on the ridge. She wondered about them, knowing that her gran was proud of Uncle's book-learning. "What's he going to be, Grannie?"

"Alisdair? Well, I can't say. He probably can't say right now, either, at that. But he's got a bright future, that's for certain."

"Do I have that as well? A bright future?"

Grannie stopped in her brushing and folding of the dried clothes and looked fully at her. "I 'spect you will, little Mairi. A smart lad for a father and a good woman for yer mother, with a solid farm at your back to support you—yes, I'd say you had a bright future as well."

Mairi beamed. Grannie's expression softened.

"Now go on and see if yer da needs anything in the field, why don't ye," said Gran.

Her father was spending the hottest hour of the afternoon walking the furrows, preparing for harvest by marking on a paper in his hand and counting days and ticking off his fingers. She didn't know that he needed anything, but without her uncle as deputy, she would try to be useful.

"Da! Is there anything I can fetch for you?"

"Mairi! Ah, wait a moment, like a good girl." He glanced across to the east and made a few more marks, then folded and shoved the paper into his pocket. "Now. Have you been pestering yer grannie, is that why she's sending you down here?"

"No, I'm being useful. Until Uncle comes back."

"Ah, of course." Da gave her a smile, one of those half-smiles that moved his chin and nose and cheek, but didn't reach his eyes. "Well, I've no mission for you, but thank you for asking." The smile disappeared.

"Do you know when Uncle is coming back?"

"I don't, Mairi. Soon. Why?"

"Well," Mairi needed her uncle as a link; he helped Grannie bring her father closer to her, made them feel like a family. "I want him to teach me to read."

This made her father blink a couple times. "Read? Well. I could—that is, tha's a grand idea. You already recognize the letters from the blocks, isn't that so?"

"Reck-o…"

"Recognize. It means you know all the letters. You'd know them if you met them, that is." Another grin split her father's face. She didn't understand the joke but smiled with him.

"A good idea. I'll find Alisdair's old books, the first primers, for you to practice on. And he'll help. Yes, a very good idea. But you know his first duty is to the land, just like mine." He seemed ill at ease with himself, turning this way and that to look in all directions before meeting her gaze.

"All right, then. Back to the cabin. Don't want you shriveling up in this heat."

Mairi blinked up at the tall shadow in front of her. She turned to go, feeling that her victory, her 'good idea,' had somehow gone wrong. She'd got what she wanted: more time with Alisdair when he returned. But she sensed she had lost something else without knowing to fight for it.

A frown clouded her expression as she reentered the yard where Grannie sat with the clothes.

"Ah! My Mairi. Would you carry these in there now like a good girl?"

She dutifully picked up the tall pile of folded linens and went into the dark cabin. She heard Grannie clunking her way in behind her.

"Sure, and I've not seen such a long face in a while," said her grandmother when she'd sat and accustomed her eyes to the dark.

You mean since Mam's funeral or the baby dying or Auntie leaving? Mairi thought, but did not dare speak. That would have been sass.

The place felt so still, at a time when the farm should be at its busiest. She hoped her uncle would return soon to enliven the place. Or Mrs. MacGregor! Why hadn't she thought of visiting their neighbors? Her heart lifted. She turned to ask permission but found her gran staring at her with a serious expression.

"It's no use sulking until he returns, Mairi. We will often be apart from those we wish to be near. But your character is set by how you act in such situations. You want to have a good character, don't you?"

"Yes, Grannie."

"Then sing some hymns for me. Or go out and thank God for the good weather. Or—"

"Yes, Grannie." And she shot back out into the sunshine. "Thank you, Lord," she mumbled glumly. Mairi thought of the lovely trees surrounding her mother's grave and how inviting they were, how protective as she lay there. But she mustn't go and fall asleep again; they'd never allow her to wander on her own again. Well, until she was at least ten. That seemed the magic age.

For now, she repaired to the byre, where she sat on the cool stone cross-legged and stared into the large, liquid eyes of Darien. Blackie mooed behind her. Darien's bell tinkled as she gave up the staring contest and lowered her great head to snuffle around the floor's leavings.

They'll see, Mairi thought. *I have a bright future.*

And she spent a solitary hour imagining all the bright things her future might contain: lamps, gold, white cloth by the yard, and a closet full of pure wax candles.

July 1833, Halifax

Alisdair bore the painful farewell with dignity, and saw his sister off with Mrs. Hambly—not the warmest woman he'd met. But then, perhaps it was crucial to her duties that she retain a distance from people. What did Alisdair know of paid companions? Nothing, of course.

After watching the boat ship anchor and be guided out of the harbor, he sought out a shabby inn, of which there were scores by the harbor, and secured a room. He changed into his best clothes, a suit of black worsted, and stuffed his other effects under the bed while he went out for the day. After gulping down spiced sausage and a crusty roll from the proprietor, he felt charged with energy. What could he not do, this day of freedom granted to him?

His first aim was the shipping companies, which was convenient as their offices were the closest to the harbor. He patted the left breast pocket of his jacket, where his reference lay. Alisdair approached a group of buildings on piers. The old wood rumbled with traffic at the nearer one to his left, while the farther one had no one about. Less than an hour after Sheena's ship passed out of harbor, and the place looks half-deserted. *Why is that?*

He raised a hand to a navvy passing.

"Excuse me, but is the pier usually this busy?"

"This? Busy?" the man said. "Slower and slower it gets, mate. And this is supposed to be high season."

With that dismaying but useful information, Alisdair nodded. The man touched his cap and went on his way. Alisdair proceeded to the busier building, and, since it seemed more like a shopfront than a place of residence, he steeled his nerve and thrust himself through the door. A bell tinkled.

Two men on either side of the narrow room sat on high stools, bent over thick bound logs of some kind. One faced him while the other craned his neck around to look behind. This man quickly dismissed Alisdair and turned back to his work. The other rose and sauntered toward him.

"Good afternoon, gentlemen. I'm here to inquire after a job."

"Afternoon, Mr. —?"

"Mr. MacLean."

"—Mr. MacLean. Is Mr. Wicke expecting you?"

"No, but I only happened to be in town suddenly, you see, and—"

"Quite." The man was several years older than Alisdair, in his mid- to late-twenties. Pale skin, light brown hair, the line of which receded to the top of his head, giving his face an open look even though he was frowning.

"Well." The man let a deliberate pause hang for a long second before continuing. "What line of work were you looking for, sir?"

Alisdair felt a little fizz in his chest at being called 'sir.' He stuffed it down to answer calmly. "I am seeking a clerkship. I'd heard that Wicke's was first in its field, and I believe my education has prepared me for quality workmanship. I've brought a reference from a—a professor in New Glasgow, where I went to school."

A small lie, a white one. Why not call a tutor a professor?

The man's eyes slid toward the clerk, who was no doubt listening, though he posed with his head turned to his page.

"Mr. Wicke is not in today, Mr. MacLean, but shall I leave your card?"

"Oh—no card. I've forgotten them. Do you expect him in later?"

"No, I'm afraid."

"Well, is he the one who makes all the hiring decisions?"

"Yes. Sir."

The man was building up steam, taking umbrage at Alisdair's mild insistence. He'd better go.

"Thank you, sir. Another time, then."

The man bowed slightly and turned his back. Alisdair did likewise. He got through the door, but it had not fully closed before he heard a howl of laughter behind him.

His heart shrank in its cage of ribs. *Idiot. Of course I should have written out cards.* He took a deep breath and walked slowly to the quiet pier. No one passed him. Indeed this wharf looked empty of all life and activity. Emboldened for a look 'round, Alisdair pushed at the door of the low warehouse.

Locked. He glanced around for lookers-on, saw no one, and cupped his hands around his eyes at the window. A vast dark stretch of ground yawned toward the back, where piles of rope and barrels lay stacked along the wall. *Tar, probably. Old storeroom, now in disuse. Must be really slow going these days*, he thought with some surprise.

He walked on, stopping in at Forbes', then Mitchell & Dexter's. He was finally seen by someone of importance at the last place.

"Well, Mr. MacLean, I have just lost a clerk today, so my mind is open. What do you know of ship cargoes?" asked Mr. Dexter.

"I know a little of trade, sir. And my mathematics are in top form. I'd like to be able to start at the bottom and learn as I go, make my way up, you see."

"All right. Let's see your reference." He took the offered note and unfolded it, not remarking on the oft-folded creases. His eyes scanned it quickly through spectacles then looked up to Alisdair. "This sounds very much like you are expected to go off to university. Was there trouble?"

"No trouble, sir. But the only university in Nova Scotia is Church of England, to which I do not belong, and I couldn't go farther out, not with my mother as she is, sir."

Mr. Dexter gave a small nod of acknowledgement. "I see. New Glasgow——that's where you're from, is it?"

"We've a farm just southeast of it, sir, which my brother manages very well."

Another white lie.

"Hm. Well, Mr. MacLean, I'd be inclined to give you a start, but I need someone right away, and I have to infer from your circumstances that you're not able to start right away, is that correct?"

Excitement and gratitude leapt within Alisdair's chest, quickly burnt to ashes.

"It is correct, sir."

Mr. Dexter measured his heavy tone and long face. "I'm afraid you'll have to wait and try again, young sir. Luckily, you've got plenty of time. Not yet twenty?"

"Nearly eighteen, sir."

"Ah, well, there you are! Plenty of time. Perhaps our interests will coincide more precisely when you come again." He rose to shake Alisdair's hand and sat back down, dismissing him.

Alisdair left, more miserable than when he'd been laughed at. Someone had given him a chance, but he couldn't take it. *Because of duties at home. Because of our circumstances. Because I've no father to run the farm. Because of Mam's stroke and debility. Because my sisters have both married and deserted us. Because—* Alisdair stopped the bitter stream of accusation. His mind was racing, as he stood there on the wooden sidewalk.

He had time. Another year might well see the farm flourishing. He'd made a promise to Mam. And Neil. And Mairi. Thinking of her wee, wan face softened his disappointment a bit. Well, if he couldn't accept an offer right away, he'd stop asking about employment: there was a lesson learned. So why not enjoy the rest of the afternoon?

Still in his good suit, he strolled away from the docks toward the high street, and made an effort to appear in good humor, with the world at his feet. First came whitewashed houses, then clapboard houses, then a commercial area where he could stop and look at all the window displays. Then came the finer houses and government buildings, in grey and white, marble and stone. His stomach began to rumble, and he looked around for a tavern or street-seller.

But this was Halifax, not Glasgow, and no street-sellers seemed to inhabit the place, at least in this posher part of the capital. He walked uphill a ways to satisfy his curiosity about the town plan. Viewing it from above, he enjoyed the sea and her gulls, the masts, and the large buildings just below that obscured all the little ones. *There's the truth*, he thought.

Something to the right caught his eye as he gazed. Red— brick? Sandstone? The clink of hammers on stone then caught his ear. Something worth inspecting up close, he thought, and turned to the west to descend the hill. In about a half-mile, he came upon the site, which was all movement, with more people than he could espy from the hillside.

One man in dusty white smock passed by him with a long barrow full of churning grey mud.

"Excuse me, what is this site to be?"

"School, mate. Big, bloomin' school. Old Dalhousie and Dr. McCulloch's pet project." He didn't take a hand away to touch his cap, but nodded and hurried on with his burden.

A university? Could it be? He stood watching the construction for a few moments, his mind racing, his body humming with the need for activity, some action to express his ridiculous hopes being raised again.

Alisdair backed away, crossing into the street to imagine how the whole building would come together. As he did so, there was a shout. He felt the wind of a passing vehicle, and the whip of a horse's tail as he jumped forward out of the road.

"Watch where you're going! Idiot!" the driver yelled. A bumping noise soon made him stop, however. Alisdair was about to apologize when he saw an older man—white beard and tall back hat—exit the carriage.

"I'm so sorry, sir." Alisdair directed his apology first to the elderly man, then glanced up at the driver.

"All right?" said the man on the ground, who also looked up to his driver.

"Aye, she's all right, Dr. McCulloch, sir. Not that a nasty scare can't take years off a horse's life!" He said this viciously in Alisdair's direction, then looked away, muttering to himself.

The older man ran his eyes over Alisdair's frame. "All right with you then too, young man?"

"Yes, sir. Fine, sir. Are you—are you Dr. McCulloch who owns the school to be built?"

"Owns! Ha!" The man gave a bark of laughter but kept his face stern. "I am the caretaker of this pile of rock, but not its owner," he admitted. "Why, are you interested in purchasing said rock?"

"Purchas—no! No, sir. I hope to go to university next year and I wondered if it might be open—"

"Is that so?" The man's blue eyes sharpened in on him. It wasn't a twinkle he saw there, but an eagle's eye, a gaze of predator on prey. But perhaps the man's beak-like nose called forth that aspect unfairly. The driver pulled away.

"Would you care to take lunch with me, young man?" He'd apparently made an abrupt decision in Alisdair's favor.

"My name is Alisdair MacLean, sir. And I would be honored to…speak with you over lunch."

"Very good, Mr. MacLean. Let us walk a way. There is a fine tavern on the street behind the courthouse. Yes, yes, this way."

Dr. McCulloch shepherded him along until they arrived at said tavern. They sat, and he ordered beef rolls for them both. A couple tankards of ale appeared quickly. Alisdair felt not a little dizzied by all this unexpected attention.

"Now then, sir. Why have you not applied to King's College? Why must you search the province for a rubble pile that is not yet ready to receive anyone?"

"I did try to apply. They refused to accept my application. On account of my religion."

Dr. McCulloch smiled shrewdly at that: a knowing, tired smile. "Of course they did. I know all of the men who sit on the committee, and not one would give a non-Church of England man the time of day."

"Is that why you're building a new school, sir?"

"Oh, the school's already built. That is an addition you saw today." He waved his hand in dismissal. "The real question is funds, Mr. MacLean. Funds for instructors, for materials. For fuel to keep scholars from freezing in their seats during the winter. The Council," and here he paused with emphasis on the word, "does not believe non-Church of England men need an institute of higher education. We Church of Scotland folk —you are Church of Scotland, are ye not?"

Alisdair let that pass without committing himself either way. He clutched the tankard for a long sip.

"Yes, well. We should be happy to continue to receive our instructors from Scotland, where they are already watched and spied-upon, so that the colonial government here may not be put to the trouble of doing the same!"

Alisdair's face must have shown some shock, for Dr. McCulloch quieted his temper.

"Excuse the outburst, Mr. MacLean. When you have been fighting for something for over twenty years, having it almost within your grasp so many times…"

The beef rolls arrived at that moment, and Alisdair was again surprised to see the older man dive in with fork and knife. With relish. What an interesting man, a man of intense energy. He could well imagine what such a man might have done in his earlier years.

Alisdair likewise dove in, chomping hungrily down on the meat and bread.

"Is there anything to be done about the Council, then, sir?"

The man's face grew serious, and he chewed more slowly. "Anything to be done. Besides abolish it, you mean?"

Alisdair scanned the room, anxious lest someone should hear such seditious talk. Dr. McCulloch watched him appraisingly.

"Mr. MacLean," he finally said. "I am a man of some posi-tion in this colony, despite my enemies in Government. If you wished to study with me in the interim, while I am politicking to get the school opened, you would be in good stead to matriculate when it opens. What do you think of that?"

Alisdair had no idea why the man would show him such pointed favor. He grasped for a motive as he tried to show his gratitude at the offer.

"Sir, you are very generous. I would no doubt be in your debt—but I can not pay fees. My family own a small farm on the other side of the island. We've only been here ten years, but—"

"Ah, I know the story. Your story. My story. Many people's story. My fellow countrymen's story." He glared at Alisdair then dropped his gaze. "It is that very discrimination, my boy, which I hope to do away with. If we stand on equal footing of opportunity, what can we not do, eh?"

His voice was quiet as he spoke thus, and Alisdair guessed that such talk was considered more dangerous for overlisten-ing than that of doing away with the Council. So this was a patriot? A reformer? A Radical? Alisdair still felt unsure where or how to place him.

"Do you have an idea of when you might open your… university, sir?"

The man waved the hand with his fork irritatedly. "Could be next year, could be a decade from now. Politicians are fickle. One never knows when they might respond to the sting of the gadfly."

Ten years? He could not wait that long to start his career. But a year of interim study might place him well enough, and Neil may recover well enough by then, and—

"Would you be available for the course of university study I want to initiate—" the man's eyes scanned the tavern's roof, "—the fourteenth of November?"

The exact date was a surprise, but Alisdair ducked his head and replied with some hesitation. "I would welcome such a program, sir. But I must consider my responsibilities at home. My mother recovers from a fit from some years ago, and my brother has just lost his wife this year. Things are…a bit muddled."

"Of course. Of course, no decision made in haste. Here is my address. You may write to me when you return. We shall see what to do about you, Mr. MacLean." The man gave another fleeting smile, shook out his napkin from his lap, and tipped his hat.

"Good day, Mr. MacLean. It was a pleasure to dine with you."

Alisdair rose hurriedly to bid him good day, then sat down again as the man disappeared from the tavern. Alisdair was sweating at the hairline, the drops sliding down his cheek and the back of his neck. Hastily he wiped away at his face with his handkerchief. He finished his beef roll slowly, considering his extraordinary circumstance, and whether it be good luck or some sort of trap.

The man behind the bar came by to tell him his meal was paid for. Alisdair rose in a daze, took a step, remembered to go back and pick up the card on the table, and left. Though it was only five o'clock, he made his way back to the dilapidated inn and lay back on his rented bed. He lay for hours before getting up to change out of his good suit. His traveling clothes back on and his bag packed, he finally fell asleep. He woke stiffly in his sweat-soaked and hardened clothes at the knock on the door.

"Coach is come, sir. They leave in ten minutes," a woman called outside his door.

"Thank you," he called back without thinking.

He took his seat in the coach hurtling through the dark, and turned his fortune over in his hands, attempting to scry the right path.

July 1833, Atlantic Ocean

Sheena had the same trouble as before adapting to the rock of the ship: she was ill for five days. By that time, the *Jean Hastie* was out in the high seas, cutting through the water like fine shears through silk. Sheena left her cabin and was immediately joined by Mrs. Hambly, who had seen to her needs while indisposed. She hadn't shown much solicitude, but fetched and carried and rinsed and fed with a brusque efficiency.

Still, she was a companion, not a sick nurse, Sheena thought. And had she been stronger and not still recovering from the loss of the baby, she might have responded better to the sea. Perhaps the woman thought her weak and worthy of contempt. Sheena put such unpleasant notions out of her head. She followed the woman, who matched her in height and frame, as they ascended the steep stairs to the passenger deck.

"Do you know our location, Mrs. Hambly?"

"I'm afraid I don't, missus."

"What about our orientation?"

"Orientation, missus?"

"Never mind." She asked one of the sailors in white passing by, who gave her more information than she was prepared for. But generally, she understood they were a quarter of the way there.

She spent the remaining two weeks restlessly walking the deck, sleeping fitfully, and trying to ignore the presence of Mrs. Hambly, who would neither be drawn out nor contribute readily to a conversation.

Once they began to sight land, she felt the thrill of both anticipation and doubt. Fear worked its way into her chest to stop her breath and into her bowels to cause all sorts of flutterings. They stopped in the port at Liverpool, but only for eight hours, and passengers not departing at Liverpool were not allowed off. Sheena stayed at the railing, gazing out at the harbor and all its people scurrying, crawling, hurrying through their day.

Another two days brought them to anchor finally in Greenock. A porter brought her bags out and placed them in a pile around her, as she stood to one side of the line of people debarking. Mrs. Hambly was a few minutes behind her, carrying her own large carpetbag. She dropped it at her feet with an exhalation.

"You intend to wait with me until Mr. Lamont's family finds me?"

"Yes, missus. I am to deliver you safely into the hands of your family." She smiled briefly, the far-away gaze avoiding her eyes.

"And how are you to be paid, Mrs. Hambly? Did my husband—"

"Oh yes, already paid me when he left, missus. Not to worry."

Sheena settled in to wait. She had no clue whom to look for. Someone resembling Gordon? But then he had no siblings, only cousins, and second cousins, in this area.

For a moment she thought of the Turners, and her sister's struggle to gain respect from her husband's family. How low his father had considered their family. Would she face a similar disregard here? As the minutes ticked by, her stomach, accustoming itself to land motion again, started to ache. It wasn't hunger, nor yet was it indigestion. She laid a hand on her waist, and took a deep breath.

When the long line of people had disappeared, Sheena saw a tall, broad woman coming through the crowd. She limped a bit but projected an image of strength. Broad shoulders, a bold red and blue checked dress and blue bonnet, and a reddish face that turned this way and that, looking for someone. *That must be her*, Sheena thought. *But who? How do I even call out to her?*

She waved a hand gingerly. The woman's attention was caught and she narrowed her eyes at the pair of them before hobbling over.

"Mrs. Lamont, is it?"

"Yes, that's my name. And you are of Gordon's family?"

"Yes, ma'am. Mr. Lamont is my mother's cousin. I'm up from Motherwell with my husband to see you to Ardkinglas." She said it a bit gruffly.

"I hope it isn't too much of an inconvenience," Sheena said, for courtesy's sake.

"Eh, no. We're both out of work." The woman swung her

gaze to Mrs. Hambly. "And you're the companion. Well done. You can be off on your business, then."

Mrs. Hambly nodded. She shook hands with Sheena and wished her luck, in a perfunctory way. *Where is the heart of these people? Are they all merely business transactions waiting for a bit of bread?*

But she smiled at the large woman. "And what is your name?"

"Marjorie Clemons. Let's get you sorted, then." She swung two of Sheena's heavy bags up, her shoulders pressed down into an even more triangular shape. Sheena's smile faded, and she hurried to scoop up the remaining bags and follow the red and blue check through the milling crowd. They went about a quarter mile before stopping at a warehouse. A large wagon stood by, with a man in his shirt sleeves and a chestnut horse with its head down to graze.

"Hello, Mr. Clemons!" the woman shouted. He grimly pursed his mouth.

"How d'ye do, Mr. Clemons," Sheena ventured. He looked over at her, scanning briefly down and up. *He's out of work*, she thought. *Surely there's some bitterness in his situation. We'll make allowances for discourteous behavior. His wife at any rate seemed unfazed and more matter-of-fact.*

The two women settled themselves in the bucket of the wagon, facing each other. Marjorie seemed to stare at Sheena's chest, until she felt compelled to look down to see if something was amiss.

"Gotcher there," said the woman promptly. Sheena looked

up. She was smiling wide, a sort of delight spreading across her face that Sheena associated with a child. She felt a little wild, trusting herself to these people. *But I am no better. Whenever wild folk come to the city they learn new manners. These are Gordon's family, helping him out. I must be forbearing.*

The trip to Ardkinglas took four long days and nights. They camped on the road once, the women staying in the wagon while Mr. Clemons slept on the ground. They bunked with families two nights near Loch Lomond, where Sheena could distract herself from the company with the beautiful views over the water that made her ache for home.

And the last night they stayed in an actual inn, in Inverary. The exchange at the ship had happened so fast, Sheena had only remembered that she should send Gordon a letter of her arrival the second day on the road. At the inn, a willing messenger was found and dispatched that evening to give him at least a day's notice.

When their wagon finally arrived back at the sea, Sheena felt a clutching at her breast as if sobs wanted to tear out of her. She made a small noise of distress, trying to keep it in, as she raised herself to look more fully down the slope to the see the expanse of water she could hear crashing onto the rocks.

"Firth of Lorn," said Marjorie, ignoring the noise she'd made.

"Yes," Sheena breathed. She'd looked at maps that Alisdair had studied. Had gazed and gazed at their home island, and she knew the Firth of Lorn separated the mainland from Mull. She saw some dark specks along the horizon but couldn't be sure it was Mull. The mist over the water played tricks on her. And the wind was picking up, lashing locks of her hair into her eyes.

They passed over a stone bridge and descended into a village. The wagon slowed to a stop, and the driver craned his neck in all manner of ways to look about him. "Ah!" burst from him finally, and he jumped out of the wagon. His lively steps took him toward the building on the corner, with a sign swinging in the wind. It was bleached and faded, but as Mrs. Clemons motioned her to follow her husband, she drew closer and could discern perhaps the outline of a pig.

"Are we meeting—"

But the door was open and she was thrust into the noise and light of many lamps and a good two dozen people talking in a mood made merry with drink. Mrs. Clemons' hand was on her shoulder guiding, or pushing, her forward along the right wall toward another doorway. Sheena had a fleeting worry for her luggage out in the wagon unguarded, then she was through the door, into the dining room, and Gordon's lovely face was right over hers as he embraced and kissed her.

"Oh, my dear," he groaned. "I am so glad to have you safe."

"Gordon!" The shock of seeing him so suddenly made her feel faint, and his embrace tightened around her as she swooned. A shaky breath slid out and she hugged him close. Recollecting where they were after a moment, she peeked around his shoulder to look at the dining room. It was empty except for two men talking on the other side of the room. Sheena smoothed her dress. Her legs were still wobbly from sitting in the wagon so long. She stretched her back as covertly as she could and reached up to cup Gordon's jaw in her hand. "I am glad, too."

"Everything went all right? With Ms. Hambly and the Clemonses? I've so much news to tell you, but I must assure myself of your health before I proceed with any of it." He glowed with his tidings.

"Just a mite sore from the travel," said Sheena gamely. "And I might use the privy before you start…"

Gordon laughed. "Of course! It's twenty paces out the back. I'll fetch your luggage. We'll stay here the night and proceed to Ardkinglas in the morning."

She nodded, anxious to relieve herself and let him dismiss the Clemonses. The evening wind whistled as she walked unsteadily to the back. She exited the privy and peered westward, where the dark blue of the twilight touched the darker blue of the water. *Home*, Sheena thought. *I'm finally home.*

Gordon's news was that all had been made ready, the gentleman who was his employer had much work to be done that was exactly in Gordon's way. They were guaranteed the house for two years and promised nineteen shillings a week, with the possibility of improvement after six months.

Sheena enjoyed the glow from her husband's face as he told her all this with pride. They didn't speak much of others that night, falling into each other again shyly, first for comfort, then with a surprising amount of energy, at least on Sheena's part. Their union hurt like the first time with him, a short searing fire, then numbness, then the dribbling back of sensation.

In the morning, Sheena rose slowly to wash and dress, her aches and pains from the journey magnified after their lovemaking. Gordon whisked through his ablutions, darting about the room to rearrange his effects.

"Hurry, Sheena! I want to make a smart entrance onto the estate this morning. It will take less than an hour to arrive there. I'll have them ready the horses." He smiled quickly before disappearing downstairs to the bar and dining room. *Would the proprietor even be up yet?* She doubted it. *But maybe, for the Laird's representative.*

Horses. *Oh, God.* She'd never learned to ride a horse. She'd only been on one a few times in her life, under periods of strict emergency.

As she descended the stairs, she spied no one in the dining room, but low voices drifted from the bar room adjacent. She stood at the doorway and quickly saw Gordon wasn't there, either. She tried the street front; there he stood, saying something to the boy holding their horses.

"Gordon?" she called. "I'm afraid I never—"

"What is it, my lovely woman?" He came closer to her, grinning down from his full head of height advantage.

"I can't ride properly," she whispered.

His eyebrows went up.

"Oh," he said.

"Yes, oh," she agreed.

"Well, we shall go slowly and I shall help accustom you to the practice."

What else could she do? She shrugged her shoulders, settling a little flutter of nervousness in her stomach.

"How do I get up on it?" she asked quietly.

"Charlie, bring the little one over to the block, please."

The inn's stable boy led the smaller horse over to a two-step stair. *Ah. Easy enough.* His expression was carefully blank. He must have heard her, or read her hesitation. *Well, it did not matter now. Just hold on to your dignity. And the horse.*

She stepped into the stirrup and hooked her knee around the place where her leg went. She took Gordon's instructions, glancing at his saddle.

"Why is yours so different?"

He looked shocked for a second. "Because ladies can't ride *astride.*"

She watched how his waist and legs moved as he urged his own mount forward and back to come alongside her, and concluded that no, it probably wouldn't be proper to have her legs doing something similar. Not in view of everyone. Not even in a full skirt.

"We'll get you a riding habit and give you lessons," Gordon said happily. "You've got good balance already. Now…"

They set off for the estate, the luggage having been sent forward by wagon last night. Gordon spoke in low tones to her most of the way, commenting on how she sat, where to look, what to pay attention to. As the horse moved, she lost some of her fear of the giant animal, rather liking the slow rolling of bone she could just sense below the hard leather.

A short hour later, she had managed to trot for a few steps and had not fallen off. She was a bit seized with panic but quite ready to try it again soon. They came to a view of a loch and turned right. Sheena rode with her neck craned to the side, glimpsing every now and then a view of the far shore, where white buildings were visible.

"That," said Gordon proudly, "is Loch Fyne." Sheena gazed through the many trees and flowers, vines seeming to creep across every living surface. They came to a neat house with creamy plaster and a central peaked roof with two chimney stacks, smoke curling from both.

"We are very close to the Laird's house now," Gordon said. "And shall stop here after presenting ourselves."

"Who lives here?" Sheena asked quietly as they passed.

"We do," Gordon replied, grinning.

Sheena looked back. A very solid house. Two stories! And fires already stoked for their arrival. A track leading to the front door. A thriving vegetable garden of greens shooting into the sky. Large buckets and troughs out back next to a pump— *good gracious*. She craned her neck again to see more as her horse continued up the path.

"Oh!" She smiled almost tearfully at her husband. She couldn't wait to enter. "But we are going to see the Laird first?"

He nodded.

"And I'm presentable? I won't smell of horse?"

"Not too much, after only an hour in the saddle."

She took a deep breath and raised her eyes skyward in exasperation at his teasing, and saw the bluest sky, the arch of mature trees, and the drift of an eagle, high, high up. She gaped; Gordon glanced up to see what held her attention.

"An eagle! What a happy coincidence."

They continued another half-mile to the estate house, which spread to their left as a solid mass of masonry with a motif of peaked dormers. The modest approach was on a path of whitish sand, in between decorative sections of lawn, with a fountain at the center. The scent of the honeysuckle wrapped around the entrance gates tickled Sheena's nose.

"Isn't it lovely," she murmured.

They rode to the back courtyard, where they were met by grooms to take their horses.

"Thank you, Davey."

Sheena nodded mutely to her groom.

Inside the back door was a servants' parlor to the right, and a gun room to the left. They were made welcome by the housekeeper, a Mrs. Slant.

"You just go on right ahead, Mr. Lamont. He's receiving in his study, and has time for a brief visit."

Sheena straightened her bodice and patted her hair, useless gestures of nervousness. A footman led them through the central hall, which was beautiful and simple, to the study. He announced them as they were ushered through the door. Sheena had an impression of rich reds and blues before her feet found the rug and she was staring at the Laird of Ardkinglas.

"Good morning, sir. May I present my wife, who is just arrived."

She dropped into a curtsy, her eyes down, then raised them solemnly to see quite a young man, pale-haired with deep-set eyes, behind a solid oak desk. He sat crookedly on his leather armchair, one leg over the side, as he leaned toward the opposite end of his desk. She did not betray her surprise at this informality with anything more than a movement in her throat.

"Sir," she echoed.

"Ah. And you had a good journey, I trust," he said. His eyes didn't leave the sketches in front of him.

"Yes, sir. Thank you," she answered as gently as she could.

"You'll be helping Lamont in some of the organizing of the ladies who work at the loch. Have you told her yet, Lamont?"

"No, sir."

"Well, should do. Everyone must earn their keep." He smiled, a curl of nastiness breaking the facade of disinterest.

"Of course, sir." Gordon's voice behind Sheena sounded neutral. Unruffled.

"I suppose we shall have a welcome supper in the house, now that she's come and is meant to be a retainer."

The man's cavalier contempt and backhanded courtesy struck a nerve in Sheena. She could feel her pulse quicken in response as she gazed downward, drew a constricted breath.

"That would be most kind of you, sir."

Please, let us be gone.

"We shall await the invitation with pleasure. But now, we must settle in, and I must show Mrs. Lamont her new home."

She heard the Laird sniff. "Of course. Carry on."

She curtseyed again and they crept quietly out the door. She turned her head to look at her husband once it closed behind them. His gaze was shuttered, contemplating something. She waited until they had made it back to the gun room vestibule.

"Gordon," she said, her voice wobbly, "Is he usually——? Did I——"

Gordon placed himself in front of her and placed his palms on her shoulders. His eyes drifted down to the top of her bodice. She watched as his gaze turned gentle.

"Don't worry, Sheena. You were perfect. I know it must be a shock to your hardworking soul, but many of the people I work for have been similarly…indifferent. They are busy, or worried, or——" his voice sunk to a whisper, "——just plain indolent. It is we who will help this estate run smoothly, and that is both a privilege and an opportunity."

Sheena turned his words over in her head. "Let's go home," she said.

He tucked one of her hands in the crook of his arm and led them out into the daylight. Gordon steered them in the direction of that delightful house they'd passed on the way. Their house. As soon as they could not be overheard, Gordon spoke again.

"He is absent most of the time. He spends a good portion of time in Glasgow managing his overseas enterprises, and there's the season sitting in Parliament in London. He doesn't like to travel abroad much, but we can expect to see him at most two months out of the year. I am charged with managing his local contracts, tenants, and commerce, including the mill, fisheries, and relations with his various Campbell relatives. And they—" He cocked his head to emphasize the name. "They are the people of most consequence in the area. It may be I shall find advancement in one of their concerns farther west." He took a few steps, his brow furrowed and lips puckered, and Sheena saw him playing through the possibilities in his mind.

"I see. And what was the part about my organizing ladies on the loch?"

"Oh, one of the ways they feed the workers—make them catch their own supply of fish. It is a small operation to preserve salmon and trout and mackerel and such for winter. There has been some difficulty with some of the women, and I agreed you could inquire about suitable requirements when you made your rounds to meet the families."

He smiled, and Sheena allowed herself a smile back, meanwhile wondering why the women had been difficult. She wouldn't go looking for trouble, not when she was close to realizing everything she'd dreamed of since a child: being back in Argyll, almost in view of her own dear island, with a strong, able husband and his secure position. And a house! It came once more into view, emerging from the ferns and green boughs as though in a faerie story. *This, at least, I can enjoy. Right now.*

August 1833, The Ridge

The reprieve was over; Alisdair was back at the farm again, and without the sister who understood him best. Their sleeping arrangements became fluid, with Mairi gravitating more toward the big cabin, and Neil more often sleeping alone in the smaller cabin. Mam talked with him sometimes at night, but Alisdair didn't approach his brother for fear of the powder keg that might blow if he hinted at any type of neglect.

No, Alisdair stayed away from his brother except in the fields as they harvested the oats. He spent more time around his niece, just being near while she played out-of-doors, and prodding her with questions when she made grandiose pronouncements.

"No more going to town. Everyone should stay here with Grannie and me."

"But how would we get our tea? And our fish? And grind our grain? You know yer da goes down to New Glasgow with the winter wheat to make our flour. You don't want any more bread and cakes?"

"No…"

"I thought so. We do have to travel sometimes for important reasons, Mairi."

"But why travel and never come back?"

"Well." Alisdair chewed his lip. "Yer auntie got married and her husband had to go back for his job—he's an important man, is Gordon."

Mairi's lip still jutted out stubbornly. He wasn't going to win her over on this one easily. Probably because he didn't understand Sheena's desire to go back over the ocean either. He hoped she would write them and stay close; he wished Gordon success but couldn't imagine crossing the ocean again for a mere job. He caught himself: *Aye, and making a living for one's family is surely important, but I'll find a different way than leaving.*

Another day Alisdair mended a part of the byre wall that had been eaten away by the years of dirt and ice gnawing at the wood. Mairi worked in the vegetable garden a stone's throw up the hill, gathering the beans and leeks, exclaiming when she smelled a melon that was ready.

"A melon for Grannie! This is a good 'un!"

She hoisted aloft the prize, and Alisdair looked up to shout in reply. "A big sweet find!"

Mam poked her head out to investigate, her cane in the right hand to steady her progress over the dirt.

"Come here with that, Mairi—let me see."

Mairi scampered awkwardly with the weight in front of her, and Alisdair recalled Sheena's awkward waddle when she was pregnant. He frowned. Mairi was the bright star of their little circle now. Without Letty or Sheena, the men were too stalwart and Mam didn't have any women to talk with. He wondered whether hiring an extra hand or two might not be a good solution.

Clearly, Neil wasn't in a place to consider remarrying yet. But if they could get a good laborer for the fields, perhaps with a wife to help Mam, Alisdair could perhaps take up Mr. Dexter's offer, or accept a position with Dr. McCulloch. He considered all the ways this might help their situation, as well as some of the dangers. He knew Neil would be stubborn, and so prepared his rebuttals for several days before posing the possibility to him.

Where would he find a labor for hire? In town. Maybe better in Pictou than New Glasgow, as new arrivals were still coming by ship. He could offer them the smaller cabin and a contract of a couple years, while he was away. It was the third week of August already, so he'd have to start making inquiries immediately if he wanted help with the final barley harvest and the processing.

He wrote to Muirne and Edward right away, asking for them to check with the grocer in Pictou if there were a couple that were looking to hire out soon. Then, all his arguments marshaled, he waited til the end of a day of planting the winter wheat.

Neil was silent as usual, wiping his brow with his sleeve. They stood in the shade of the apple trees and gulped down the water from their ceramic jugs.

"Hard work for just the two of us, eh, Neil?"

Neil frowned as if at a tasteless joke.

"I've been thinking about the barley, Neil, and how it might be better if we hired out this autumn."

"Hired out?"

"Aye—had someone to help us. Our family isn't enough to cover all we've planted alone, and we can afford it with the sale of the oats and some of the barley. And Mam—"

"The only reason we wouldn't be enough is if you wanted to bolt."

"Well, I might do more good if I did, y'know."

"More good for whom? For you? Oh, aye," Neil said with sarcastic vehemence.

"No, I mean I wish to study the law and fight for what's right. Against the people who always have their thumb on the scale, like Brown."

Neil considered that, twisting his hand over the lip of the jug. Alisdair hoped mentioning the man who'd ordered their father beaten to death would work to his advantage rather than sink Neil into the low spirits he'd maintained for months after the sham trial. When Neil spoke, it was in a soft, controlled voice.

"I just don't think you haring off like Gillan is going to come to any good. Mam needs—"

"*Haring off?* Da was not escaping from us—he was trying to find a better life! And just because you and he had a different opinion, does not mean he deserved to die!—"

"—Of course he didn't deserve it, Alisdair—that's not what I meant—"

"—And Mam needs help—more help than Mairi."

"What do you mean by that?" Neil's voice had gone from placating to sharp.

"She's getting older, and not improving her left side… she's still doing all the cooking, with no one around during the day. I'm worried something will happen while we're out in the fields. I was hoping we could find a couple to hire out—a man for the barley and a woman to help with the preserving for the winter."

Neil grimaced, which Alisdair read as an attempt not to cry. He felt bad for his brother, losing Letty and all the future plans they had conjured up. But they had to face reality as it was now.

"Mairi can learn and be a real help in two or three years. But ye can't expect her to do the work of an adult."

"Don't tell me how to raise my daughter!"

Alisdair looked away. He could hear the tears in his brother's eyes.

"There is no call to invite strangers onto the Ridge. We will manage just fine. Just need to get through this year."

Alisdair took another gulp of water to fill in the silence.

"We can scale back the barley and winter wheat if necessary. We'll stay together, Alisdair."

The words again reminded him of Neil's accusation that he was just escaping family responsibilities as Gillan had. He felt the flame of rage and shame at the reminder from his brother.

Just another year. It's what Dr. McCulloch says; it's what Neil says. Well, then. I shall give it another year.

August 1833, Ardkinglas

The first month flew by for Sheena in a rush of new names, routines, expectations, and pleasures. The well-appointed house was provided with a housekeeper: a widow at forty-three, Rhoda helped them settle in. She had a spare frame, bright blue eyes under swept-back black hair, and a gentleness about her. She had no children, and when her family had succumbed to the flux in 1829, she'd been hired as the house-keeper for the factor's house. She'd been there ever since, through three different factors. Sheena noted her efficient habits in the kitchen and blessed her stars to have such help.

Sheena visited all thirty-one families living on Ardkinglas estate. She tried but failed to remember all eighty-three chil-dren's names. But the families of the eight women who worked at the salt barrels: those she could recite. She learned of the seasonal work underway, how the women worked quickly because the faster they put up the Laird's quantity, the sooner they started on their own larders, as allowed by their tenancy rights.

The first couple of weeks, Sheena listened intently with a smile on her face, learning the ropes. Most of the women dwarfed her in stature, their powerful arms reaching past her face almost making her eyes goggle. But a few were as runty as she was, and made their worth known by declaring with pride the number of fish gutted each day. Although Sheena enjoyed the rough camaraderie, for the sake of Gordon's ambition, she stayed carefully respectable and didn't join in the lusty work songs. She was meant to learn the process and manage the accounts, that was all. She marked the women's tendency to gossip, and that Rhoda's name was bandied about rather dismissively.

By the end of July, with the season well underway and the Laird's salmon accounted for, the men started bringing in creels full of sea trout with smiles on their faces, and Sheena could see the interactions among the women and their husbands. One woman named Rose was there only part-time, on account of her duties as the village midwife. As the women cleaned up the small workshed for the evening, Sheena saw a chance to ask her about the difficulty Gordon had mentioned one Saturday.

"Rose, come here for me, will you?"

"All right, there, missus?"

"Yes, Rose. Just come sit for a moment."

Rose was one of the sturdier ones; when she sat down on the barrel in front of Sheena, Sheena found herself leaning back to look up at her.

"There's two more good months of this work, is that right?"

"Aye, missus. And mostly for ourselves, although when the crab and the mackerel come along, the House will have their share of them as well."

"Of course. And it's not too hard, is it? You have that special salve to help heal the cuts?" Sheena gestured to Rose's forearms, which were covered with half a dozen nicks from fish scales, slathered with a milky-white salve.

"Aye, that's Mellie Coates who does for us, a right good job. Heals in a day or two. Good, cuz they only ever get the Sunday off for Kirk." Rose looked back and nodded to some of the women who were leaving by the door, laughing and chatting.

"True. So, I was wondering, why did some of the women leave at the beginning of the season, if it's such good work?"

Rose's attention came back to Sheena and her expression darkened. "I canna be talkin' ill of those women, missus. It weren't their fault, and they done well as they could, is all I can say."

"But they left the Laird in a lurch, didn't they, at the beginning of June?"

"And didn't he just do the same!"

Rose's voice had got high, almost the whine of a dog that doesn't want to abandon its master. Sheena kept her voice low and gentle. "What do you mean?"

"They were sisters, two of 'em, and Katherine their mother. Daft clod probably never realized they were two different girls. In the same house every night. Katherine out visiting her sick—no, I'm not tellin' no more o' this, missus. They was sore done by, that's all, and had to go away, for the shame of it, is all. Weren't no trouble at all, with us."

Rose's eyes shifted all around the dark interior of the

workshed, and her legs swung her body to and fro on the barrel, obviously uncomfortable. Sheena blinked and closed her mouth after the recitation, astonished and not, at the same time.

"Of course, Rose. It's no matter, I just wanted to understand, and now I do. Thank you."

Rose twisted her hands together some more before ducking her head in acknowledgement.

"And I meant to ask about Rhoda, as well. I heard—well, some of you said she was wicked for not coming to Kirk. There were some remarks that sounded even jealous—"

"Jealous! Of Rhoda Sudbury! That'd be the day. No, missus, nobody's jealous of your housekeeper. She doesn't mix with us, though. So we can say what we like, can't we?"

The woman shrugged, the light of cruel sport glinting in her eyes. Sheena remained stern.

"No, I daresay if you listened to the minister's sermons, you'd know otherwise."

"The minister! Pah!"

Sheena saw such contempt there that she let it go.

"There has been a visiting preacher for the past month, but he left last week, isn't that so?"

"Aye, missus, you'll be hearing our regular minister tomorrow, if ye go."

"Of course I'll go, Rose. See you in the morning."

Sheena walked home the half mile in a grim mood. Should she confront Rhoda about the gossip? *No, better just observe. She seems a good woman to me and I wouldn't like to upset her with such prattle.*

So the Laird had got two sisters with child. And they and their mother had fled the neighborhood in shame. Even strong working women, and they hadn't been able to defend themselves. She wondered what could stop such a man. Clothes? Manners? Threats? Cold steel? She wondered if Gordon knew about the Laird's wandering eye.

She arrived at the door and relaxed a couple notches, grateful again for this comfortable abode. It was humid outside, and the coolness inside was a relief. She went through the parlor to greet Rhoda, who stood by the back fire, where the cooking pot took pride of place.

"Evening, Rhoda. Potage coming along?"

"And the greens how you like them, and the brown bread getting nice and toasty." Sheena sniffed appreciatively and gave her a quick smile.

"I'm so glad you know where to find that wild mustard…"

"And so frustrated I won't tell you where? Sorry, missus. Can't."

"Then I won't tell you when I find a grove of the most perfect mushrooms, will I? Just you wait, I'll have my revenge!"

Rhoda laughed. Sheena *tsked* as she climbed the stair, her smile loosening and then disappearing. She entered their bedchamber and removed her apron and work sleeves, which were damp with sweat. She unbuttoned her cuffs and the top of her blouse, lying back on the bed for a moment to blow softly down the front of her bodice and cool her skin.

A warm, heavy weight pressing down the length of her body woke her abruptly.

"Gordon!"

"Sheena—good evening, wife." He grinned.

"I must've fallen asleep. But Rhoda didn't call me—"

"She said it's only been a quarter of an hour, you must be having trouble with your buttons. Well, are you?"

And Sheena realized he was unbuttoning more of her blouse. "Sssh!" She batted back his fingers. "Honestly. Do behave. I'm sure she's got supper already on the table—"

"Almost. Stay a minute." He paused. "You did look lovely all undone on the bed."

"Oh, then I forgive your squashing me, if I was so lovely —"

Her lips were immediately silenced, and her chuckle gave way to an earnest embrace just as he pulled away. "I am starving in more ways than one, wife."

He sighed expansively and regretfully, then reached out a hand to pull her up and helped her redo the buttons.

"But I can wait."

They sat down to eat, Rhoda wearing a knowing grin. At that moment, Sheena didn't care if the whole world knew how happy she was.

"And how was your day with the women at the loch today?" asked Gordon.

"Fine, fine," she replied, although the news revealed that day came back to her, suddenly and painfully. Gordon narrowed his eyes at her then changed the subject.

"And the vegetable garden thriving still, I see."

"Yes, I am most pleased with it. The heat and moisture here—no wonder anything in that soil shoots up." The meal passed in similar chatter until they had finished supper and bid Rhoda good-night. The sun was finally sinking behind the isles to the west when they repaired to the upstairs bedroom to shuck off their clothing. Gordon asked what she knew he would, ever since her brusque reply. She told him of the unpleasant revelation about the Laird's conduct.

"…Rose thinks they've left the district in shame—sister, sister, and mother. I suppose these sorts of affairs go on all the time, but it's disturbing to be working for someone who so obviously fails in such a matter of character."

"I agree. Well." Gordon sat on the bed in his shirt, its sleeves billowing. "I haven't heard any other tales of the sort around the place but that may well be a woman's secret. I'll keep an ear out, and an eye open, in case. Though, in truth, what could I do?"

He said the last bit almost to himself, sounding doubtful of his role as protector. She came to stand before him in her shift, pushing his legs apart with her hips.

"You will do what you must," she said softly.

August 1833, Ardkinglas

As the summer passed, Sheena felt the nights coming in faster.
She grew more confident as a horsewoman. She knitted hats
for all the newborns that summer and distributed them per-
sonally, committing to memory a few more names in her
rounds of the tenants in their cottages sprinkled along the
banks of the loch and around the river valley to the south.

She asked Rhoda about the great ruin, which occupied the
field south of the current residence.

"Oh, the old laird had just passed away when there was a
great fire. It consumed the old hall."

"How long ago was that?"

"Oh, just two years ago, missus. There were some plans to
build a new hall, but—" here Rhoda lowered her voice, even
though they stood in the back kitchen with the door closed.
"There was talk of *debts*."

"I see. So what is the house where I met with the Laird
last month?"

"They converted the stables. Took quite a while—"

She was cut off by Sheena's laughter. *A fitting home for that
wastrel of a master.*

"Missus?"

"Oh, I'm sorry, Rhoda. I just find it amusing that the

gentry sleeps where the studs once stood. Now, you've been here several years, I know. You have friends up at the—the stable block, then?" She smiled to make her tease less barbed.

"No, missus. I don't talk much to anyone up the road."

"Then—but how do you get your news?"

"I go into the village every week, and the tradesmen there are very kind."

Sheena sensed a hardening of the barrier between them, and decided not to press any further that day. The thought hovered over her shoulder for several days afterward. *What kind of social pariah have we got in the house?* But she proved so gentle and capable that it was hard to give the fishwives' gossip or her reluctance to talk to the hall servants much weight in her judgment of the woman's character.

She learned of Gordon's duties as he came home each night and talked. After maintaining such strict composure all day around the master, his relief at expressing his own views was obvious. While she listened to him, she could feel proud of the position he held and the respect it commanded. She also monitored her courses carefully, newly disappointed every time she anticipated a stoppage only to bleed several days later. She tried not to feel she was failing as a wife each time the blood confirmed she had not conceived.

One morning's sunshine brought a series of great booms and crashes. Sheena looked up from her sewing seat in panic, wondering if it was a storm or a flood or what—before recalling Gordon's description from the night before.

"His Honor has decided to experiment with some of the

powder-shot he has in the storehouse and the cannon rescued from the old fort. In short, he plans to raze the rest of the old hall tomorrow. So don't be surprised to hear the great Waterloo happening outside the window."

Sheena ran out to see the spectacle where, less than half a mile away, the Laird was instructing his ghillie and his butler and—yes, there was Gordon—on where to lay the charges before yelling, "Stand back!" and signaling another man-at-arms to light the fuse. She hurried up to watch as blackened masonry clattered into mushrooms of dust. Others had assembled as well, and she glanced curiously at their expressions. There was more than a little head-shaking.

When she looked at Gordon, who was shaking ash out of his hair, she saw his grim expression, and the covert nod. She looked across the field and saw the ghillie had a similar set to his mouth that said, "I don't like this at all." Well, it *was* dangerous, but as the Laird did not have many servants, they were called upon to serve. She asked Gordon about it at dinner later.

"It's the folly of it—the danger—for his good fun that is hard to take. A soldier can face the fire of battle for his captain knowing the battle is just, but exploding an old house because it is faster and a good spectacle, though it cripple a good man? It makes both Ben and me uneasy."

Sheena felt the uneasiness in her own belly, but tried to keep it contained. *The women, the explosives…but at least the wastrel will soon be away in London.*

September brought a new intensity of rain, and they had

to barricade part of the garden path with bags of stones so the flood wouldn't enter the house.

"Always happens, spring and autumn," Rhoda assured them.

The petulant management of the Laird did not seem to influence his estate's productivity. What had once been mired in debts was slowly climbing out of them with each year of better weather and faster communications, each quarter of solid interest in the Four Per Cents and calm stability under King William IV. Then came unimagined news from London.

"His Majesty has given his Royal Assent to the Slavery Abolition Act," Gordon reported one night in early September. "And what has Master Callender in a froth is that there is to be an immense fund to recompense all the owners of slaves in the Crown Colonies. He only has a controlling interest in one sugar plantation in Jamaica, but I'm damned if he won't be there with his tin cup, begging the Crown to pay for all those 'highly skilled Negroes' he's lost in the bargain."

Sheena gulped a bite of sausage a little too quickly and swallowed again before speaking. "You mean the slave trade that was abolished before I was born? They're getting compensation now?"

"Yes, for it was only the trade that was done away with twenty years ago. Now it is the state of slavery itself; everyone is—instantly—free."

Sheena crinkled her forehead, shutting out Gordon's carefree look. "Of course. It still goes on in the United States, so there is still slavery. I had—had forgot about it—here. But it's not done away with until everyone is free, everywhere."

"In a way, that's true," said Gordon slowly. "But I can see why they've done it this way in Parliament. Hell, the Government's made up of slave owners, you know. They wouldn't be pushed off that ledge without ensuring a wagon full of down feathers was right below."

Sheena noticed Rhoda's silence and glanced over. "Rhoda, are you finished? I can do the wash-up if you're not feeling well." Truly, she didn't look well: her color had fled and she looked peaky, almost excited to the point of giddiness. "Can Gordon walk you back?"

"No, missus. Thank you, sir," she said as Gordon rose. "But I'll be fine. It's just a shock to hear of—such things. Sure and good night to ye both." She drifted out, bumping the door-jamb as if lost in a fog. Sheena was a bit worried but let the woman's pride have precedence.

"And the *owners* are being recompensed. Of course, because they are the Government. Makes *perfect* sense," Sheena muttered to herself as she closed the door and went to scrub out the pot.

Later in bed, Sheena's mind was still racing with the implications of such a major scheme.

"The Laird's an M.P., right?"

"Yes."

"So he will go right along with his tin cup." She scoffed in disgust. "And is there any proposed fund for the slaves, since by abolishing slavery, we admit we had no right to own other people in the first place?"

"Well, no——"

"No, of course not." Her voice softened and she imagined all the rich folk who had prospered here in Scotland, wearing silk brocade and slaughtering hundreds of sheep for feasts, squeezing tenants for their shillings in rent, trading in thousands of pounds of sugar and molasses and rum…all the while knowing they owned slaves on those islands, and they good-as-owned them back here at home, too. She didn't think about her courses the next morning.

September 1833, The Ridge

Mairi was writing on slats of scrap wood with a piece of charcoal. Waves of the black sooty stuff showed her hand was getting steadier. She blew carefully across the top of the wood and was rewarded with a fine row of beautiful M's.

"Mmmmm," she read.

"Are you writing something delicious, Mairi?"

Grannie's voice came over the garden wall behind her. Mairi raised the wood so she could see.

"Ha! I see, very nice. Now can you come in and help prepare the carrots ye brought in?"

Mairi leapt up and followed her gran into the cabin. Blackie had stopped giving milk in preparation for a calf in December, while Darien had just given birth and would keep them in milk and cream for the autumn. The bull would be brought over early in December to serve Darien and start the cycle again, so they'd have plenty of milk after the new year, when nothing else would be growing. For now, they'd put up as much cheese as they could, and churn as much butter and cream as they could. It was hard going, for the churn handle was still above Mairi's head, but when she stood on the bench it was doable.

"Carrot pudding?"

Grannie nodded. One of Mairi's favorites. She filled the cauldron with water to boil the carrots then refilled the bucket from the stream.

"Almost full!" she cried as she set it down.

"That's a braw girl."

As she waited for the carrots to cook, Mairi peeled some of the butternuts that Alisdair had gathered in.

"Mairi, dear, how are yer bones feeling these days? Are we to see another growing stretch?"

She wiggled a little on her stool. "They feel fine. But my feet sure seem to be growing."

She stuck out one foot, wiggling to show where her toe was pressing into the shoe leather.

"Ach, that's no good. We'll have to get you some new ones o' them. Next time Flora is over, I'll ask her."

Mairi smiled her thanks and curled her toes back down so they wouldn't hurt. She liked these times with Grannie. It felt like she was there just for her. They sat companionably working until the carrots yielded to the knife. Grannie helped drain off the broth into a bowl and Mairi set to mashing them with the back of a spoon.

"Mairi, my love." She looked up at her gran's voice. It was gentler than usual. "You know your father's doing the best he can, don't ye now?"

"Of course, Grannie."

But she mumbled it into the cauldron, bending further into its depths and stabbing with the spoon a little harder.

"There is a lot to do around here, and he's trying to do it

all without help. Because he's lonely. Can ye understand that and be kind to him?"

"He's not alone. You're here, and Uncle Alisdair is here, and—I'm helping—"

"I know that, *mo chaileag*, but without Letty he's feeling alone—"

"Me, too."

There was a silence, and Mairi pulled herself up slowly. Her gran wrapped her good arm around her and held her close. "Of course, Mairi dear. We've all lost people. But we're not alone. We're here for each other, no?"

Mairi let herself be hugged. *Fine. I will try again for Grannie's sake.*

They labored for another hour at the hearth, Mairi going to the stream twice more. She was tired, but satisfied, when her father and uncle returned for supper and the smell of the carrot pudding wrapped itself in the rafters. She flung a cloth over the handles of the bowl in the ashes and tugged it out. The beet greens were drained and set out, next to the fish chowder, all crispy with the bannock crumbs. Mairi bit her lip and enjoyed the smells and steam while Grannie distributed the plates and the men washed their face and hands at the basin.

"What special feast hall have we tumbled into? This can't be our very own cabin!"

Uncle Alisdair's eyes sparkled. Mairi squeezed her hands behind her back, and looked towards Da.

He was sitting in his chair, already chewing a mouthful, his fork dangling from his hand as it pressed to his forehead. He looked down at his plate. Mairi darted to her stool next to Grannie, who said a quick grace. Mairi dove in, savoring the salty greens and the rich, creamy chowder.

"Mmmm," she said with her eyes closed.

"Just like what you wrote, eh, Mairi?"

Mairi's eyes popped open at Grannie's nudge, then she caught her meaning and laughed. "Yes!"

"What's this?" Alisdair asked.

"Oh, just Mairi, readin' and writin' in one afternoon!" And Grannie gave her a wink. Sure, it wasn't a real word, but it was a sound—and she'd written it!

"Knew you'd be an early bird," said Uncle. "I'll set you on my lessons next, so be careful."

Mairi bathed in the glow of their regard. She dared a look at Da again. He stared at a place on the table above his plate, his jaw working fast like he was hurrying to finish. He took another helping of chowder.

"Alisdair, can ye take a cloot and—aye, there ye go. This is the nice carrot pudding we made. Mairi practically did it herself. She'll have all my receipts memorized by the time we send her down to Muirne's."

Mairi's smile froze. "Send me to Auntie Muirne's?"

"Not for quite a while, but there are lots of receipts to learn," Grannie teased.

"For school, Mairi," Alisdair added. "You can go with Kitty."

Oh, Kitty. Mairi vaguely remembered her cousin, a year

older, and didn't much like to run. She kept quiet but wondered how long 'quite a while' was. It was one of those phrases that grown-ups used when they didn't want you to ask, she knew.

Alisdair served the pudding, and Mairi's first bite made her close her eyes again. The rich eggs and milk and sweet carrots and currants almost made her teeth ache. It was still piping hot, though, so she opened her mouth to breathe out the hot steam.

"Don't be vulgar; close your mouth, Mairi."

She looked up to see her da taking a drink from his cup. She closed her mouth, even though it made her eyes water. Gulped down the pudding to get it out of her mouth, even though it scorched her throat. She hesitated, heart pounding, panting from the thrill of pain that was already starting to subside.

Her eyes still stung. She picked up her fork again and looked at her plate without hunger. The table was quiet.

"Is that nutmeg?"

Uncle was screwing up his mouth in an odd way. He put two fingers in and pulled out a speck of brown.

"Didn't know we had any left." He sounded surprised. "Must be why it tastes so good, eh, Mairi? Well done."

She didn't know what to say. "I tried to grind it all up, Uncle. Sorry there was—"

"It's no problem, dearie. Wouldn't kill me, at any rate. Why—were you hoping?"

She giggled. She took another bite. It was good. She finished her portion and was looking up to see whether it was time to clear away plates when she saw the look her uncle gave her da. As if he was looking at a mountain, puzzling about how to climb it, and a little exasperated at having to.

September 1833, Ardkinglas

As September waned, Sheena took full advantage of the dry days, pulling her chair out of doors to work with the wool. She went to check on the ladies lochside each Friday, having found two more recruits who were learning to scale the fish and pick the whelks at half the speed of the more experienced women. Sheena had not returned to the subject of the sisters who'd got with child and left, so Rose had come to see Sheena as discreet, trusting her enough for a habit of amusing conversation most days before supper. Rhoda was usually inside at work during these visits. Today, the Laird was down in London for the season, and Sheena was happy to be chatting with Rhoda in the late green sunshine spilling through the foliage.

"Rhoda," Sheena began a new subject. "You were taken ill the other day, at the news of the Abolition Act. What was it that affected you?"

"Was nothing, missus," she replied, but her neck had gone pink.

"Are you an abolitionist?"

"Aye, missus. Have supported them for many a year."

"That's very good of you. From here, do you mean? Sending money?"

Sheena wondered how Rhoda, a widowed housekeeper in

this tiny place, could have sent extra money to a cause, but she sensed there was something to unravel in this story and couldn't stop herself digging.

"No, but I spent some time helping the demonstrators when I was in Hull, missus." Rhoda looked down at her knitting, and away from Sheena nervously. She'd never displayed such behavior about anything in the few months they'd spent together. *Helping the demonstrators—I wonder if that means participating in a riot. Well, it is long past and I don't need to know of poor Rhoda's youthful misdeeds.*

"Oh? I have never been to Hull. Tell me of it."

Rhoda hesitantly told her of the canals, the marine trade, the excitement of the whaling vessels and their ever-revolving crews, and gained confidence as she did. Sheena relaxed when Rhoda was back in her normal spirits, until she saw Rose's burly frame coming up the walk. *Well, this is as good a time as any to extend the olive branch.*

"Rose is coming. Fetch a chair and we can be a little party here below the hawthorn tree."

Rhoda went in for the chair. When she was in hailing distance, Rose bellowed a good-natured "Howd'ye do, missus? This is a night and no mistake."

"It is lovely, Rose. Will you join us for a bit? Mr. Lamont should be back right soon, but even he may join us out of doors, it is so pleasant."

"I surely will. Stop my stravaigin' long enough to give you the latest news." Rose winked as she gathered her skirts and stained apron and sat upon the stool Rhoda brought out.

"News! Oh, do tell," said Rhoda.

"Well, there's Jenny May as got married, and her husband leaving for Glasgow on the horse he bought with her dowry, which is a shame on her father for giving it away."

A clucking sound from Rhoda indicated this Jenny May was to be sympathized with.

"And then there's the Daltons who took over the lease on the Old Ferry Inn but have brought their own serving staff and send for meat over in Lochgoilhead—can you believe?"

"Shocking," came the commentary from Rhoda, to which Rose clucked her tongue against her teeth.

This seems to be going rather well. "That seems rather stingy. Where do the Daltons come from?" Sheena asked.

Rose's face lost its disapproving cast and she looked apologetic. "Nova Scotia, I believe."

Sheena felt her face flush. "Well, perhaps they will learn to be better neighbors," she said.

"Aye, let us hope so. And then there was what come with the post from London." Rose paused, and Sheena felt her own embarrassment evaporate. There was obviously something big that she'd been saving for last.

"What is it, Rose?"

"That man that struggled so long against the slavery, he's died."

"Wilberforce?" Sheena figured that's who she meant.

"Aye," Rose said, looking at Rhoda with a queer, cruel expression. "And his family's got him to lay in rest in the big cathedral itself."

Sheena glanced at Rhoda and noticed the woman had gone pale. What was she missing?

"But he got to hear the announcement—the declaration, at least?"

"Aye, he did that," Rose admitted. "May he rest in peace as a sincere Reforming soul."

There was a silent moment of prayer, and Sheena was trying to form a question for Rhoda when Gordon's figure could be seen on the road.

"Finally!" Sheena said, standing up and waving. She turned back to Rose. "Thank you for the gossip, Rose. I'll see if there's anything Gordon knows to add to the stories and pay you back in kind on Friday."

"Nae bother," Rose said, rising and shaking out the folds of cloth about her person. "Might be he knows more about the politicking than I heard. Obliged." And with that short pronouncement, she set off, nodding at Gordon, but otherwise: full steam ahead. *She must have a pudding to get home to*, thought Sheena, before setting her face in welcoming lines. He greeted her with a nod and followed her and Rhoda in with the chairs.

Sheena let him wash up while she put away the wool and brought out the dishes for supper.

"Almost dark! That *is* a long day in September," said Gordon.

"It is, and what profit have ye made of it?" she asked her husband.

He trotted out a tight smile. "Oh, a few things. The minister was out about the Statistical Account, first I'd heard of that. Quite an interesting undertaking. And no doubt, as I saw Rose leaving, you've heard the news from London."

"Mr. Wilberforce dead? We did."

"Beyond that, the government man is refusing Callander's submitted claim. They've still a month or two to appeal, but it appears the man has already spent on the promise of a substantial sum. Unwisely."

"Oh, no. He is indebted again?"

"It's not quite that bad," Gordon hurried to say, glancing at Rhoda. Sheena got the message: *even if it was, she shouldn't say so in front of any of the other tenants.* "Just another unfortunate management mistake, in some people's opinion."

"Hmm," was all Sheena could think of to say. *A management mistake.* Is that what they'd called it when they'd run her family off their land?

There was a constrained air about supper that night. Sheena wanted to question Rhoda again about what had given her such a shock, but the housekeeper excused herself early with a headache. Sheena could do nothing but take her own self to bed.

Her wondering state was quickly dispelled by Gordon's cooing attentions. Sheena mentally catalogued his actions since they'd come to Loch Fyne, counting his confident management of the first harvest as a positive and his doubtful execution of the explosives duties as a negative, before all the mental notes slid into a pile and she felt the yearning fire start within her. She moaned.

Gordon's enthusiastic thrusting came to a halt. Sheena opened her eyes. Gordon was just above her, eyes squinted shut. Then came the immense exhalation of breath and clench-ing of jaw. And his eyes opened.

"Sheena, my love," he managed before scooping his hands underneath her waist and rolling over until they had switched places, she on top of him.

He was all over sweating, which Sheena was not. Her little yearning fire pulsed another note and gave up the ghost, and she went back to examining her swept-up pile of thoughts.

"Is Callander *very* indebted?" she asked in a low tone. Gordon's tongue was silent, but she felt his still-racing heart and gave him the time to come back to himself. She traced a finger down the inside of his arm, which twitched.

"Debts? I don't know, Sheena. We seem to be in a fair way until the bills come up from London, when we're set down to nought again. Everything must be dear there—or else he's living it up."

There's been no building here since they converted the stable into the main house, Sheena mused. *So he's not putting any money into the property up here.*

"Perhaps he's spending to find himself a wife. I hear that can run up quite a bill," she said drily. She saw the wry smile come and go on Gordon's face.

"I don't know about that. Mine came quite cheap!"

They laughed together, then Gordon brought up his head to kiss her. Sheena moved off to his side and lay on her back.

Gordon sighed.

"How are you feeling, wife?"

Sheena furtively straightened her shift so that she was mostly covered again. She had a suspicion, a humming sort of feeling that felt like a new babe, but she wanted it confirmed before she raised Gordon's hopes.

"Quite strong, actually. Those fishwives prove that even the littlest can be hardy." She tried to smile placidly but gave it up. She felt the mattress shift as Gordon shifted closer.

"Not so hardy you don't need quiet and rest, and none of that gunpowder excitement," he said. "Funny your brothers and sister should have such rude health—"

"They grew up with a man in the house," Sheena interrupted. "So they had enough to eat. Just as our children shall —plenty to eat, and a father to protect them."

Gordon stroked her cheek gently with his thumb.

October 1833, The Ridge

Sheena's second letter lay in Alisdair's hands. Morrissey the postman had delivered it the day before. Alisdair read it again, searching for something between the lines that would show more of his sister's wry humor and less of her superficial wit. It worried him, even though he knew Gordon was a good man and a worthy husband. *And this is what she wanted, after all.*

They wouldn't have another word from her for quite a while, he surmised, as the first winter there would keep her busy, and the ships wouldn't cross the sea as easily in the stormy season. Or maybe he simply felt as if she was drifting away. He would write her back, but he had another letter to write first—and a question to ask before that.

Alisdair glanced around the cabin, where various jobs lay in states of half-completion. Mam sat just inside the doorway from the kitchen shed, plying a needle through a string of garlic bulbs in the bucket at her knee. Mairi sat nearby, peeling apples ever so carefully.

Neil was out somewhere. It wasn't snowing, but was mighty cold for a stroll, and Alisdair thought he knew exactly where Neil had gone: Letty's grave. Why he didn't take Mairi when he visited it, he didn't know. He knew she'd snuck back many times since that time she fell asleep in the sunshine.

Only natural. But why they didn't go together…It seemed strange to him. It was too far in the mud for Mam to get to easily now that the chill rains had mired the creek bed in perpetual rivulets.

Boots sounded on the board outside their door, placed there over the mud. The door whined on its hinges outward. Neil humped in, his cheeks red from the cold and his nose dripping. Whether it was from rain or a cold Alisdair couldn't say, because he hid his eyes from him. He'd bet the horse he didn't have they were bloodshot from crying. He looked away.

After the heavy noises of disrobing died away, Alisdair spoke his brother's name.

Neil looked his way. He warmed his hands over the fire.

"Come here. I've something to ask ye."

Neil rubbed his hands together another few times. "All right."

"Let's take a keek at the byre," Alisdair suggested, since there was no way to speak without being heard in the cabin.

Mam and Mairi heard him. Mam stilled her hands but kept her gaze down. Mairi looked at him, biting her lip. Alisdair already felt like a heel.

The brothers proceeded down to the cows, checked on the hay and the water trough, then shoved the manure out of the way of the cows' feet into a corner pile to dry. Finally, Alisdair stopped the distracting movement and folded his hands over the top of the rake he held.

"You know the man I spoke of meeting in Halifax, the man building a school?"

"McCulloch?"

"That's the one. He also invited me to study with him while he was getting the political votes for funding his courses. He mentioned a date—"

"Oh, aye? So you're ready to leave, like that? Think Mairi's up to handling the horses and cows and mucking out *now*?"

The bitterness in Neil's tone surprised him. He must have felt the request coming. Alisdair regretted having waited.

"Nay, but—"

"Think our mother's up to handling the sledge? Load it up and set off by herself in case of another illness?"

"Neil." Alisdair's voice cut sharply into the heat of Neil's. One of the cows twitched her ear in his direction. "I'm sorry for your loss, and the poor circumstances we find ourselves in. But it's not impossible, if you make adjustments—"

"Adjustments!" The dun cow jerked her head and rolled an eye toward him. "What do you mean by that? Hire out? Marry again?"

Neil looked worn out, battered. The side light of the lantern set by the door made him look even more like a ghost, or demon. Alisdair held his peace, letting the echo of Neil's bitten-out words fade away.

Before he could form a suitable reply, Neil let go the *cas-chrom* he held and sank onto the milking stool. The metal clanging against the stone reverberated through the dirt and up to Alisdair's knees. Neil was clutching at his hair and sobbing.

Alisdair knelt beside him and put a hand to his shoulder,

but Neil ignored him. They stayed that way for several minutes. Neil drew in an abrupt breath and folded his arms tightly across his chest, rocking forward. Alisdair felt the tremors go through his body and kept his hand where it was to reassure Neil he was there. But these weren't tremors of rage or feeling; Neil was shaking uncontrollably.

Alisdair sprang up. "Neil!"

His brother didn't look up but kept rocking forward and back. He called to him again, then bent to wrestle his arms apart and hook one over his back. His older brother, once so strong as to seem unassailable, now shook with cold and hung on him with unconcern. Alisdair shook him, angry that Neil would abdicate his responsibilities and take refuge in this childish behavior. He flicked off the guilty thought of his own responsibilities and jumped into action.

"You can't do this to your daughter," he whispered fiercely. "You need to be well for her."

Bloodshot eyes now turned to him, watery and bleak. "I know."

Mute helplessness remained in those eyes as they roved over the room.

"Well," Alisdair finally said. "We're getting you to bed."

He hauled his brother back up the path to the cabin. When he entered with Neil dragging at his side, Mairi shrieked in panic and flew at them.

"Da! Da! What's wrong?" She beat at Neil's legs, crying already.

"Shh, shh," Alisdair crooned at her until she subsided a bit.

"He's just overworked himself, Mairi. He's too cold for my liking and needs to get a good rest. So why don't you help me tuck him up in bed…"

She whipped the sheet over the tick mattress, then went to fetch all the blankets in her little nest by the fire. Alisdair tugged off Neil's outer clothes, surprised to encounter a resistance in his breeches he had not counted on. Drying his brother's wet hair roughly, he quickly piled on the blankets Mairi offered. She chopped her hands pointed like blades to tuck the covers around Neil's body.

"Snug as anything, thank you, Mairi," he said. She looked up at him, her eyes saying both, "Don't you dare let anything happen to him," and "I trust you to make him well." Alisdair swallowed uncomfortably. She made a bee-line for Mam and asked for help making broth for the invalid.

Alisdair gazed on the unconscious expression on his brother's face. *Ill. Damn him.* Could he write that letter now?

He sat down to compose himself and realized he would not be able to leave for McCulloch November 14th starting date. Not only would he not go to university this year, it looked like he would not graduate to this miraculous tutor, either. He'd told Neil he would stay the year, and he'd been there for the plantings and harvest. But it looked like his winter would be spent holed up here as well, with little to do. Would this paralysis spread to another year, and another? Would the new university be built in two years, or ten? Which decision led to advancement? Which bolstered his family's health?

He chose his words carefully.

> *Dear Dr. McCulloch,*
>
> *I am conscious of and thank you for the great honor you do me by inviting me to study with you this term. With regret, I must write to inform you that my situation is not such that I have leave to stay in the city this winter. My brother's family is still grieving and my mother can not be left alone in her condition. I would be neglecting the family that raised me at great cost to themselves were I to leave at this time.*
>
> *Therefore I implore you to keep me apprised of any progress with the university. If my circumstances change, I certainly intend to take you up on your generous offer. I also consider your words about the Council with gravity, and whether my views may lend support to your cause of Reform. I remain,*
>
> *Sincerely Yours,*
> *Alisdair MacLean*

October 1833, Ardkinglas

It was a doubly happy day: Sheena had received a letter from Nova Scotia, and she couldn't wait to reply, because of her news—finally with child! The letter detailed all sorts of inconsequential news that made her feel at once included and homesick. Mairi was learning the alphabet from Alisdair. Mam was showing Mairi the proper way to turn a heel, even though the wee girl could hardly yet control the multiple metal wires.

Better keep her to the drop spindle, thought Sheena with a smile to herself. She read the lines with all their mishmash of handwritings by a crackling fire. It was mid-afternoon, cold, and of course wet. The bumpers were back on their garden path to keep the rains from rushing in, and the last harvest was snug up in the barns. Gordon's duties were more riding visits and writing correspondence than supervising the field hands at work, which meant he left later and came home earlier, pleasing Sheena very much. She'd told him about the change only yesterday at breakfast.

"Gordon, there's something I've been longing to tell you."

He'd looked at her from his chair by the fire, alarmed.

"What is it?"

She glanced at the level of hot tea in his cup to ensure it was not too high before continuing.

"I'm with child again."

He leapt up from his seat, tea splashing the carpet and making the fire hiss.

She'd teased him about his exuberance, even though she'd been just as beside herself when she suspected and started monitoring for signs. She hoped to tease him about that cup of tea in the good years to come.

She reread the letter one more time, then closed her eyes briefly to wish them all safe before opening up her writing box and starting the reply. The incessant rain lent a sort of hush to her motions inside the house. She suddenly realized Rhoda hadn't come back from her noontime errand to the big house.

Well, perhaps she's been countermanded to help the cook over there. Och, if only the laird would stay in London. Things are going so well. Even as she thought it, Sheena made the sign of the horns with her fingers to ward away evil. The steward and staff had been given notice that he planned to return in six weeks and stay for two. Sheena held out a tentative hope that he would bring back some countess or other who would take up his attention. *After all, he's rather past thirty—isn't it time to be getting an heir for the place?* Unless he had married and become a widower before she knew of it, stashing away the young heir someplace eminently more suitable than the laird's own household. She would have heard of that, though, surely?

She put down the quill and went in search of Rhoda. She called her name a few times and poked her head around to the kitchen, the byre, the kailyard. Where had she got herself squirreled away?

Sheena tsked at the housekeeper's mysterious absence and went back to her letter. By the time she was finished—five closely-written pages later—it was past four o'clock. She was surprised to see Rhoda still not back, but she set to work on the bannock batter. She'd set the dough to rest and moved on to the onions when Gordon arrived home. Cutting onions always made the tears flow, and so it was a blurry face that came in to greet her.

"Evening, husband. Have you seen Rhoda? I——"

She was engulfed in his embrace and struggled to blink away the onion tears to see what was the matter.

"What's wrong? Has something happened? What is it?"

Gordon let her go gently, not meeting her eyes until he had positioned a seat beside her and made her sit upon it. She blinked furiously and wiped her running nose on a hankie. Gordon spoke quietly, watching her face.

"Rhoda went to the shed where the fishwives were mencing nets. There was rather an unfortunate scene, but it's clear that some news upset her terribly. That Mr. Wilberforce? One of the women told me that she boasted of some relationship with him when she was a girl in Hull. True or not, she was deeply disturbed, and…"

"What is it?"

"She's drowned in the millpond, Sheena. Tillie McGann thinks she was going down there to talk to someone, but seeing as how she was so unbalanced…"

Sheena felt her mouth hang open—the skin on her face

rigid like rock. She put a hand to a cheek to feel it.
Unbalanced.

"The poor woman," Gordon muttered. "She was probably fine until someone mentioned it. Kept it locked away in her mind. But Tillie and the others said she was sobbing like a wretch, like it happened yesterday—whatever it was, or wasn't."

Sheena recalled the conversation that had made her suspicious—when Rose had seemed to glare at Rhoda when she announced the man's death. *Cruel.* Poor Rhoda. Rhoda with no family, who had only this house and its revolving strangers to look after.

"Of course it happened. Something. Must've." Sheena honked into the hankie and stared at Gordon defiantly. "You should write to Mr. Wilberforce's solicitor, to see if she was mentioned. We should believe her. Set an example."

She didn't like how out of breath she sounded, as if someone had just punched all the air out of her.

"How are the fishwives taking the news?" she asked, Rose's red and satisfied face startlingly clear in her memory. She'd had no idea of that level of animosity between them. *I thought it was gossip that could be cleared up with more gossip. What a fool.*

"I don't know. I haven't gone back down. I came here straight away to tell you and look after you. The coroner will be out, and a burial…when he determines whether she fell or jumped."

"Och, how awful!" Sheena crinkled her face and turned

away. She saw the fire was dying down and jumped up to feed
it.

"Sheena—you're all right? I can do that. We can find
someone to help you—I don't want you—"

"I am perfectly in health," she said. She took down the
bread basket rather too early so she could punch down the
dough. "I'll just get back to making supper for us. Don't
worry about us for a few days; I'm up to it. Go tell everyone.
Tell what you believe happened."

The sour-sweet smell of cut onions in a stuffy house hung
around them. Gordon hesitated.

"Go on," she prodded. "No, wait! I finished the letter for
my family. Since you're going down Strachur way, you can
post it."

She retrieved the envelope and put it in his hand.

"All right, I'll go. Be back in about two hours and a half."
He picked up his hat and squinted at her again. Sheena murmured something like a goodbye and turned her back, ostensi-
bly to gather up the onions for the pot, but she hadn't yet set
it in the fire or put the bacon grease in to warm. She grabbed
at the upended pot and wiped it out. The door opened and
closed behind Gordon. She put down the pot, feeling Rhoda's
hands over hers as she hung onto its rim and bowed her head,
felt the rough iron bite into her forehead. *On Samhain, poor
soul.*

She took the big turnips from the basket under the table,
seeing again Rhoda's ghostly hand that had chosen each one
for making lanterns. *Coroner, indeed,* she tutted, shaking her

head to clear it of cobwebs. *She was a good woman. And if there was some sort of early foolishness, well, that was long past. Not a rioter, but a lover!* Sheena scolded herself for not seeing the truth and confronting Rhoda when her words might have done some good in easing the woman's grief. She would pray for her soul tonight, though, and light the turnip lanterns for her, too.

She wondered if Gordon would take her seriously enough to write to the solicitor in London. Probably not. Should she do it herself? No, they'd throw away any letter from a woman attempting to direct them. If Gordon didn't ask, no one would. She would pester him after supper. In the meantime, she meditated on what she might encounter next time she went to count the barrels of fish left. Whether Rose would come up the road to chat. How could she be so cruel, knowing Rhoda's past history—to bring it up, like nothing? And why hadn't Sheena followed her suspicion with more action? Guilt lay upon her for the next hour as she picked the kale for the soup and set the table for the two of them.

Supper was mostly silent, even more so as the rain stopped for several hours. Gordon fidgeted with his pewter spoon, drawing out each bite as if the activity required all his attention. Finally, Sheena ended his misery by opening the subject herself.

"If you're still afraid I'll break down, dinna be. I am very sorry about Rhoda. She was a good woman, a kind friend. I do feel upset by the rumors, but I'm sure you'll be able to sort them out when you write to London."

Gordon cleared his throat several times, finally replying with, "If you like. I'll make it a general request so that the solicitor won't think I'm mad."

"Oh, but you must mention her name!"

"Oh, very well. But in my opinion, she was a poor, lonely woman whom none but we will remember!"

"Gordon!"

"I'm sorry."

Sheena took her time with another swallow. *Here I am in my perfect life, where I wanted to be*, she thought somewhat bitterly. *And it is the sorrows of others that manage to upset me.*

"And what of Rose and Martha and the other fishwives? Did they look contrite when you told them about it?"

"Contrite? I didn't tell them. Davy did; I went the opposite direction. What do you mean, contrite?"

"That scene Rhoda made in front of them. I'm sure they made her more distraught by not believing her."

Gordon raised his eyebrows. "Ah. Well. For that, you will have to conduct your own interviews, as that is your purview."

Sheena was taken aback. He'd just recognized an area in which she was in charge. *Well!* She nodded and took a sip of tea.

They finished the meal in silence. A quiet night followed, though Sheena did hear the wind whipping the trees against the roof in the middle of the night. By the following morn, the rain was steady again, and Gordon was off to confer with the coroner. Sheena felt the heaviness of loss, of unsure grief, of sorrow unshared. She walked the mile to the lochside shed where the fishwives gathered together each day.

There was a clamor of voices raised in argument as she approached. She stepped in through the doorless entry and removed the thick shawl from over her head. The din of voices abruptly stopped. It felt less like a respectful silence and more like a wary one.

"Would someone please tell me what you all knew of Rhoda Sudbury's past?"

Awkward shuffling of feet echoed off the tin roof. Breathing that tried to remain silent became ragged, as the women inhaled through their open mouths.

"Please," she said flatly.

Isbell, a buxom middle-aged woman, finally raised her head.

"We were just talking about that, missus. Whether that ol' tale Rhody used to tell might be true."

What old tale? Sheena almost spat in frustration. Instead, she raised an eyebrow.

"Her meetin' that Wilberforce when they were both young, when she worked at a mill in Hull. Her family sent her there, and she was gone almost two year before coming back —looking rather ill, my mother said. By that time, her family had died of the flux. Anyway, she told Kathleen, who told Aidy, who told me, that she'd been with child, had lain with a right fancy young gentleman. Someone who went to university and was a moral philosophizer, she said. He'd end up bring-

ing about the end of slavery, and wasn't she proud of him...
Anyway, she never got no letters, so if it did happen, he
must've forgot all about her, that's what we was thinkin'."

Isbell's long speech went unanswered, so Sheena guessed
the women had hashed this out as the most probable sequence
of events. She spied Rose, as far away as she could be from the
door.

"Rose, why did you deliver the news of his death like
that?"

Rose glanced around at the other women, whose eyes
widened.

"I didn't think her story was true. I feel awful for it, truly,
missus. I've prayed about it and all."

The woman looked cowed, but not truly *guilty*. Perhaps it
was the pressure of the crowd that made her confess so
readily. Sheena, now that she'd got the confrontation over, had
no more desire to point fingers.

"Good. Mr. Lamont is writing to the solicitor in case—"
Goodness, what if the child is alive? "In case anyone in connection
with Rhoda was mentioned, but you are probably right, and
the man in his greatness has forgotten all about a silly young
woman who loved him. But we won't. Will we?"

"No, ma'am," they chorused.

"No," she murmured. "Do any of you know how Katherine
and her daughters are faring? Come now, she was here for a
whole season, and I know how familiar you get."

"Aye, ma'am. She's awa' to Glasgow and workin' for a
piecer, as are Myra and Anne. They've a brother sending 'em

money to keep the babes, for they be comin' soon."

"Good." Sheena nodded at the smaller woman who'd responded, and left.

December 1833, New Glasgow

It was mid-December, the snows were piling in hour after aching hour, and Alisdair felt his composure slowly slipping. Knowledge of the clipped reply from Dr. McCulloch burned like a new brand on his brain. It was civil as could be, yet he sensed disappointment between the lines. He knew it to be disappointment in himself that grated most, and he brooded over it as he did his chores in the frigid dark. *When will I be able to strike out on my own?*

The farm did fine; he and Neil had managed to finish harvest and store everything sound and tight, with a sheep slaughtered and hanging in the smokery and their salt fish barrel full up. But their *home*—the cabin felt bleak. Neil had stayed abed for two days by Mam's command, then insisted on returning to his rounds of the property, his turn at the farm chores. The pink to his cheeks did not return, but a new grey-blue settled under his eyes. Alisdair offered once to take over his chores, the second day he'd been up, when he'd stumbled coming out of the byre. But Neil had shaken his head once. It was his pride. Alisdair left him alone for Mam to tend and Mairi to comfort.

Pride goeth before a fall, echoed in his head. Alisdair walked the fence line, testing the poles to make sure they would hold beneath the snow. On his return sweep to the byre, he heard one of the cows making a racket and came in to find Mairi struggling with a bundle of cloth. She looked up at his shadow blocking the poor winter light, and the cloth in her hands opened up at two ends, spilling crowdie down her front and into the muck.

"Aw, Mairi!"

She clutched the cloth against her, trying to hold up the forward end.

"Hold it. Right there. Now give me that—let go your finger, girl. There." Alisdair wrested free the warm bundle, twisting the top quickly and setting it on a pile of clean hay.

"What are you after, anyways?"

"Grannie wanted the crowdie for a—for a pudding. It's my—my birthday soon and she—"

"Aw, Mairi, come away here." Alisdair squatted to one knee, with one knee upright. She came and put a hand to his, and he gave her a quick hug, then settled her against his leg.

"I'll help with the cream. I've got bigger hands. It's harder with smaller hands to gather all the cloth, see?" He held up a hand to show her, and she was distracted from her hiccuping enough to match hers to it.

"You didn't spill but a little. Some mousie'll sure thank ye." Her cheek moved a little, wanting to grin but not quite ready yet.

"And you're coming along well with your studies. Your sounds are better than mine, and your rhyming is better than yer da's, if ye don't tell him I said that." He was rewarded with a full grin this time. "So dinna greet over spilt cream. I'm sure yer grannie'll be able to bake something wonderful for ye. Almost a week off, though, isn't it?"

"The day after Midwinter Day," Mairi replied.

"Ah, yes. And then Christmas. And then Boxing Day. And then Hogmanay." The litany of holidays lined up to depress him. What did he have to give? The work of his body. The bitterness of his soul? It wouldn't do. But he wasn't ready to simply leave. He sighed.

"Let's go away in. I'll follow you, make sure you don't slip under a snow bank."

Mairi grinned and popped up. When Alisdair rose, he marked how she'd grown in the past few months. Another inch or more, if he wasn't off his mark. He gathered up the cloth and they hauled themselves back up the snowy hill to the cabin.

When they reached the safety indoors, Alisdair saw Neil was missing. A small ball of heat pressed against Alisdair's gut as he took off his heavy coat and hung it by the door. Lord Almighty, what was his brother off doing now?

He raised an eyebrow at his mother, who stood over the fire with her cane, using an iron rod to poke the coals. She saw him and shrugged her right shoulder.

"We've fetched the cream for your pudding, Mam," he said, instead of bothering to enquire after Neil.

"So you have. And what pudding is this, again?"

"Mairi said it was for her birthday—" He whipped around to glare at her. "Was this all your idea, ye little terror?"

Mairi looked worried until he called her that, when she ventured a smile. A tiny nod.

Alisdair stood with his hands on hips, and laughed. His mother merely smiled. Never would he or his siblings have done such a thing. Well, maybe he might. He softened toward Mairi, and felt a little more hopeful that her pluck would survive such a somber household.

When the solstice had come and gone, and Mairi had been covered head-to-toe in new-knitted clothing, a note was delivered that Muirne would be coming up with the children in a great sleigh they had borrowed to fetch the family down to New Glasgow for Hogmanay. This produced unrestrained joy in Mairi's shining dark eyes. His brother sighed as he read it, and Alisdair had to wonder whether he felt dismay at the social duties to come or simple exhaustion at running from himself. Muirne wouldn't let it continue, that's for certain. Alisdair hoped she would talk some sense into him.

Mairi's excitement could not be contained, and Mam had a heap of trouble keeping her out of the way as she tidied things up and wrapped and stowed and battened down for their departure. Alisdair volunteered to go to their neighbors' the MacGregors with the news and the request to look in on the cows and sheep and hens and to feed them while they were in town. Mam was staying home, but she wouldn't be able to do the outside chores. It would be good to have her looked in on, too. He enjoyed the chance to talk with Lloyd and Fred, the two older brothers who helped their aging parents farm the land. They weren't close enough to confide secrets, but they were good-humored lads. Alisdair left them with best wishes for a tall, dark stranger to grace their door for luck in the new year.

"Aye, so it's good you and your brother will be as far away as New Glasgow!" yelled Fred to his back as he departed. His brother still had fairer hair than he, and both would be considered bad luck. Alisdair laughed and waved back.

The Turners arrived without Edward but with great fanfare. The sleigh had been outfitted with silver bells and gold paper stars, was pulled by two enormous shire horses, and had two broad rows for seating. Muirne's cheeks were rosy, as much from shouting warnings at the children as from managing the horses, who seemed to look after themselves a sight better.

"Who on earth owns such a wagon?" was Mam's unbelieving shout. Muirne laughed.

"A man name Downs who is a solicitor with aspirations to be in Government. Edward met him at a gathering and we had him to supper. A very generous man."

Alisdair observed his sister's scattered management of her five children. A flash of a feeling made him think about Sheena being with child again. He sent up a quick prayer for her safekeeping, then smiled broadly as the two older children, Mollie and Gil, descended to run into the cabin and fetch the bags to be brought down. It was a short stay, only a week, but two bags were needed for the spare clothes and small gifts.

Alisdair took over the driving.

They made their way down the mountain, onto the road, over the various frozen creeks until the land rose again, only to descend into the fertile valley where towns dotted the landscape. Even under the blanket of white that covered all, there was more color and motion to a town, Alisdair noted with pleasure. He felt some of his worries, tightened in solitude, start to loosen. He turned to catch Neil's eye in the seat behind him and found him squinting off into the far distance to their right, perhaps to the bay. Next to him, Mairi was occupied with whispering to her cousin Kitty across the seatback.

When they arrived at the modest house on the main road through New Glasgow, much noise was made during their debarkation, with Gil's perhaps the loudest voice in the melee. Edward came out to greet them and whisk them in to a warm supper. He clasped Neil's hand as the children ran about the sleigh. Alisdair smiled at the chaos, and nodded at Edward's request to put away the draft horses. He unhitched them and led them forward, looping round to the barn. Their backs steaming, he took them inside immediately but put several warm blankets on them so they wouldn't take a chill as he cleaned their feet, gave them water, and then finally brushed them down.

He used the Tilley lamp to guide him through the dark mist of the snow-lined road. He found the traces easily and made sure all the pieces were put away properly. A sound attracted his attention to his left. He lifted the lamp and called out.

"Hallo?"

Nothing. But when Alisdair returned from the barn to cover the top of the wagon, he swung the lamp around again and could make out, to his right this time, a dark figure backing away quickly. *Quickly, in these drifts?* Alisdair shook his head. Perhaps it was just shadows. He secured the cover over the sleigh with cords, stretching them tight. Ignoring the itching feeling on the back of his neck, he walked into the house and smiled at the bright light and warm fire. He glanced at Neil, who sat somberly in one of the two high-backed chair, untouched by the children's merriment.

Alisdair let out a deep breath. This would be a rough one to navigate. Everyone had helped themselves to the soup over the fire, but Muirne served him a piping hot bowl as he came to sit and exchange news.

"The colony keeps healthy, by the fruit of your hands, eh, Edward?"

"Outside the isolated cases of smallpox and one of cholera, yes, I think we are keeping healthy."

"Where was the cholera?"

"Oh, a traveler from Halifax found himself all the way in Truro before feeling any symptoms."

"Nasty cities."

Alisdair kept quiet during this exchange. *Halifax is exciting! Somehow the city will be the making of me, I can feel it. They can't see it yet, but they will.*

"And Mollie and Gil, they do well in the village school?"

"Not quite the student Alisdair was, but they do well enough." Muirne shot him a grin, which he acknowledged with a bow from his seat.

They discussed the contents of Sheena's last letter, where she had relayed the news of her pregnancy as well as her efforts with the fishwives, which led into a discussion of the old croft. Alisdair thought of Sheena, always homesick for the place, whereas he had been just that bit younger enough when they emigrated not to remember the old island house almost at all.

Finally, the children were calmed enough for sleep, and Alisdair followed them quickly, tired as the journey had made him. Christmas passed with dancing and music, games and laughter. Then Edward went out again on his rounds, and Alisdair and Neil were free to walk around the village and take their leisure in front of the fire. Alisdair seized the opportunity to do the former, visiting his old haunts from his schooldays, while Neil preferred the latter, even adding a smoking pipe to the picture.

"Edward surely knows his way around a pipe," Neil said to Muirne one evening. "I thank ye for the loan of it. 'Tis marvelous liberating."

Muirne smiled, but Alisdair perceived a bit of brusqueness in response to Neil's comment. *Impatience? Regretting her generosity? Worried about the tobacco's effect on our already moody brother?* Alisdair steered clear of Neil's moodiness. He managed to murmur to Muirne that she should talk to Neil, try to get at the core of his melancholy and draw him out. But whatever force he had hoped Muirne would exert to get Neil back into fighting shape, it seemed not to be having any effect. He thought about discussing his predicament with Edward but never had time alone with him when he returned from his doctoring visits.

Finally Edward was home for Hogmanay and they shored up their preparations for the night, setting out their gifts of salt and whisky to share. They were to stay home this time, so Muirne had stashed away small mincemeat pies and honey tarts to offer their visitors all the night long. Just after midnight, a knock was heard on the door.

"Someone's here first!" Up went the cries of Kitty and Gil. Mollie had the honor of opening to this first visitor, one of the near neighbors who had dark hair. He cupped Mollie's cheek and wished her a happy new year before striding in and shouting for good fortune for the Turners through 1834.

The rituals were observed: food shared, drink consumed, and songs sung, with over a dozen folks from the village, until the children were dropping onto the floor with fatigue and Alisdair had to blink rapidly to keep himself aware of the goings-on. Ed sat with Muirne on the new sofa, canoodling with wee Thomas and baby Dugal between them. Alisdair looked around for Neil but he was not in the main room. He checked the bedroom in front, then the one in back: no Neil. A shaft of cold air sent him to the back porch, where he found his brother standing in the doorway, leaning against the jamb with his head bowed.

"Neil!" Alisdair had a moment of heart-pounding fear

when he thought his brother was with fever and out of his head again. He saw his brother's back hitch up, as though guiltily hiding something. Neil closed the door and turned to face him. His face was crinkled up in grief and red with the raw wind that was blowing. He opened his mouth to say something, but struggled.

Alisdair extended his arm. Neil gave up trying to say whatever it was and reached out to embrace him. Alisdair felt his brother's forehead grind into his shoulder as Neil yielded to his frustration silently. *The new year will be better*, he thought at his brother. *I promise you.*

December 1833, Ardkinglas

The sickness this time seemed to hang on longer, and Sheena was reduced to bending over a bowl each morning through December. Almost a year past it was, the last time she'd felt this helpless as soon as she stirred each morning. Then, she'd had Mam to sweep her hair away and hold a wet cloth to her face. This time, Gordon was usually there by her side, stroking the bumps of her spine as she crouched. Some level of herself appreciated his tenderness, but most of her was given over to embarrassment as she tried to wipe her mouth of spittle and cover the bowl quickly. The embarrassment felt silly, but she'd never had to bare herself like that before a man. It was worse than taking off her shift.

She also noticed herself filling out as never before. *And isn't that odd?* She poked the flesh of her upper arm, enjoying the soft roundness of it. *God be praised, it's the right time and the right place.* She heard her mother's tones in her own mind, the soft burr of her *r* and the sharp hiss of her *s*. A pang of home-sickness came near, but she batted it away. *It's a good thing I've got the extra meat on my bones, as I've all the work of the house to do myself.*

Rhoda's presence, company and good humor were hourly forgotten and remembered, each time with a sigh or a bitter smile. Sheena missed the help almost as much as she missed the woman. She persevered for the first few months, then appealed to Gordon for help when her back started to seize up at the end of each day.

In late December, she went with the rest of the tenants to the village chapel for the service. Upon her departure from the chapel, she noticed a matronly woman, hatted and caped against the windy weather, was waiting for her.

"I am Mercy Campion, the midwife from Cairndow," said the figure encased in brown. Outside with no lamps, Sheena could not see her face, and she couldn't very well squint at someone.

"Good evening, Mrs. Campion," said Sheena, guessing a midwife would be married.

"Mr. Lamont asked me to look in on you, and I thought tonight might be convenient for us both."

"Oh! Very well. I won't dawdle, then. Pleased to meet you."

The two women silently wrestled their way the mile and a half in the wind and rain with hands on hats and collars, saving their attention for the slippery path. They reached the trees next to the loch and Sheena felt the wind die down, blocked by the trees. She let her hand drop with a sigh of relief. She shared a look of weary triumph with Mrs. Campion, but the woman did not return the sentiment. No, the figure in brown kept her attention on the ground. Sheena quickly extinguished her hopeful expression.

Finally they reach the cottage and ducked inside.

"It is quite wet," Mrs. Campion said, removing her coat and hat.

"Aye. I'll get a kettle started. If you would stir up the coals? Thank you." Sheena poured cold water into the tin kettle and set it on the short, thin stove that had been newly installed. She glanced at the woman, a bit surprised she had not offered to help. But then she was a guest, this first visit at least. Sheena finally got a good look at the woman.

She was sturdily built, with lustrous chestnut hair topped by a black lace cap. Her face was lined but still fair, and she bore a look of unflappability. She jabbed the fire with the poker and warmed her hands as it crackled to life. Sheena wondered at the woman's brazen self-assurance.

"So you've carried a child before?"

Sheena froze. Her hands which held the spoonful of tea leaves and the tea pot lid arrested and shook ever so slightly. Then she carefully poured the tea into the pot and put away the chest.

"Yes."

"But I don't see any bairns running around, so you must have lost it."

"Yes."

"Aye, missus. That's a pity, that is. But it shows at least your body knows what it should do. I've got less of a worry for ye, then. I thought it would be disease. One of mine went that way—diphtheria at six months old. It's hard that, too, but…well."

Sheena cleared her throat and resisted bracing her hands

against the table. Her throat felt suddenly dry. It scratched as she spoke.

"I was at my sister-in-law's funeral when I went into labor and we lost the babe when I was six months gone. This past spring."

Saying it to a stranger made the scene come rushing back: the funeral, Letty, the pain, poor Neil…Sheena gasped. She blinked quickly and tried to remember all that had happened since: the voyage on the ship, coming to Ardkinglas on a horse with Gordon, getting to know the fishwives, losing Rhoda.

"Excuse me," she apologized. "It's only—"

The noise of the kettle starting to whine allowed her to abandon her unformed thought. What had she been about to say? Sheena picked up the kettle with a cloth and poured steaming water into the pot. She replaced the pot lid, then sat to wait.

Sheena tried to match the stolidness of the midwife, who maintained her poise while waiting. The swelling in her throat made any attempt to converse unwise. She forgot about the midwife, and her own cold feet, and where Gordon might be. She thought of Letty, and how alive she'd seemed just the day before her labor started. Did she name her baby that died? She didn't recall. And Rhoda, how warm she'd been the day before she was drowned.

She came back to herself as Mrs. Campion cleared her throat, and she peeked at the tea to make sure she hadn't been woolgathering long enough to make it stew. Too bad if so. They weren't so well off they could pour out stewed tea.

Increasingly discomfited with the silence, Sheena spoke. "I'm sick in the mornings still; I suppose that's normal."

Mrs. Campion nodded.

"Anything else I should watch for? Or have ready?"

"When did your courses stop?"

"Oh," Sheena blushed a little. When had the baby been conceived? She pictured that night in September when Gordon had been so happy for the last of the winter wheat being sown.

"Late September."

"Let's see, then: you're almost three months along. Sickness is normal for some. Baby should be coming in late June. Wouldn't worry until the sowing time, just don't tax yerself overmuch, missus."

"Of course."

There were a few more questions about her routine health, and then Mrs. Campion gave her a final skeptical once-over. "You might want to have an extra cup of beef tea in the mornings, and an egg, just to strengthen that constitution You know Betty down south a little ways? She'll be happy to trade you for beef tea, as her brother's the butcher in Lochgoilhead. And find you some chamomile. Good for the stomach. So, have you any names in mind?"

"Names! Oh, em…well, no, not really." It wasn't true: Sheena *had* thought of a name for a boy: Gordon, for his daddy. But it was bad luck to say the name aloud before the birth. The name Fenella came to her, one she'd heard from something Alisdair last read to her. Something may have flitted across her face, because Mrs. Campion pursed her lips and raised her eyebrows.

And with that enigmatic mark of disapproval, the midwife stuffed her hat on her head and swirled the cape over all. Sheena thanked her and bid her good evening.

"What a baggage." Sheena said it out loud just to feel some vindication for herself. The woman was quite proud, quite rude, and—on top of all that—disapproving. Whether it was for Sheena's keeping the name secret or for her being too lean, she neither knew nor cared. *I'll show that baggage.* She helped herself to a bowlful of farmer's cheese. Afterward, she felt faintly sick but settled carefully by the stove with her work bag. After knitting all those caps for the tenants' children, she realized she had better start laying out their wool sock supply, as wet feet through winter would always invite illness.

The bloated feeling went away and she made good progress for over an hour, until her gut got a whiff of the cheese. Her belly started in with some disturbing gurgle noises. The second hour her rate slowed, until she just curled over the tenth sock, waiting for her body's uproar to finish. It was at this point that Gordon returned. His cheeks were pink and his hat dripped in his hand as he stepped into the living room. Sheena lifted her face and gave a pained smile.

"Tidings of Christmas…what's wrong, wife?" His pleased expression immediately clouded over.

"I've overeaten," she said sheepishly. "Let that be a lesson to you for Hogmanay—"

Gordon's expression came out sunny once more. "Well, if that be all—"

"'Tis."

"—Then I will just part with a kiss and leave you be. I am tired!" He gave her a quick kiss on the top of her head then swept toward the stairs.

"But!"

"What?"

"Just look at you!" Sheena spoke in exasperation. "You'd do well to lean over the tub as you change."

He grinned, shaking his head. Drops flew from his rain-darkened hair.

"Oh!" Sheena exclaimed, but she was laughing.

He grabbed at a cloth on a line strung along the kitchen wall. Rubbed his head vigorously. Sighed expansively. Fell into the upholstered chair across from her.

"Oh, indeed," he repeated softly. "Oh, Sheena."

"How's the day?" she asked.

"Fine. New peat field marked out for those who need it. New shipment of cloth gone out, good price, too." He put a hand out to feel the thick grey sock in her lap.

"I'm getting better by the tenth," she told him. She snatched up the first sock to show as proof. Gordon forebore laughing at the difference, which earned him a smile.

"Did you keep one of those caps for ourselves?" he asked.

"Of course. A nice blue one."

"Do you think it's a boy, then?"

"I've no idea. But I like blue. And—I've a name in mind for it, either way."

"Have ye now?"

Gordon stood and bent over her for a kiss. She enjoyed the contact until another cramp in her belly told her she shouldn't. She groaned and excused herself to the privy, grabbing the oilskin coat Gordon had come in with.

After she had dealt with that difficulty, then come back in and got dry and warm once again, it was quite late. Sheena told Gordon of the midwife's visit, leaving out none of her impressions. He had a pipe in his hand by this time and studied the fire with a furrowed brow for several moments.

"I'll see about a doctor anyway, by the time summer comes."

Gordon could read her so easily sometimes. It was a strength she leaned on often enough. She clarified that the birth was expected in June. Gordon nodded and changed the subject.

"Now, are we ready for Hogmanay?"

"Almost. We will be, in another two days. You've secured the whisky?"

"Yes."

"You'll be the perfect First Footer."

"Will I indeed?"

"Yes—your height, your dark hair." She leaned forward to rustle her fingers through the damp mass.

"And do those make any inroads with you?"

"Oh, aye, to be sure."

He pulled her wrist from his hair and toward him, bringing her body along with it. He leaned forward.

"Wait!" Sheena called out. With her other hand, she carefully laid aside the knitting needles from her lap to the floor. She turned back to see Gordon silently laughing.

"Thank you for that, madam!"

"Well—"

Excuses were forgotten as his lips met hers.

January 1834, The Ridge

Shivers ran up her spine but Mairi stayed as upright as she could, bringing in the bucket of ice. She wore the mittens knit by her mother, and they cushioned her fingers where they curled around the iron handle. Normally, she took three rests from the creek to the house, but today she was trying to take only two. She felt strong and happy and buoyed from the visit to the Turners for Hogmanay, and she tried to hang on to that feeling. The bitter cold seemed to be winning, however.

She was in sight of the cabin, but the burning in her palms and behind her shoulders made her stop, panting for breath. She grunted mightily in frustration. *I* almost *made it.* She sighed, then a voice popped up in her head: *There's always tomorrow.* This pushed aside her disappointment for a second, but then it came back.

But there isn't always a tomorrow. Not for Mam.

Setting her jaw and bending over for the final climb, Mairi struggled carefully up. She came in through the back shed where the water was kept and set the bucket down. As she slowly flexed her fingers, she wondered where that voice had come from. It hadn't seemed like anyone else's voice. It was hers, just different. *Odd.*

When she entered the main room, Grannie looked up

briefly to smile.

"Thank ye, dear. Full this time?"

"Almost," she replied. Da did not look up. He was absorbed in a letter. He used a set of spectacles to read the big looping script very carefully, his mouth grim. Mairi sidled closer to Gran.

"Money?" she whispered.

"Aye," Gran whispered back. "Some new trade laws. He needs to know when things change so we don't get left in a lurch."

Mairi bit her lip. Uncle Alisdair had stayed in town after the new year holiday, and she already missed him.

"I can tell you the rest of what we did, Gran," she offered.

"Oh, of course. Go on, dear." She continued throwing the drop spindle, the wool twisting up and back down.

"Well, I told about the night already."

Grannie nodded.

"The next morning was a slow start, with everyone abed because they were tired."

Da gave a loud exhalation at that remark, which she ignored.

"But Aunt Muirne had cleared everything away really nice anyway, so when I woke up first, there wasn't much to help with—I did try. Gil and Mollie were up soon after me, and then Kitty started yowling."

A suppressed smile showed on Grannie's face.

"And when she did, we all decided to go outside in the snow, so we wouldn't get in trouble with waking up the old folks, y'know how they get angry sometimes."

"Indeed, very thoughtful."

"So we went out the back and shoveled a bit. Then Mollie and I started a snowball fight with Gil—which we won,— even though it was a bit unfair."

"Mmmm." Gran's tone agreed.

"But he's a boy, so he figured it was all right, and I'm glad we beat him." Mairi smiled. "Then we went out the front to see if other people were out, but the street was empty except for one lady and her bairn, and they seemed to be staring at Auntie Muirne's house. That was mighty strange, so Gil went over to talk to her, but she hurried away and didn't say a word!"

"Did she so?" Gran's eyes narrowed. Mairi looked at her father, who was glaring straight forward, his face a mix of white and unhealthy red.

"Da?"

When he switched his focus to her, she saw his effort to calm himself: a swallow, a double-blink, a slow let-out breath.

"And what did the bairn look like, Mairi?" asked Da.

"We could hardly see him, he was wrapped up in leathers like a—like a—Indian boy!"

Her father's eyes widened at her description.

"Perhaps he was sickly, so she wrapped him up against the cold. But then why would they go out?" Mairi wondered aloud.

"I don't know, Mairi," her father said quietly. He lowered his head into one hand, which scrubbed and scrubbed at his scalp. She looked back to Grannie, who watched her son with compassion. She turned the look on Mairi, her eyes sad and wondering, then picked up her drop spindle again.

"After that, we went back to the Turners'. Aunt Muirne was cooking for breakfast the food left from the night before. She made it into a great big feast with new bread and mounds of butter, and it was all delicious!" Mairi finished with a flourish of her hands.

"That's very good, Mairi. I will tell Muirne that I've heard a fair report."

"And next year you should come down with us," Mairi said. But her grandmother protested about the house being left alone.

Mairi said nothing. Perhaps it was something between Da and Grannie, the way they exchanged glances. Or perhaps Grannie just hurt too much to move these days. She watched as her grandmother's good hand pulled the fleece down and spun the spindle, her bad hand supporting the rest of the fluffy batting. Watching it made her miss Mam.

"May I go down to see Mam? I'll be quick, back before it gets real dark," she asked.

"If yer da thinks it's all right."

Mairi looked to her father.

His eyes in the firelight glinted, but the rest of him looked tired and flat. He started to say something then checked himself.

"Aye, but go canny and quick," he said.

"Yes, Da."

Whatever was troubling him, she wasn't going to let it get in the way of her visiting Mam's grave. But she could go canny.

February, 1834, The Ridge

"S-H-O-E. Shoe. S-H-O-P. Shop. S-H-O-R-E. Shore."

"That's excellent, Mairi, very good."

Alisdair took the book from his niece and flipped forward several pages, looking for a harder set of words.

"How come none of our words from home are in there?"

Alisdair found the page and put his finger in as he attempted an explanation of language.

"Because our words from home are a different language, called Gaelic."

"So…things are spelled different?"

"And spoken different."

"Then how do you know what means what?"

Mairi's exasperation made Alisdair smile a little.

"Well, take a book."

"B-O-O-K."

"Or?"

"*Leabhar*. But I don't know how to spell it!"

"Dinna fash, Mairi. It's enough to know both words, and be able to write in one. That's very good, already."

She looked only slightly mollified.

"Pretty soon, you'll have a turn down in town with your cousins, just like Sheena and I did, and you will delight and amaze all the teachers with your knowledge." Her spine straightened. "As long as you don't lord it over the others, d'ye hear?"

"Yes, Uncle."

"All right. Now, if we've enough of that, let's keep going."

Reading and spelling with Mairi kept Alisdair's mind off the reply from Dr. McCulloch he was waiting for. He'd written again to ask if there was any movement on the committees where the doctor had been campaigning, or men likely to change their minds. Even with Dr. McCulloch's dim view of the Council, Alisdair had caught the man's optimism that eventually he would be granted the money to hold classes at his university. Alisdair wanted to be in that first class to enroll.

Even if there were to be no classes that year, Alisdair still entertained the possibility of going to study with Dr. McCulloch before the spring plantings. The older man had impressed him with his talk about the larger situation in Nova Scotia, the depressed state of education for the masses—meaning the poor—and the selfish parochialism of the governing body. Alisdair felt a tingling in his fingers, hearing that. Like he wanted to change it all, upend all the stuffy old men in their collars and replace them with energetic young men: all pitchforks and pens and pointing fingers.

This is what he thought when he went out on his brief, frosty walks to care for the animals. Most of February was spent indoors, with the heavy weather and socked-in conditions. Since returning from town after Hogmanay, they hadn't had a visitor and weren't likely to until the spring melts started. Unless someone had some good snowshoes.

A thought rustled in the back of his mind at that. *Snowshoes?* But he couldn't place what had made him stop at the word.

When Mairi had finished the harder list of words, he said that was enough for the day.

"Can't I read a little from one of your novels, Uncle?"

"Novels! Who's telling ye I read novels, eh?"

Mairi darted a glance toward Neil. "Nobody."

"Leave him alone, daughter."

Alisdair looked at Neil sitting in the firelight, carving a little bit of wood.

"She's fine, Neil. Here, let me fetch you one of those 'novels'…" He fished out one of the tracts on government reform he'd been handed in Halifax and held it out to her, smiling broadly. "Feast yer eyes on that, Mairi."

She took it and turned toward the fire, her mouth working to sound out the long chains of letters. The writing would be hard enough, with its official flourishes and tails and bobs across the lines. He grinned at Neil, who grimaced and dropped his head to whittle some more.

"Sure that's suitable for a young girl, Alisdair?"

Alisdair scoffed. *As suitable as such a father in such a life*, he thought, then felt badly. Neil was lonely—he could see that—and turned neither to his daughter nor his brother. *Maybe he talks to Mam.* Alisdair looked over at Mam, at her regular place on the stool by the table. She leant her elbows on its edge and wound the last of the yarn into a ball.

A knock on the door interrupted his first words to Mam. He got up to answer and led in the snow-encrusted postman, Morrissey.

"Phew, man, what you doin' out in this?" he laughed, knocking off the ice and kicking it out the door before hurriedly shutting it again. The post! He tried to be extra civil because he knew the traveler must be carrying his letter.

"Oh, it's cold but all right if ye k-keep m-moving," Morrissey chattered as he rubbed his hands at the fire.

"Important letter, then, I imagine? Or just earning yer keep?" Alisdair kept up the banter as Neil hadn't offered anything.

"Oh, aye, there's that, but I thought you'd be wanting your news from Halifax." Alisdair took the letter from the proffered hand, quickly folded it, and stuck it in his waist band.

"Here, have some tea to warm up. Are you making for anywhere else tonight?"

Morrissey took a quick sip and exhaled in relief. "Ahh, yes. The Frasers' place. I'll put up there for the night. And if I'm lucky, I'll be there before they finish supper and get an eyeful of that daughter of their'n."

"*Mister* Morrissey, I'd appreciate if ye didn't take on so in front of our Mairi," Mam said, stern enough to put ice back on his coat.

"Sorry, ma'am." Morrissey glanced at Mairi, who watched the interchange with fascination. "Beg yer pardon. Well, it's near six, so I should be going. Thanks for the tea, Alisdair." He set down the mostly full cup and quickly got gloves and hat and muffler back on before scooting out the door.

"Aw, Mam."

"Aw, Mam, nothing! I'll not have it. We shall have respect in this house. That's all." Mam stuffed the ball of yarn into her chest of sewing notions and yanked out knitting needles, the yarn hanging off. Knitting was still difficult for her to master, so Alisdair felt even worse. Mairi sidled closer to her, his tract wrinkled and twisted in her hands.

"Give that here, Mairi. Go on and help yer gran with the knitting."

The family members formed a new constellation in the room, and Alisdair had some space to read his letter alone.

> *Dear Mr. MacLean,*
>
> *You are right to hope, young man. That is the only road which leads always to eventual success, with the help of Our Lord. I have been working these past twenty years, as you know, in those same hopes, and have watched as several sets of men have managed to lose the veneer of egalitarian hopes for reform as soon as they enter office. Perhaps it is the initiation rite, or the Oath that they swear, that does it.*
>
> *But it truly cannot stand, in the field of Education, which is the only way we have to improve the situations of so many striving for Excellence such as yourself. The monies I used to collect as principal in Pictou were a pittance, and yet I counted myself happy to have made a dint of Progress in that town and its people's education. Now, in the Capital, there is the potential for so much good, I can not but contin-*

ue to hope in the Lord's Power and mysterious ways.

There is always the possibility of work that would give you a foothold into the industry of your choosing, Mr. Mac-Lean, as you suggested. But I find that there is an end to that ladder, which can not be traded for another unless a man have an University education. I, who was so fortunate to attend the University of Edinburgh, found it opened many doors, and I would encourage your Patience on that front, rather than any attempt to batter down the doors of the Institutions by untutored Genius at Industry.

A few years are not looked upon as an insurmountable obstacle, especially if they have been put to profitable use. If you cannot travel due to family responsibilities, then you may avail yourself of newspapers and examine the policies of the Crown, with an eye to Improvement and Efficiency, so that when the time comes, you will be well prepared to seize such Opportunity.

I shall wait for the autumn session of the Council to write to you with news. Until then, I am Cordially Yours,
    Dr. Thomas McCulloch

Hope, hope, and hope. Profit, profit, but with no idea from where. It was more of the same, and Alisdair felt heartily sick at the empty words. He respected the doctor's opinions and appreciated his confidences but felt cut off at the knees. What was he to do to profit from this listless, frozen time? He was young and strong and could work like an ox for his brother. And make sure his niece was literate. And help care for their mother. But what *else?*

He looked up to see Mairi watching him, next to Mam.

"Mairi," said Mam in a mild voice, setting down her knitting. "Go fetch us another tray of fish, would ye, dear?"

"Yes, Grannie." She flung her large coat and new mittens on and dashed out to the smoke shed, where the layers of salted fish were stored in the barrel.

"Ye are disappointed," Mam observed. She put out a hand and Alisdair came to sit by her, squeezing her hand before clasping his own together between his knees.

"Aye." He glanced toward Neil, but his brother had moved away from the fire and toward the bed. "It's that doctor fella I was telling ye about, ye remember?"

"The one you met when you brought Sheena to ship?"

"That's the one. We've exchanged a couple of letters since then. He's built a university but can't seem to get the money to run it. He's a Presbyterian, but it's for any Church."

"Well, that's a pity. He sounds like a great man."

"Aye, I think so. He's advised me to travel or, barring that," he hurried on, "to keep myself informed of political affairs—to do something to add some polish to my record. Only I'm not sure how much I can do from here, and I feel so —so frustrated!" His whispered voice was raised a little, but Neil didn't turn.

"You could go abroad, as others have done," his mother said after a pause.

"I couldn't go that far from ye. It wouldn't be right."

She smiled at him. "My boys and girls, so unwilling to

leave me. Did I do something right or something wrong?"

He stayed silent, ruminating.

"It might be that he only needs you this year, Alisdair," Mam said softly enough that Neil wouldn't hear. "To make it through without Letty, or Sheena."

"Aye."

Alisdair knew his brother needed him, even if he didn't always show it. Maybe that's what grated: that Alisdair was making this choice to remain for his brother's sake, who couldn't even acknowledge the sacrifice. But things could change after this growing season. The university could open; Mairi could go to school in town. And Mam? The place would be verra lonely with just her and Neil in the winter, but the family would be back. It would only be for a short while.

Alisdair kissed his mother's cheek and stripped to his shirt for bed. Mairi returned with the pan of fish and noisily wrestled it into the cabinet in the back room. She and Mam said prayers together then smoored the fire. Alisdair was left to his own, prating thoughts.

February 1834, Ardkinglas

February in Ardkinglas was cold and wet, wet and cold. Sheena sometimes felt she'd never be warm and dry again. She couldn't remember a winter like this when she'd grown up on Mull, even though it was only two days' journey to the west. But her misery was eased by the fact that Gordon didn't travel so far in winter; her rest came easier when nights fell early and she settled against him to fall asleep. She began to feel the baby more clearly inside her, and sometimes to feel even grateful for the terrible weather out-of-doors, when she was snug inside, singing softly to the quiet.

Most days, Gordon's work took him only to the manor house, where he would work on figures for the estate, copying bills of sale or deeds of ownership by this or that cottar or merchant. He often arrived home from the short walk drenched, but in good spirits.

"Happy to come home to you, wife," he said.

And Sheena would smile and embrace him while he was yet sopping wet, and they would have a good laugh over his imprint left on her apron. Rose had been asked and accepted the post of housekeeper, at least temporarily, until the fishing season started again. Sheena believed her remorse over treating Rhoda shabbily was genuine and forgave her. She was a rough cook but a dab hand at cleaning, which Sheena noticed and gave thanks for. By February, while no longer hurling up her suppers in the morning, she had lost her good sense of balance and saw stars when she bent over or stood up quickly. Mercy Campion came by once a month with chamomile and a face like she'd been sucking on a lemon. She listened to Sheena's tentative reports of dizzy spells and told her with a nasty smile not to bend over. Sheena kept as much dignity as she could muster for these interviews.

The first time that Mrs. Campion visited, Rose was cleaning on her knees by the stove. Neither woman took notice of the other. Gordon was away at the main house, and Sheena, now with a well-rounded figure, submitted to the battery of questions and probings.

"You switch that chamomile to the night-time as I said?"

"I did."

"No headaches?"

"No more than usual. Only two, in truth."

"Moving your bowels all normal?"

"Aye, Mrs. Campion."

Sheena almost sighed in exasperation, then thought of Letty. Mrs. MacGregor was a fine herb-woman, and yet nothing she did could save her sister-in-law. She humbled herself in her mind.

A few more pinchings of the wrist and palpatings of the back and she was pronounced sound.

"And I'll leave these with you for a tea when the babe starts moving and your body's all needles and pins, you hear?"

"Thank you, Mrs. Campion." She took the little bag and put it on a shelf, then led the way to the door. Once it was closed behind "the baggage," Sheena turned to find Rose sitting back on her knees, regarding her with an injured air.

"That old hag! Excusin' my language, missus. There's never no way she should be a-treatin' you li' that!"

"Like what? I figured she just forgot how to smile at anyone, ever."

"Well, there's some as can be more solemn, it's true, but she's just bein' a heavy-handed shrew. No call for that old—"

"Do you know her, Rose?" Sheena gave her friend-cum-servant a meaningful look. If she didn't know her, it was better not to cast aspersions. And if she did, what was her story? Sheena didn't want to be caught out of the local gossip as she had with Rhoda's situation.

"Not past noddin' terms, though I will say—that is—the boatman that comes down to our wee pier, he said that Mercy Campion was thinking her man would get the job your husband has, but 'e was passed over. I'd not be surprised if it's preyed on her mind and done her a bout o' jealousy, missus."

Sheena's breath became short and hitched. *Of course. Of course there was bound to be someone looking to move up and who got passed over in favor of Gordon with his experience and connections in the government.* Oh, why hadn't she even thought of that until now? She wished there was someone else who could help her through the birth. At least there would be a doctor in a few months, as Gordon had promised.

Sheena took a deep breath and told herself there was

nothing to worry about, nothing to be done in any case. She listened to Rose as she spoke of the Campions' social standing at the village to the north of the big house. She wondered if there was a way to get the woman onto her side.

Mid-February, Gordon came home with a storm on his face. Sheena saw it immediately and attempted to divine its cause and win him over to a good humor.

"Happy to come home to me, husband?"

He looked up at her and wiped a hand over his face, changing the storm to a scowl. Another scrub brought him almost to neutral, but instead of genuine pleasure, he seemed to be forcing a levity he didn't feel.

"Of course, my darling. Come here." She came and he took her head in his hands, imparting a much longer kiss than usual. Sheena opened her eyes to him, expecting to find his good humor restored, but instead saw a sort of desperation. He was even chewing his lip. She started to worry that it was bigger than some argument with a farmer.

"Is everything all right at the manor house?"

"Of course. We've had some bad news on the debts. I've been tasked with thinking up the solutions, and they are—we are in a bit of a tight spot. That's all I should say for the moment. Now don't you worry. What's on at home?" he said with an attempt at a dashing smile.

Sheena placed her fists on her hips.

"Well, what is it? Maybe I can help."

"No, no. It's to do with agreements with banks down in London, nothing to do with you."

"That reminds me, did you hear back from the solicitor about Rhoda?" Sheena had read the letter he'd composed to send back in September and approved its perspicacity. It had been sent four months ago, but Gordon had reminded her that the estate was probably large and its settlement complicated. The settlement didn't matter now that Rhoda was dead, except that Sheena had an attachment to knowing the truth.

"Oh, yes, actually. The man finally replied to say that the name Rhoda Sudbury does not appear anywhere in the Wilberforce will, but that there was a small annuity for a Mr. John Sudbury, living in the vicinity of Hull."

Sheena's brows shot up. "The child?"

"I've no idea, but I don't feel called to write to him to demand entry into his affairs."

"No, of course not," Sheena said softly. So perhaps there had been a relationship, and the boy had taken Rhoda's name, even though he was fostered out? It didn't make sense, but Sheena was not ready to travel down to Hull to prove her belief, either.

"I simply choose to believe her. The story she told the women at the loch, I mean. What a tragic end."

"Yes, well." Gordon loosened his collar and cravat. "Tell me something of your day. I don't want to think about estate business anymore."

"My day? You mean the scouring of pots and ripping of hemlines and—"

"No, no," he protested, with a laugh. "What were your thoughts, my love? Those are always beautiful."

Sheena looked back at him, feeling her heart simmer with love for the man.

"Oh, what occupies most of my thoughts these days: I thought about the future for the baby. How he'll be well-fed and go to school, perhaps with the other children being born right now on the estate—"

"Ah, yes. That is a good thought," interrupted Gordon. His face did not match the sentiment, however. His jaw was locked, and he was chewing his lip again. Sheena's mind scattered in multiple directions, leaping from one horror to another and trying to guess what was making Gordon so jumpy. *The children of the estate? Was there illness?*

"What other thoughts did you have?"

"Well…I thought on the last Sunday sermon, when the minister spoke about preparing for the privations of Lent, how we must give up our comforts to seek the True Way, but—"

"Oh, enough!" Gordon practically shouted. He turned away from her for a long moment. "I'm sorry, Sheena. I'm feeling poorly. I shouldn't subject you to this mood. Excuse me for a moment. I'll return shortly and be in a better humor."

He sighed and turned to face her. He gave Sheena a quick kiss on the cheek, lingering close enough that their eyes didn't meet, before heading out the back gate toward the wall around the estate.

He'll only get wetter, and his humor blacker, Sheena thought.

Can't see as what's bothering him will dissipate that way, but what do I know? There was obviously some deeper matter about the estate, but what was it?

Gordon returned half an hour later, no wetter than before. *So he spent his time steaming in the shed. Hmph. I'll have an apology before I bend to please him again.*

He didn't look at her but peeled off the wet layers in the middle of the room and hung them up to dry on hooks by the hearth fire. When he shucked his breeches, Sheena turned away, fiddling with the sheet she was folding. She listened though, and heard the sound of a cloth being rubbed against skin to dry off.

Good. Can't have him catching cold.

The rubbing sound stopped and she tensed again, waiting for her ears to tell her what to expect. They failed her, as his arms wrapped silently and soggily around her and she gasped in surprise. She felt his chin, then his cheek, rest lightly on the top of her head. A few drops fell onto her shoulders, and the heat of his body radiated through her clothes. He relaxed against her, finding solace in the embrace.

Sheena grasped his two chilled hands in hers. After a moment she turned and let out a little gasp to see he had not replaced his clothes. She placed a hand on her heart.

"Rose is already come and gone, no?" he murmured.

"Yes," she replied. "It's only—I wasn't expecting—you are a shock of a sight for a cold evening."

That got a genuine smile out of him. His arms curled her closer.

"I hope I always am, Sheena. As you are to me."

Sheena turned her face to rest on his chest and let the hairs tickle her skin for a moment. They stayed like that for a good while, Sheena letting the good feeling build up in him, measuring his mood by the gradual relaxation of his grip. Finally, she lifted her head.

"It is well past supper time, but I'm sure the soup has kept. Shall we have a bite?"

"Yes. I will regret it tomorrow morning if I don't. And I shall regret it sooner if my wife has anything to say about it!"

Sheena shot him a look, but the teasing threat was a facade. He was hiding something, and she had not the courage to ask what, just then. She felt a flutter of movement and pressed a hand low to her belly. It was like a call with an echo inside. She closed her eyes to listen to the echo, feel it in the twitch of her hands, then opened her eyes and let it go. Gordon was watching.

"I love you," he offered.

"I know," she said. "Now go on and have yer pipe."

He sighed, then went up to put on dry clothes. She set their table and broke up the bannocks from lunch, slathering them with butter. She set out the cold cooked celery root, the new dish she'd tried from a tenant farmer's wife's receipt. And she plunked down two bowls of thick barley broth. No smell of pipe smoke reached her, but she saw the back of Gordon's head in his soft chair, where he must be "just thinking." She called him to the table and said a quick grace. Sheena had picked up her spoon and blown on a first mouthful—*I am hungry, let him go on and be dainty about it if he will*—when Gordon reached for her hand across the corner of the table.

"The matter of the debts—Sheena, it troubles me, and because it troubles me, you won't let me be. I see it." She put the spoon in her mouth, unsure what was coming and suddenly flooded with fear in her bones about what could make her Gordon this agitated.

"The Laird is in difficulties—we knew that. He is behind in expenses, mired in new debts now, too, and denied the quick solution of a settlement on his Jamaica plantation, he wants something done *now*. He sees only one way of rescuing his accounts: creating private grazing out of the commons and importing the Leicester Longwool from the South."

"The commons? But that's where everyone grazes their cattle! He'd be robbing the poor tenants to pay his own bills, as if their rents weren't high enough! And what's wrong with our own sheep, that he has to replace them with Leicester sheep?"

"I don't know, Sheena. But he also intends to evict those that couldn't pay in cash at the Candlemas reckoning."

"That's almost a half of the folk on the land!"

"I know. I have tried to show him other ways to retrench, but he is keen on what he sees as an easy transmutation of empty land into profit. It seems he's to be one of those landlords that is a pox on their tenants."

"But he can't do it, can he? Don't they have protections against such a thing, that happened to us?"

She could feel the buzzing start in her ears. Flashes of red seared her vision. It wasn't alarm for the tenants, although that had a place in it. And it wasn't simply fear for their own prospects. No, it was the rage about her own displacement coming flooding back. She fair choked on it, feeling the power of its howl against her throat. Gordon was standing over her, a hand on her back, saying something she couldn't make sense of.

She tried to swallow it down, drinking the glass of ale Gordon pressed to her lips. Fast, quick gulps couldn't get past the lump in her throat, and the ale ran over her chin onto her apron. She shut her eyes, but they squeezed out tears all the same.

"…thought you were out of the stage of being ill?"

"I *am* out of—I was much—better—but—"

The memory of their home's roof timber in flames was before her again, blending with the red of her rage. *How can this be happening still—again? And with me here, a witness once again, powerless to stop the powerful or protect the weak, just like Mam was?*

Sheena stood up abruptly. Gordon stood by her, the half-empty cup still in his hand, a look of alarm making his eyes seem whiter at the sides.

"I should lie down," she said, gripping his forearm for aid. Gordon put his arm around her waist and walked her carefully up the stairs to their bed. She lay down in her clothes. The fizzing along her skin stopped, and the heat next to her heart turned cold. The sudden squall of emotion passed and she felt empty. She gazed at the ceiling, the clean staves and boards all of a length and width exactly the same. That sameness she had marveled at when they'd first arrived. That sameness which now housed her comfortably, while others would soon be on the road starving. She closed her eyes, and heard Gordon move away.

February 1834, Ardkinglas

When Sheena woke, it was another day, and the roof timbers faded back into the scenery. She turned a stiff neck to see she was alone in the room, and the light was the dark grey of morning. She got up slowly, feeling a sour dryness in her mouth. She noticed the clean water in the basin and limped over to splash her face and neck, then padded down the stairs carefully, so fragile did she feel. Gordon was poking an iron in the hearth. He was muttering to himself.

"Gordon, what *are* you doing?"

He looked up, surprised, then guilty.

"I was trying to make some bannocks for when you came round. I mixed and shaped them well enough, but I seem to have lost them to the fire."

"What?" She was torn between laughter and exasperation. She smiled, then the unreality of the scene brought back yesterday's news. Gordon continued to clang metal against stone.

"Ah well," he said. "I've set out the cheese and pickle and porridge, if you're up to it."

"Do you not go to the house today?"

"No, I sent a note you were feeling poorly and I was worried for you. I said I would be detained for the morning. It's barely eight o'clock. If you're well enough for some breakfast, we can take it together and then I'll—go up to the house."

Sheena let her gaze rest on Gordon's waistcoat, the good one, that he had changed into for today. Was he dressing himself with courage to talk to the Laird? Would he tell her what he meant to do before he made the decision for them both?

She caught his eye, and he met her gaze evenly. She sensed him breathing deliberately to calm himself, steel himself, and her heart beat a little harder in response.

"What will ye do?" she whispered.

"I will try again to dissuade him from turning people out. If I cannot, then…I will have to look for another situation."

The heaviness of admitting such a defeat struck Sheena as she gazed at her husband's face. She knew it was all he could do, and the pained helplessness she had often felt in herself recognized its twin in her husband for the first time. Sheena broke eye contact, her breath heavy and stuttering.

"Is there not a solicitor we could engage, on the part of the tenants?"

Gordon considered the possibility grimly. "If we could do so in secrecy, aye. But I don't see how it could be done. I'd be blacklisted."

Sheena cast around for more ways to help. "Do you know any solicitors who might undertake it for them?"

"A solicitor, and then a barrister," Gordon murmured. "I can ask one solicitor about the matter, but whether he knows a trustworthy barrister, I cannot promise. And neither can I promise that we will be able to find as good a situation elsewhere, if we are known to be troublemakers."

Gordon's grimace showed his frustration. *It feels like Us or Them to him, when what it should be is All of Us against the Laird.* Sheena stretched out her hand, and Gordon grasped it.

"Let us take breakfast together before you must go, since you have already sent your excuses."

Gordon still studied her with a tortured air. His hand was warm and clenched hers painfully.

"We will do what we can, my love, and then what we must. And we must go without scones this morning, it appears." A slight smile accompanied her words.

"Yes," he said, loosening his grip.

A few weeks later, March brought endless rain and a pervading heaviness. At times it felt warm, at other times as if the cold damp would not leave her bones. Sheena sat by the hearth, almost oblivious to the noise of rainfall on the trees outside.

The Laird had not changed his mind, and had left again for London. Gordon had contacted the solicitor Jones, but after a few introductory hints, Gordon knew the man would not champion their cause. He would run straight to the gentry, expose the upstart, and bask in the ensuing favor for as long as he could. So Gordon started to send letters of inquiry out to some of the industrial concerns with which he had done business in the course of his nine months as factor.

They had quietly sold some of their cookware and linens,

as well as the new desk and clothes press. Gordon had told someone that a present from a family member was coming to replace it, and so far, their lies had been believed by the manor house staff. They were preparing for flight, but being as conciliatory as possible to the Laird and his staff.

"Can you at least tell the folk on the land what is coming?" Sheena asked him one evening.

"What good would that do?" he muttered.

"They would at least have time to make their choice and prepare for leaving, as we are doing!" Her voice came out a bit sharper than she intended.

Gordon looked reproachful, then mournful. He nodded. "I will do that."

Sheena listened eagerly for his reports each night. He missed dinner most nights to talk to the tenants and cottars, and when he arrived home, worn and weighed-down with the little good he tried to do, she would ask about the tenants' plans. Many seemed prepared to head to Glasgow. A few seemed willing to brazen it out and stay on their ancient leases. And more families than she thought were prepared to emigrate across the ocean. Each morning when she woke and remembered the day's tasks, she cursed the landholding system, so obviously broken.

While she urged Gordon to seek the best options for the tenants, she took the coward's way out and pleaded weakness to avoid joining the fishwives at the loch. She felt the tingle of guilt every time Gordon came back from one of their cottages. *I no longer want to care about them. They will quickly forget any part I played here, at any rate. Oh, Rhoda.*

Sheena sewed the coins they had got in exchange for their goods into a long, narrow, interior panel abutting the seams of her dresses. When Gordon had suggested somehow concealing their cash instead of using a purse, she'd told him the idea.

"Good as gold, you are, Sheena, dear. And twice as devious."

She laughed at his nonsense. "Not devious forbye, just think: you will have all the more reason to keep me close!"

The joke still made her smile as she sewed, until she remembered the risk they ran of being turned out, or brought up on trumped charges, and how important their duplicity was.

It is only for a little longer, she reminded herself. *Then we shall be free of this oppressive secrecy.* Gordon had figured that the orders would start to be delivered at the end of April, and he was scrambling to secure his next employment. He had been hard at it, burning the candle at both ends, writing his correspondence in the early mornings and continuing the secret visits in the evenings.

Sheena suddenly wondered if they might return to Nova Scotia. Her stomach dropped, and with it, the child moved. *What if we did? I would be at home, in a way, but we would have failed…Gordon would feel miserable, as well as outcast by his social circle…Och!* It roiled within her, and she couldn't decide whether she was terrified of returning, or excited. *Would we have failed, in refusing to be part of such oppression?* She wanted to hear Gordon's opinion. Tonight when he returned, she would ask him about the possibility.

She turned her attention to the letter she had received from Alisdair. The family was well, and he was hopeful for a place in a new university to be opened in Halifax, an institution open to all religions. He hoped to make the right connections there to be in a position to make life better for future settlers to Nova Scotia. His yearning bubbled through the measured expectations. Sheena wished her brother well in the career he was embarking on. She wondered if Gordon's presence in their lives had influenced him, made him consider politics for himself, for it surely would have seemed impossible a few years before. *Gillan's son? A politician?* The two ideas together were preposterous. But Gordon's example as a civil servant might have shown Alisdair a new possibility. *There is so much to be thankful for*, she mused, *even amid such turmoil*.

The panel seams were finished. She pulled the inside out and folded the dress so it wouldn't let loose a telltale clink or clatter, then set it in the chest. She took her cold supper of lamb and spring onion shoots while sitting at the table and absent-mindedly resting a hand on the slight curve of her belly. A knock nearly caused her to lose her knife across the table. She recovered it and answered the door.

"Mrs. Campion!"

The midwife stood with dignity. "Evening, missus. Thought I'd drop in for a wee visit... What, yer man not home yet?"

Her voice dripped with suggestion. Sheena ignored it pointedly and offered her a seat.

"Would you like some supper? He's out for something or other."

"Something or other. Aye. Well. If ye've enough, I would-na mind…"

Sheena gritted her teeth and went to the kitchen to cut another slice of meat from the cold joint. She placed it on a plate and returned to the main room, where she saw Mercy quickly closing the lid to their chest. Sheena pretended she hadn't seen, but her heart jumped and wriggled in an erratic march.

"Tea?"

"I'd be pleased to join ye, missus. That rain, it'll do for ye."

"It will, indeed." *May it do for you*, she silently thought, then blotted out such a hex from her mind. She heated more water in the kettle over the hearth and sat, waiting, focusing on maintaining poise while her visitor shifted uncomfortably.

After she'd served tea, Mercy dove into her cold meat and vegetables, stuffing herself in the way Sheena had in the years before she'd known satiety. Her heart softened a bit. *Perhaps she is having a hard time making her way this year. Perhaps she is on the list to be evicted.* Then her mind took a different direction. *What if she found out about her eviction and turned informer on the rest of the workers, in order to keep her roof?* Sheena narrowed her eyes at the woman. She could well believe it.

As her guest was finishing, the door opened to admit Gordon, whose hat miraculously still held its shape against the downpour. He didn't say anything as he hung it and his oilskin coat on a peg, placing a bucket underneath.

"Good evening, husband. We have a visitor."

Gordon's startled eyes took in the table, sizing up the situation. Sheena hoped this would give Mercy her cue to depart. And she did, in fact, take one last swipe of her bread over the plate.

"Yer wife was kind enough to host me for supper," she said. "Many thanks."

"Most welcome," he responded. "I've been entertained by the Guthries tonight, so I hope my portion was big enough for you." His smile sparkled. Mercy melted only a little, and only for the moment.

"Aye, tasty. Mrs. Lamont be a good cook."

Sheena inclined her head in acknowledgement, though Mercy paid her no heed.

"What you want with them Guthries? In this weather?"

"Oh, stock details to be tallied up and new purchases planned. Estate business." He smiled pleasantly and she nodded slowly.

"I'm afraid we've no heart for entertainment, do we, dear?"

"No, I'm fair tired after the day," she replied.

"S'all right. Appreciate the food, missus. You're looking in fine health. I'll be on my way."

She gathered her shoes, drying by the hearth, and disappeared out the door. Gordon let out his breath in a long, controlled hiss.

"She's either on tae us, or suspects you," she said, rinsing the two bowls and cutlery in the large bucket.

Gordon still stood by the door, gazing into the air, deep in thought.

"Anything to keep her in the dark," he muttered. Then his eyes lit up. "News."

"Oh?" Sheena clenched her fist, squeezing the horsetail brush she used to scrub the bowls.

"I received a reply from a Mr. Stirling. He is acquainted with Mr. Longnoth, whom I wrote a week ago. Stirling is undertaking to build a new bleachworks and believes my recommendation from Longnoth suggests I am a good man for the job."

"Oh?" Sheena repeated.

"Yes. And it is a very exciting project, indeed." He looked excited to continue but Sheena scrunched her brow and interrupted.

"Where?" Why was she limited to one word responses? She felt weakened, a-tremble all over as she focused on her husband's reply.

"It would be southwest of Glasgow, in Barrhead. Stirling writes of a large flat on offer, part of some new terraced housing. It's near their other businesses in cotton, linen, and wool manufacture. You see—"

"But what can you do, in that sort of place?"

Gordon came around the half wall to scrutinize her. "Sheena. You're getting upset. What's the matter?"

There was some impatience to his tone. Of course, he couldn't comprehend the panic that accompanied her memories of living in Glasgow for months and choking in its coal dust. She hadn't related that small window of her experience, and so he had no idea of her fear of the city.

"Never mind. Where is Barrhead, then?"

"South of Paisley. Some five miles, I believe. But come, tell me why you're in such a state. I understand the—the distress over the evictions," he almost whispered the word. "But what is this dithering over being near Glasgow?"

"It's the smoke, and the air," she said softly. "I was in Glasgow half a year before we took ship for Nova Scotia. It was—bad for everyone's health. Gillan's. Neil's. They worked in a cotton mill and had it worse in the lungs, but I didn't do very well there, either. Oh, Gordon, don't tell me I'm going to have a baby in that smoke!"

She turned away from him, angry to learn that this new opportunity that had heartened her husband so took them back into that city. There was a long silence behind her. She didn't want him to think she was disappointed in him, but such a place—! She turned back and saw him struggling.

"It is the best position, for now, and time is getting away from us," he said softly.

"Would you ever consider," she started, but couldn't finish. How could she ask him to leave the cities where he thrived and knew his business to return to the backwaters of provincial Nova Scotia, where he would scrape along, never getting to grow his talent?

"Nevermind."

"Go back to your family? I think not, Sheena. I hope not to have to depend on them, strapped as they are at the present. I don't want to be an albatross."

She rather felt she was the albatross, but forebore saying so. At least he'd said they might return if necessary. She drew herself up and nodded. She would go with him to Barrhead, if need took them there.

April came on, blustery and strange. Gordon still went to the manor most days, and to tenants' houses most evenings. One of those evenings, after Sheena had weathered another tense visit from Mercy, she was surprised to hear another knock at the door. With her now-customary hand on her expanding belly, she rose from her stool by the hearth and opened the door carefully.

It was not raining that evening, but it was rather late, and too dark for Sheena to see the woman's face as she looked down at her.

"Yes? What is it?"

"It's Silla, missus. From the fish house."

"Oh, of course. Come in, where we can talk." Sheena hustled the tall woman inside as much to be courteous as to keep the cold air out. Besides, what was she going to say to her—it was sure to be about the evictions. *Now who was Silla married to?* Sheena cudgeled her brains to remember any of the woman's gossip from last autumn.

"Thank'ee, missus." Silla had to duck her head to enter like Gordon did. She walked to the middle of the room and turned, her arms clutching opposite elbows as if she was cold.

"Sit by the fire, now, and tell me what errand you're on," Sheena cajoled.

"I needn't stay long. I'm just the messenger from the fish house, come to say thank'ee for your husband's visits and his efforts with the solicitor fella. We've all had a talk 'round and figured it was right decent of him to look after us, even if…"

"Even if?"

The woman tensed even more. "Even if you'll both still be in a nice, homely spot like this!"

After she spat out the hateful jibe, Sheena's jaw dropped. Gordon wasn't telling the tenants that they were leaving, too?

"Some of us thinks you don't care for us anymore, after how poor Rhoda went, but some others had thought you was really good and kind and should've done more for us women, as your husband's doing." Silla sniffed, obviously uncomfortable being the messenger of such emotion.

"Silla, I——" Could she explain how they were planning to leave, if Gordon hadn't? She didn't want to endanger their leaving by discussing it where she shouldn't. But those women, and their families, must think her so callous! How could she defend herself?

"Of course I feel as you all do. My family was evicted from Mull twelve years ago. I——we have thought through all that we can do, and Gordon is doing what he can. I am more sorry than you can know."

Sheena felt her cheeks quivering and clenched her teeth to keep her countenance. "Please tell the women that, Silla."

"Better if you came to tell us yourself, as the factor is

doing," Silla replied.

"I couldn't. This one—I need this one to survive. I can't go about as I used to." She rubbed the top of her belly, her voice hardening.

"Well. Good night then, missus." Silla was brusque as she showed herself out.

Sheena's gut squirmed, then the baby was moving—circling all her most sensitive spots. She sat back down by the fire, wishing they could leave right then and forget everybody.

March 1834, The Ridge

March meant more wretched snow for *Sealladh Cùil*, the Gaelic name for their mountain cabin which Mairi had just learnt to spell. She was happy enough in the cabin most days, but the months of confinement with only brief forays allowed were wearing her down and making her head feel numb. She wished for more variety and found an escape in the stories she continued to make up, but they began to have a sameness that made her feel trapped and dull.

Uncle Alisdair was not happy, either. He didn't delight in teaching her anything much anymore. She'd learned her alphabet straight off, and practiced her hand a little each day, but needed his help to read much of anything. The nights that were getting shorter, they'd sit side by side at table after supper, and Mairi would spell and sound out the words of a book of his, while he gazed at the paper, hardly seeing anything. Often she would have to ask him directly if she'd got a word right.

"Strand? That can't be right, Uncle."

"Oh? No, that's a word."

"What does it mean, then?"

"A single, long piece of something. Like hair. Or a long, narrow beach."

Mairi didn't see how a piece of hair and a beach could be

similar, but stored away the comparison and continued.

Later that night, she sat at Grannie's feet by the fire. The knitting needles were lax in Grannie's lap and her eyes were closed, but Mairi could tell she was not asleep: something about the purposeful look on her face. Da and Alisdair were out in the barn again working with the tools.

"Grannie, why is Uncle so quiet these days? Is it because he doesn't have a wife, neither?"

A startled kick from the leg next to Mairi meant she had been almost asleep. Grannie smacked her lips. Mairi repeated her question. When she replied, Grannie's voice gave Mairi an ache inside, it was so pained.

"I don't think that's the reason, Mairi. I think he has a dream that he wants to pursue, and a family he wants to support, and he doesnae see the way to do both."

"Is his dream to go away to school?"

"Aye. I think even more than that, he wants to change some of the rules for people like us. He's got a heart of iron, that one."

Mairi noted the pride in her voice. "Doesn't Da have a heart of iron, then?"

"Oh, perhaps, but it is broken for yer mother just the now. He needs time to sew up the edges of the hole she's left. Just gi'e 'im yer love, like a good girl, and he'll be back with a lion's heart; you'll see."

Mairi scooted closer, and Grannie put her good hand over Mairi's head. She stroked her fingers through her hair, and soothed away Mairi's worry.

Mairi tried to be the good girl Grannie wanted, but found herself crossed at every turn. She asked Uncle politely for help the next evening, and he continued with the same sullen stare at the page as before. She even made up a few words and slid them seamlessly into her recitation. He didn't notice. She stopped and stared at his face, looking for evidence of this big dream of his that Grannie knew was there. Was it rotting inside him? Is that why he smelled so bad?

"Ey! Why'd you stop?"

"So you'd notice," she pertly replied. He raised his eyebrows at her. "Sorry, Uncle," she quickly excused herself.

The next morning she elected to follow her father around. She tried to hang back and not be a bother, but after an hour of her shadowing him on the hill where he measured and marked trees for removal, he turned to her and barked. "Come here!"

"What are ye playing at?"

"I just wanted to be near ye, Da."

"Why don't ye go along home and help yer grannie with the breakfast, there's a good girl."

"But, Da—"

He held up a gloved hand.

"How am I supposed to be good when no one wants me?" she shouted. "Not you, not Uncle Alisdair. Nobody wants to be happy here but me!"

Da stood still, with one leg cocked on the rise of the hill

for balance. His head dropped several notches, until he mumbled into his shirt, "Go back home, Mairi. I'll talk with ye later."

He walked deeper into the woods and after a minute she couldn't even see him for the shadows. She turned around and followed their tracks home, huffing frustrated air and sputtering tears all the while. No one did want her. Would she be any less burden if she stayed with Auntie Muirne? Or was shipped away to live with Auntie Sheena, who had no children, yet.

She popped into the cabin and let her eyes adjust from the afternoon sun to the fug of smoke and dark inside.

"Grannie?" she said hesitantly. She knew she'd be in for a tongue-lashing when she saw how soaked her petticoats were with forest mud. There was no answer, and the air felt still and cold. She glanced at the hearth. Embers gleamed back at her, but nothing cooked over its heat. She went to the cool shed.

"Grannie?"

She made the rounds of the outbuildings: the smokehouse, the byre, the sheep pen, the chicken roost, the privy. Nowhere. Was she in the fields with Alisdair for something? Or by the creek for washing? Mairi wiped a sleeve across her face and trudged down the hill, squinting out over the rolls and dips of their croplands, not seeing any wee figures moving down the rows. Where was Uncle?

Her heart sped up a bit as she realized they were both not in their normal places. She hastened her step toward her mother's grave and arrived at the grove in a pant. No one.

"Alisdair!" she yelled as loud as she could. Da might hear

her, which would be just fine. She was starting to be afraid. She had to find one or the other of them. "Gran!"

Mairi started back up the hill toward the cabins and heard shouting; she increased her pace until she was gasping for air and felt like she might fall backwards into the air. The hill leveled off and she was able to run flat-out. She saw her uncle's blond head coming over from the road; he was carrying something awkwardly. Her da was already running, crossing in front of her from the woods to help him with his burden. She slowed as she got close enough to see the awkward burden wore skirts the color of Grannie's. They disappeared into the door and Mairi stayed rooted to where she was, panting, wanting to scream, wanting someone to tell her it would be all right. *Mama. Mama.*

Mairi swayed, torn between staying away and going toward the house. She crouched, still twenty paces away, and hugged her knees. She watched and wept for a stretch before she saw Uncle Alisdair coming out, his head twisting this way and that, looking for someone. She popped up and limped over, aware now that she'd hurt her foot running. Alisdair's eyes narrowed in on her. He waved a hand, beckoning. She grabbed it as she came up to him. His eyes were reddened and his hair a-scrabble.

"Oh, what has happened to Gran, Uncle?"

"She's had a sort of fit. It's happened once before, and we have some of the medicine she needs, but we'll need more. I'm off to the MacGregors. I was going to send you, but I see you're limping."

Mairi's heart burned that she wasn't able to help. She shook out her ankle. "It's all right, I can still run. I was just sitting too long—"

"Never mind it, Mairi. Just stay here."

And without another word, he dashed off to the west, his shirttail flying behind. Mairi felt her living family slipping through her fingers like sand. She hiccuped her way slowly back to the cabin and paused a moment on the threshold. A wail broke from her and she let it fly. She couldn't hold it all in, not anymore.

It only took a minute before she calmed down. *Da is in there. And he'll have heard me.* She gulped, ashamed now at letting the sobs fly out of her when her father was already worried and scared inside. She darted in.

"Sorry, Da," she whispered, moving toward Gran's bed in the dark.

He sat on a chair by the bed, and she knelt next to him. His arm crooked out and hugged her head to his hip.

"'S all right, Mairi. It'll be all right."

But she heard the desperate wheeze behind his words. He wanted to wail just like she had! She could feel it trying to push through his words. She peeled off his hand and climbed into his lap, where she hadn't been for months. He hugged her with one arm, the other stretching toward where Grannie lay. She stayed rolled up tight as she waited with him, as the front of his shirt turned damp and salty.

March 1834, The Ridge

Alisdair ran, ran, ran. The buzz and drone in his blood had not stopped since he saw Mam slump on her camp stool. They'd been out by the road, discussing improvements to it and wondering about the mail wagon that day. He'd brought the camp stool for her, for they were going to share a flask of tea before heading back. Alisdair was thinking such exercise would be good for her, help her coordinate her walk better in time.

But after she'd had a sip and sat for a moment, he was in the middle of describing the new harvest schedule to her when he heard her grunt, and lean inward, like the stuffing had gone out of her.

"Mam?" He stepped around the stool to squat before her. Her chest was sunken in and her eyes closed, but still she balanced on the stool. He saw her lips tremble with air and spittle, but she gave no sign of hearing him.

"Come, we've got to get you help." He had a moment of indecision, when he wondered if he shouldn't go to the Mac-Gregors' now when he was closer, but he did not care to leave his mother alone as she struggled to breathe.

"All right, back to the house, then," he muttered. He swung her up in his arms. It was a little awkward, and her weight grew the farther he walked, but thankfully he made it back to the house before his arms gave way. He shouted for Neil, not knowing where he was, and eventually saw him come up over the bracken hill by the cabin.

"I think it's her heart," he gasped to Neil. "I'd use the tincture Ed left last spring. Send Mairi to the MacGregors' and I'll head to town."

"All right, let's get her in," Neil replied. He took charge of Mam's shoulders, hooking his arms underneath, while Alisdair shifted to put his arms round her knees. They stutter-stepped into the cabin, the door hitting both of them as they poked at it with elbows and hips. Alisdair made her comfortable in bed while Neil rushed to find the wee bottle Edward had left with them after Letty's passing. *Never know when you might need a spoonful of laudanum. Good to have a little handy*, he'd said.

It wasn't on the shelf with the other glass things, evidently, because Neil was clanking them all together and cursing the while.

"Did it need to stay cool? Check in the cold cabinet," he said to Neil. Neil rushed to the back room, where more noise emerged.

"No! Where else?" Neil came back in, looking wildly around. Alisdair stood up as well. Not by the fire, surely. Nor the beds. Nor the window. Alisdair's eyes lingered on the window and then went to the space above the wall under the ceiling. He'd seen his mother climbing down from there. He took a seat and stepped on it, feeling with his hand around the tiny space. A clank, as he knocked over something. He pinned it with his hand and withdrew it. A small bottle.

"Here!" he shouted, and clambered down. Neil looked at him, bewildered, before grabbing it and cradling their mother's head to take a few drops.

"There's hope that'll dull any pain she's having, and slow whatever…I'll go now."

"Keep an eye out for Mairi," Neil said quickly. "I think she'll be about the place, and maybe scared from all the racket."

Alisdair opened his mouth, closed it. No time. "Aye."

He went out the door, giving a quick glance around to see if the girl was hanging about. She popped up in the direction of the creek, then wobbled her way towards him. Neil was right: she was scared enough for the world to be ending. He told her to be strong and stay put. He lit out himself for the neighbors' property.

He ran, recovered enough from carrying his mother to step nimbly and be alert. His brain was running in a hundred directions. *Send Mrs. MacGregor to the house. Has she got any supplies—digitalis? Take their horse to town for Edward.* A terrible flash of seeing Lloyd on that horse coming for Edward last spring came to him. It would be him this time.

What else? Send word to Sheena. Mam was lucky to survive that first fit years ago—if fit ye could call it. She'd had a hysteria over something, ran straight down the cliff, and fell the last fifteen feet or so, knocking her head and sustaining those injuries that made her left hand curl and disobey her, her left leg refuse to bend.

Alisdair would send his note to the estate where Sheena and Gordon lived. *Send Edward. Send letter. Then home again.*

It is not Mam's time to go, he begged. *Not yet.*

Alisdair scribbled a cryptic message: *Mam has had a bad fit. Come if you can.*

He broke down in the post office, turning away from the clerk, who said nothing. Alisdair threw down the amount marked on the placard and hurried back to his sister's across town. Muirne had readied her brood to travel. Ed was out on a medical visit, but their neighbor had been instructed to tell him the urgent news as soon as he returned. Baby Dugal was strapped to Muirne's front by a sling. She looked like a Native and it struck Alisdair dumb for moment, but he forbore mentioning it.

He joined them to trudge to the town stables, where Alisdair ascertained the next mail wagon would beat them up to the ridge. Night was falling, and they waited an hour in the nippy twilight before they heard the horses' approach.

"Right, then," Muirne said, motioning to her children. "Everybody up once they've changed over horses."

The children watched, interested despite the mood of uncertainty, as the four sweaty giants were unhitched and walked off in a circle.

"That's so they don't get ill from being put away cold," Alisdair said to Kitty, who stood closest to him.

She looked at him with reproach. "I know, Uncle."

Alisdair smiled to himself. Of course, an eight-year-old knew everything, didn't they? The look on Mairi's face when she'd emerged from the snow to limp over to him—he reminded himself how terrifying it could be, too.

The new horses were soon yoked in together, and the subdued band climbed into the carriage, with Gil sitting atop. The wagon jostled and lurched even on the road through the town, such was the speed urged on the horses by the driver. *Lord love him for it*, Alisdair thought, *if it brings me back to Mam in time. All those horses want is to run.*

I should have as simple a life, he thought. *Without yearning for something different. Without wanting something more, all the time.*

Hours of jostling and lurching later, they arrived at the break in the road that led to their house. Alisdair helped his sister descend carefully, the children jumped out, and the driver wished them well before slapping the rein on the horses' back once more with a shout.

The lantern at the back was visible as the vehicle swung crazily left and right, driving away. Then they were in complete darkness.

"Mind, go careful now. We know the way, don't we?" Muirne said to her brood. She sounded less tired than he felt.

They made their way slowly, hand in hand, the quarter mile up the path to the cabins. The land around was quiet. Alisdair imagined it a reverent silence, but chided himself. And why would the beasts of the forests love his mother? She'd done naught but dress their fine carcasses, give thanks for the season's acorns and lumber and clear water. As his eyes grew used to the dark, a song came to him. One that stood out in his early memory, connected to his father Gillan.

Dh'èirich mi moch madainn Chèitein,
> *Faill-ill è ill ù ill ò,*
> *Hiùraibh o na hò-rò-èile,*
> *Faill-ill è ill ù ill ò…*

*I arose early one May morning…*and "sweet was the choir" of their forest. He tried to remember other verses, but all he could recall was the lark above the moors, of which there were none here. His thoughts flashed to Sheena. She'd be near moorland. She'd be hearing larks. He hoped she heard one that told her of her mother's illness.

April 1834, Ardkinglas

There were birds singing in the tree near the house, but Sheena was too agitated to enjoy them. Here it was mid-April, and the weather as bonny as a summer day. On a day like this it didn't feel like there could ever be such intolerable injustice as forcing people off the land they'd worked for centuries. The contrast made her skin feel oversensitive and, combined with her jumpy stomach, had Sheena in an ill humor.

Gordon had arranged things with the man Stirling in Barrhead. They were expected within the fortnight. Whenever she thought of the place they were going to, Sheena had that furious squirm in her belly. Now seven months along, she felt strong and sturdy, but she reckoned she would soon feel awkward and ungainly if she kept growing at this rate. No, it was best they move before she felt like the clumsiest pig in the poke, even if they had to go back to Glasgow. She'd have to find a way to put aside those memories of fleeing to the city. *Barrhead could well be a shining example of cleanliness and opportunity*, she told herself. *Don't count it out before you've even seen it.*

And we'll be better off than the tenants. Poor folk. When she'd asked Gordon why he hadn't told the men that they were leaving, he'd surprised her.

"First off, the more people know, the more chances that someone will cop to the household, and we'll be charged with incitement, dereliction—whatever the judge can think up to punish us and win his lordship's favor. But even if we aren't charged by the bailiffs, Callander could find someone to replace me and sail ahead. I want to leave him high and dry for what he's doing, when finding another factor would be near impossible in time for planting. Which is why securing employment first is so important."

Sheena hadn't known there was such a spirit of vengeance in her husband. It surprised, but moved her, that he could feel the injustice so keenly, even though he'd never been on the receiving end. She worried about the women's opinions a little less. Another gurgle that had nothing to do with the babe emanated from her gut; she clenched, grabbing a shawl to pull over her head to go out to the privy.

The rush over, she carefully gathered her skirts and walked back. An uplift of birds above the road caught her attention and she stopped, waiting. Sure enough, a rider came thundering along smartly. He stopped a few paces from her and swung a leg over in a practiced fashion to dismount.

What will I give to be able to do that in a month, Sheena thought with asperity. Then she frowned. Why an urgent rider, sent to her door?

"Hallo," she said. The man was at his saddle bag. He turned to her with an envelope in his hand.

"Good day, missus. You are Mrs. Lamont?" She nodded. "I've a letter for ye, first class. From Nova Scotia."

Her jaw dropped. No speech came.

He handed the note to her. She broke the seal and held the limp scrap of paper, reading its two lines quickly before they blurred into incomprehensibility. *Mam must be dying, for Alisdair to send for me. But I can't!* She choked.

The man put a hand out to catch her if she fell. His hand hovered above her shoulder, hesitant, afraid to touch. He was an errand lad, not yet twenty, probably hoping to be a head groom one day. He wouldn't be wanting to upset someone who could have him fired.

"I'm sorry." She closed her mouth and tried to calm her erratic heart. When she'd pulled herself together, she asked, "When?"

"Came late last night, ma'am. We almost sent it to the Laird's office, but thought——"

"No, no, that's fine," she said sharply. "Is there to be a reply? Do I owe you anything for the trouble? Would you care for a bite o' breakfast?"

"I would, ma'am. Thank ye kindly." He still looked uncer-tain. Hungry, but wary. She led him back to the house, creat-ing some noise with the griddle as she set it over the fire and made up the dough. She made small talk about where the young man was from and what it was like at the post office.

She flipped the bannocks on the griddle just as the back door creaked open. Gordon entered, surprise on his face to see a young man being entertained.

"This is Mr. Lamont, Mr.——I didn't get your name."

"Chisholm."

"This is Mr. Chisholm, Gordon. He's delivered us a letter from the ridge."

"Oh?"

"It's my mother. Alisdair wrote—she's in a bad way. Not likely to recover." At least that's what she read between the lines in the desperate urgency of his hurried script, something he usually took such care with. Her eyes filled and she turned back to the griddle.

She scraped at the bits of crusted butter on the iron. Gordon came behind her and put his hand in the middle of her shoulder blades. All he could do in front of a stranger. But his hand held his strength in it, and his sympathy. She breathed in hurriedly, dashing away tears.

"She had another fit, he says. It was a short message."

"I'm so sorry, my love."

She didn't tell him that he'd asked her to come home. What use would that be? They were leaving, she was with child, they were escaping this place—there was no room for a trip home in the midst of their calamity. But not to see her mother again—it tore at her gut, something quivering deep in her bowels. She stretched herself tall as she could and grasped the handle of the pan with her apron.

"Here's the bannocks. As good as any you'll find in Argyll." She gave a watery smile to Mr. Chisholm, made a plate up for Gordon, and excused herself to go upstairs and out of sight.

She heard the men making small talk, then Chisholm made ready to leave. He'd probably been desiring it the whole time. Poor man, regretting heeding the call of his stomach.

Sheena came down and managed a grimace as they waved him off. They went inside again, Gordon stopping just behind the door to enfold her in an embrace.

"I'm sorry, Sheena, love. That you can't say goodbye."

It was then that she let herself sob. Only when she could find a place of safety did she dare open herself up to such wolves of feeling.

Several days later, Sheena woke to find Gordon very still beside her. There was soft grey light coming through the window into the bedroom. She raised herself a little to see his face. His eyes were open, his hands folded on his chest.

"Thinking, are we?" Sheena said, easing herself down again. *Lord help us all when a man starts to thinking.*

"Yes. Tomorrow. It's on the morrow we go, Sheena."

She swallowed past a dry throat. "Need to get some water," she mumbled, and maneuvered out of bed. She went downstairs, poured a glass from the pitcher, and drank. She noticed her pitcher hand shook a bit. Set it down.

Here it is, then. He's given the word. Got to move. But—fleeing in the night, bringing a baby with us into the unknown, not saying goodbye to Mam. Is this the wrong time? It doesn't feel right.

She turned her thoughts away from useless appeals and returned to the bedroom. Gordon watched as she came, searching her face. She stood close to where he lay.

"I'm ready," she whispered.

He curled an arm around her hip and she felt his hand

across her buttocks, pulling her closer to him, until he was able to kiss her rounded belly.

He pulled back and let his arm slacken. She perched on the side of the bed.

"I have everything arranged. The horse and cart from Ramsay, the cart to be sold at Oban, the times for the coach there, the inn where we'll stop at Tyndrum. My friends will put us up by Loch Lomond, where we can rest the horse before the Erskine ferry and the last leg southward.

"I've got all the papers and cash to hand. We've got every-thing down to a bag each, and the trunk." His brow wrinkled. "The trunk is why we have the cart. We may yet have to leave it behind."

Sheena chewed her lip and nodded. *Remember when you brought it up the ridge, last year? We all felt so modern, the trunk such a wonderful shiny new piece of our future life. And now we may have to leave it behind.*

"I want you to be prepared, so it's less of a wrench if it happens," he continued.

"Yes, of course."

He got up and made the rounds of all the things he'd take, making sure they were all to hand, but not packed in case someone saw the inside of the cottage and was alerted to their plans. Sheena dressed while he thought through the day. *We are wretched, and wretched, and wretched, and my life will never be as I want it.* A stealthy knock interrupted her battering thoughts.

She went to the garden door and peered out into the morning mist.

"Is it you, missus?" She heard the whisper before the face one of the tenant women materialized close to the door.

"Come in, Edie. And how are you today?" She made her voice as matter of fact as possible.

"Oh, missus, I'm fine, thank you." Sheena lit the lamp from the fire and saw how the woman's eyes shone, betraying her worry.

"And how is your husband, missus?" Sounds of drawers and cabinet doors wafted from the bedroom.

"He is just now rising for the day. What errand brings you abroad so early?"

"Oh, it's nothing. Just on my rounds and thought you might could use a few extra supplies. We over on the hill corner made overmany bannocks and thought we'd make a present of the new cheese Betty made to go with it."

The sounds from the bedroom stilled, and the two women turned to see Gordon emerge in his shirt-sleeves, waistcoat, and breeches. Almost respectable. But she supposed that might be the least of her concerns, come tomorrow, when the Laird discovered his plans for the removals would be contested and the removals thwarted at least until planting time was past.

Gordon bowed his head respectfully. "Thank you, Mrs. Mitchell. And tell the others they have our thanks as well."

"Of course, sir. Now I'd best be on my way to the field. Good day." The woman nodded at them both quickly. Sheena saw her quietly out the door. *To the field.* She hoped they were ripping up all the winter produce they could take with them.

Two other emissaries came during the day, whom Sheena

received as Gordon was off to the big house for the last time. The kindness, the respect—it was enough to split her heart open each time. Finally, the day was over, Gordon was home, supper was eaten, and the dishes put away again.

"Time to pack," Gordon said with a sigh. He set about arranging their few tools and books among his clothes in a cotton bag, slipping their important papers in his pockets. Sheena stuffed her clothes with the sewn money into the canvas haversack and filled it to the brim with her sewing notions and foodstuffs for the journey. The trunk sat open and gradually filled with winter clothes and blankets, dishes, pots, packets of medicines, and the baby clothes already presented by friends.

The pots were the worst, as they had to be carefully padded to make no sound, and Sheena was bone-weary by the time they finished at half past eleven. *Four hours to sleep, then to Ramsay's barn a quarter-mile to the north, pulling the trunk on a canvas cloth*, Sheena went over Gordon's plan yet again.

Sheena couldn't sleep. Gordon in his shirt next to her couldn't settle down, either. After a tense twenty minutes, he turned to her.

"We need to rest. We'll not be attentive enough if we are over-tired." His fingers, rough now, caressed her temple.

"I know." She closed her eyes in resignation. "I can't seem to calm my spirit before such a—oh!"

She felt his hands at her breasts, the hardness at her thighs. *Of course, this will make him sleep.* She opened her eyes to see him looking intently at her, a yearning in his dark brown eyes.

"Please," he struggled to say. She wriggled closer, tugging her shift upward.

"I need you, Sheena. Please." His voice broke, and she was shocked to see his cheeks wince, his jaw set.

"Husband. Gordon. It will be all right." She cradled herself around him as he sought release. His grunts became her shouts as they shattered the strangling hush that had held them all day. The last drawn-out groan came from Gordon. He shook, a shiver that caused him to hiss in breath through his teeth, then fell into a boneless pile.

"I love you," she heard him say before his breathing became even.

Three hours and a half.

Sheena drifted into a restive sleep that seemed to last for a long time. She dreamed of cattle with sheep's faces, fleeces for spinning that had tiny houses mixed in with the leaves and dirt. And just before she woke, a horse bore her on a long, lonely stretch of road, but she twisted backwards in her saddle the whole time, searching for her mother.

"Ah!" she gasped. Gordon flinched beside her, then twitched himself awake.

Gordon rose to gauge the position of the moon above the trees.

"It is time." He turned from the window to look down on her in the shadows. "I love you, Sheena. We are going to make a silk purse out of this sow's ear, believe me. You're a good woman, a good wife to me, and I thank God for it every day." He bowed his head and said a few hurried words of prayer, of thankfulness and protection, of justice. Sheena's heart felt wrung out like a wet cloth. There'd be no justice for these crofters. But at least they knew the score.

May they riot and bring down that pig of a louse and his ill-deserved authority, she fumed. *And may no one come to harm*, she added, thinking of the women and children she'd come to know over the past nine months.

They washed, dressed, ate what they could not take with them, then stood for one last look around.

"Oh—will you reach that for me, Gordon?" Sheena pointed above the doorway to the kitchen. He plucked the cross of straw from its nail and handed it to her.

"It's our Brigid's cross. It should come with us."

He said nothing, nodded. They went out the door.

Forward, forward, she thought. She ignored the echoes of "Onward, Christian Soldier" that tried to muscle their way into her mind. *Forward to better things.* She remembered Mairi making up her own songs and tried to do the same, finding a tune that served—"Chì Mi Na Mòrbheanna" would do—and singing her words to herself in the locked room of her mind as they pulled the cloth with their trunk.

And we are marching, marching...
> *Making a new road just for us...*
> *Where the new house will have a garden...*
> *And the air will be as clear as that here...*

She wasn't musically gifted, and the song petered out by the time they reached Ramsay's barn. The man was already painstakingly hitching the horse to the cart, his movement making no sound, until the horse moved and there was the ethereal tinkle of chains.

Sheena had her bag heaved to in the cart, along with the trunk and Gordon's sack. She saw Ramsay shake Gordon's hand then tip his hat to her in the darkness. He helped her clamber up the back of the horse, a much bigger one than she had ridden here.

"Gordon," she whispered, clutching for his hand. He heaved himself up behind her, his arms going round her to gather the reins.

"Nothing to worry about, woman. She's as right as rain. Big enough to carry the both of us—the almost-three of us," he murmured in her ear. "She had to be. Don't worry, you'll get used to the view."

But when darkness yielded to dawn light as they rode up the coast, Sheena blanched, not liking the view at all.

"Look to the west then," Gordon suggested.

Sheena looked out to the sea, where humps of islands were visible, shady grey spines against the still-dark night. She knew when they got closer to Oban it would be *her* island they could see, and the thought gave her a bit of hope. She relaxed a tiny bit. Started a new song.

April 1834, Tyndrum

Sheena clutched her bag to her, as she had for the whole ride from Oban. Her buttocks and thighs were throbbing with the awkward balancing and clutching she'd done on the horse to Oban, and now they experienced a new torment as she bumped along the macadam road toward Glasgow on the hard wooden bench of the coach.

For a late April morning, there were fewer passengers than Sheena had expected: another man and his wife sat across from them. There was no conversation. Sheena judged the couple across from them to be about the same station—tenant farmers or smallholders, maybe. But they had not been introduced, and Gordon was not used to starting a conversation without the benefit of an introduction. *Oh, Gordon, how much will you have to bend, so we do not break?*

Her hands loosely clasped the full skirt gathers that would have hid her belly if she had been thickset anywhere else. Her thoughts bent forward to their destination, willing it to be a gentle place for their would-be family. It seemed a very long time, and she was drowsing when at last the noise reached her. A "Ho!" from the driver, the clattering of hooves giving way to quieter dirt, an answering yell.

She squinted at him. "Are we at Tyndrum, then?"

"I believe so," he said.

When the coach came to a standstill, Gordon stepped out first, then offered Sheena his hand. The other man exited and did the same for his wife. They stood awkwardly together, minutely adjusting themselves for a moment before casting around for the inn that was meant to hold them.

Gordon reached up to grab his bag and flicked a penny at one of the milling stable hands to bring in their trunk. They stood in the stable yard at dusk, the hills rising around them. Sheena caught her breath at the mournful black bulk raised against the dark blue sky. She remembered it. *But I've never been here before. Have I?*

They started for the inn to their right, and Sheena looked in the direction they had come. Something about the sloping hills on each side, the mist beyond, piqued her senses. She felt ghosts running past, felt her own desperation for a slice of a second.

"That's the road to Glencoe, isn't it?"

"I believe it is. We came from over there," said Gordon, pointing to where the road forked off to the left. Sheena looked down and nodded. *Yes, but I came that other way, years ago, no shoes and no money and no hope in the world except Mam leading us and Neil finding us.*

Like the dark times in Glasgow, she hadn't told Gordon about that part of her family's journey. It would only distress him. Instead, she strode toward the inn's front door, walked in as her husband held it and watched as he handed over money for their room.

"Mr. And Mrs. Able," he said to the proprietor. Sheena bit her lip to hide a grin. When they made it to the room, she gratefully swiped off her bonnet, relinquished her bag to the floor, and sank onto the bed. Her neck felt oddly boneless after all the rumbling of the road, even a macadamized one.

Gordon bent down beside her and kissed her temple. "Sheena. Wife. Are you well enough to take some wine? I will fetch you some along with our supper. Rest a moment."

She nodded without opening her eyes, but instead of falling asleep as soon as he left the room, she was surprised to feel tears pricking her lids. She dashed at her eyes, then gave it up to settle her hands on her belly. Her belly, that she felt coming alive more and more. *With my child*. Her child, that she was not going to lose this time. She wished it strength and encouragement.

She counted the seconds as she felt her exhaustion be filled with the fullness of her love. The baby was quiet, and she hoped that the journey had not done it harm. *No, young one, very likely you will just keep me awake all night, won't you?*

They had a quiet supper, both partaking of the wine. The trunk was delivered by the by, and the bed was found to be very yielding. Sheena woke the next morning fresher and bolder in spirit. She was ready for the next leg of their route to Loch Lomond, where Gordon had a friend. She looked forward to meeting him, and having a rest, just like their horse.

The friend, Iain Marshall, was now a prosperous factor of some lands owned by the Laird of Luss. They stayed with his family for a week, in a cottage that had more modern amenities than she'd ever seen. Sheena saw Gordon's guard relax exceedingly in his company. It made his pensiveness and worry of the past couple months all the more painfully plain to her. Saturday night, Sheena tried to find a way to speak of it. She sat next to him on the edge of the bed in her chemise.

"They are lovely people. Not proper *island* folk," she teased, "but lovely. I'm glad you've had a rest with them. It seems to have filled your heart up."

Gordon looked sideways at her. "You fill my heart up, wife. It's only circumstances that fill it with worry for you sometimes, too."

"And those circumstances will be different once we've reached Barrhead, will they?"

Please reassure me.

"Well, that's what I hope for, but there's no guarantee. We've struck out from the trodden path and must depend on friends and hard work now. Build up a good reputation anew. And I will be keeping my head down for a bit, at least until I hear of the Laird finding a new secretary and factor. But none of this need touch your head, my dear," he said, putting a hand over the one in her lap.

"Don't say that to me," she said sharply. Gordon's brow went up. "I see you happy with those friends of yours—these friends that have stayed on that *path*. And I wonder if you regret choosing me, when I seem to bring you nothing yet but sorrow—the babe, and my nervousness about—"

"Sheena, my dear, calm yourself. Don't upset—"

"It's like I'm always trying to outrun something bigger than me—the landlord, the famine, the Laird. I keep trying to be strong, over and over, but I'm afraid I just can't, Gordon. I can't!"

She gave herself up to weeping, and Gordon didn't interrupt her. She felt the anger pushing out and couldn't stop it, the whimpers turning into sobs. She didn't notice when it stopped, but woke abruptly in the middle of the night to find her husband lying with his arm cradling her head. His arm must have gone batty with the tingles some time ago. She lifted her head and gently moved his arm so it lay between them. Gordon slept on, no doubt as exhausted mentally and physically as she was. She fell asleep again, no dreams to trouble her rest.

When they woke together, Gordon coughed a few times before being able to speak.

"You," he said, in a voice so stripped he might have been suffering from drink, "are a wonder, my little wife. So much strength of will in such a fragile container." He stroked her brow with his thumb.

"Don't forget that we are one," he continued. "We made this decision together. We still have plenty of time to…raise a family, live comfortably. And we have kept our honor, the most important possession."

"Yes, but I want to see you happy," she said quietly. "That is what I want. And a family."

"And we are proceeding in that exact direction. Trust me, my dear one."

She rose stiffly to put on her clothes. Gordon sighed and bent to wash himself at the small dresser.

Trust. The word made her yearn for Mam, and Neil, and Alisdair. *Mam may be gone from this life already, and me unaware. My family doesn't even know where I am.* When she had on her petticoats and stays, she searched among Gordon's effects to find his small writing desk and the implements within. She sat down by the small side table to compose the letter to her family, realizing that having to hide the truth from them in her last letter had been more of a wrench than she'd thought.

> *Dear Family,*
>
> *We have left the cottage at Ardkinglas. The Laird planned on turning out his tenants just as we were done, and we could not in good conscience stay on under those circumstances. Gordon and I have fled to friends and plan to settle in or near Barrhead, in Renfrewshire. Gordon has a promise of a job with the new bleachworks of a man named Stirling there, and he is hopeful.*
>
> *I am well, but sick with all the concealment necessary. I hope to shed the burden of it all when we arrive and start our new life. The babe continues healthy as well.*
>
> *I am also grieved to hear of our Mam's further illness. I am sorry not to have been able to return or respond as duty demanded, but we left the Laird suddenly and under cover so his plans would be foiled for the summer and the tenants*

have a chance of recouping the winter harvest.

I will write again when we are arrived, and describe our new situation. All my love forever.

She signed it, not bothering to ask Gordon to contribute a note. She was calmer now. Gordon finished with his washing and dressing and came to stand before her. She noticed the impatience in the tilt of his head.

"Can you give this to Mr. Marshall to post after we leave tomorrow?"

"Of course." He took the envelope but didn't move.

He is resentful. He wishes I had responded with an affirmation of complete trust. A thrill of recalcitrance surged up and down her body: a shock of energy. *He waits for me to capitulate.* And she felt the stubbornness grow in her until she sighed. *Where there is no love given, there is nothing to resent*, she reminded herself.

"Gordon," Sheena finally said. "I'm sorry for not respond-ing—when you asked me to trust you." She took a deep breath, looking away. "Of course I trust you. It is why I am here. And you're right. We are taking this decision together, and keeping our pride in doing so. I'm proud to be your wife, wherever we may go."

April 1834, The Ridge

Their mother, Sheila MacLean, lingered near death for long weeks until a great fever shook her frame and suddenly, she was gone.

Muirne was there, and Edward, at the beginning, until he saw there was nothing he could do and knew he could be more useful elsewhere. The children stayed, and Alisdair took turns with Muirne and Neil watching them. He assigned them chores, and they got to work, subdued, except the two-year-old Thomas who obviously wanted just as much noise and attention as he usually got at home. Thomas was a welcome distraction when Alisdair found himself brewing too-strong thoughts.

At least the weeks were not spent in agony—for Mam. She lay quiet and still for the most part, and occasionally he saw her eyes open and a corner of her mouth twitch. She was gathering within herself for the final goodbye; he could feel it. He hoped Sheena would send word in time.

But then Mam was gone, a cold husk, and Sheena was not there, had not sent word. Mam had stopped breathing on Muirne's watch. She'd called the boys in and there they stood around the bed. *Deathbed, now*, Alisdair thought, and tried to wash away the words' touch on his soul. He berated himself as he stood by, observing silence with the others.

It's not as if this doesn't happen every day. It's not as if we didn't lose Letty last year. And Sheena's baby. It's just—Now he only had his siblings to tell him how life had been before him. And did he trust them?

Alisdair expected Neil to begin a prayer, but he just stood there, eyes squinted shut, curling his hands into claws. Muirne stood, too, after telling the children to be quiet and stay outside. So Alisdair cleared his throat and started a low rumble that grew into a rough, soulful tune:

When the soul leaves the body,
The stubborn body,
And goes, in bursts of light
Up from out its human frame,
In its final flight.
God, come and find me,
Come to seek and find me,
God and Jesus, Mary's Son,
Virgin and Apostles twelve,
Seek me and find me
When my life is done.

Muirne blinked at him, then smiled, her cheeks pushing tears out and around. She reached out a hand, which he clasped. Alisdair turned to Neil, whose head bobbed slightly, as if nodding to himself, and whose unfocused gaze lay on their mother.

"Neil?" He put out his other hand. Neil blinked overlong, and Alisdair felt him come back to himself. He was relieved, as if Neil had been about to take the same soul journey as Mam. But finally he joined hands and the three siblings formed a semicircle. Muirne's shaky sigh released them.

"Now," she said. "We shall call our friends here for the funeral, aye? No sense going to church where she knew no one these last ten years."

"Aye." Alisdair cleared his throat. "And the minister will come. And we'll have the burial here as well."

Neil twisted his head toward him. Tipped back an almost imperceptible nod. "Fine. As soon as the ground by the creek thaws."

Alisdair thought of the psalms she would want, the hymns. The friends. The flowers. The ground would be soft enough in another week or so, early May. Mam would have her favorite, soft pink mayflowers. And when he thought of the flowers, he thought of Sheena, and felt a slice through his heart yet again. Where was she? Why did she not come on the first ship? Why did she not reply?

A shriek was heard from outside. Muirne sighed and turned to go talk to the children. The door opened and a torrent of voices passed through, exclaiming whose fault it wasn't. Alisdair looked at his brother. His strong, older, defeated brother. *He'll rally once he's needed again. Although his absent-mindedness about Mairi the past year is worrying.*

"Let's go outside," he said, letting go his hand to place it on Neil's shoulder. He felt muscle tense under his hand.

They looked at Mam once more, the pennies Muirne had placed on her eyes, the linen she'd already tied under her jaw.

Love to you always, Mama.

Alisdair clapped Neil on the back and went out.

Days of preparations passed, where Mam's body was washed and sewn into its shroud, and word was sent to their acquaintances. The day before the funeral, one of the neighbors who came for the gathering arrived with a letter from town. Neil passed it to Alisdair when he came in from hoeing.

"We've both read it," said Neil. "Keep it or burn it when you've done."

Burn it?

It was from Sheena. She wrote haltingly of the newly established position Gordon had cultivated, the illness from pregnancy, and concluded with regret that she could not come.

Alisdair read it again.

"But…"

He understood the anger that had accompanied Neil's comment. He crumpled up the paper and thought of the fire, but then took a deep breath and uncreased it again. Sheena's hand was shaky and weak. There was a strike through the return address on the outside, as if in anger. And she'd signed it with, "Love, love, love always, no matter the distance."

Alisdair could understand her not wanting to lose another baby to a sea voyage; it was, after all, still a risk for a weak constitution like Sheena's. And of course they might not be able to afford to leave so suddenly. But she should have said that rather than go on about Gordon's situation if that was what she was really scared of. *No, something else is scaring her.*

He folded the letter again carefully. He would have to think about how to respond.

In the meantime, the MacGregors and other neighbors and friends were all assembled, camping outside their cabin doors, with gifts of food and sentimental recollections and sermonizing. Alisdair felt the weight of their prepared remarks, their intentions, their sadness, suffocating his. He washed up after hours in the field at the tin water basin in the cabin. Looking into it, he saw himself.

"No. Not enough."

"What's that?" Neil asked from the table.

"I've got to have a real wash. I'm going down to the creek."

"Fine. Be careful—it's dusk, and the streambed will be very dark. Don't slip, now."

"I won't."

Alisdair weaved through the ranks of tents and poles, nodding briefly at all the upturned faces. He felt like he was slinking out the back way, avoiding responsibilities, but there were three of them up there, with Ed back, and he needed some time to himself. He found their usual laundry spot, the clearing evident even in the shadows, and skirted along the bank to the right until he found the little sheltered crook of water, delineated by tree roots. He shucked his shoes and clothing and splashed in.

It was still bloody cold. Alisdair moved furiously under the surface to warm his muscles and acquaint his skin with the cold. He ran, he punched, he kicked, he writhed. Finally he splashed water on his face, for he found he was crying.

When the soul leaves the body, the stubborn body . . .

Alisdair went to the bank to retrieve the soap and scrubbed, slowly and deliberately. Mam had wanted him to go far, seek another life. And yet she'd wanted them all to stay together, too. *So should I leave the fold and go to Halifax to study at this Dalhousie College? Or just try to get into a trade concern?*

Or stay, helping Neil and Mairi, more alone now than ever? The family couldn't just leave the mountain entirely, not after what they'd been through to settle it. And neither he nor Muirne thought it wise to leave Neil alone after such loss. He'd always been so determined, so stubborn about what he wanted, but losing Letty had turned him into a coward. Alisdair hoped it would change, with Mam gone. He knew he'd resent his brother if he had to stay another year for his sake.

And when I go, will they say I was a selfish body?

May 1834, The Ridge

The guests departed, leaving homemade gifts and promises to return. Alisdair had liked the simple ceremony. The singing had gone off well, and the remembrances of Mam had been touching. Some had made him cry from grief, some with laughter. It was a solitary experience, though, as the sister he was closest to had not written; her absence felt like a rip pulling on the already large hole Mam's death had made.

Muirne and Neil talked, though. Alisdair hoped his older brother was being chided into his responsibilities for Mairi, as well as comforted. But as he watched them in the corner of the funeral tent, Muirne looked surprised. What could surprise her? Alisdair didn't want to ask. *At least there's someone to bring him to his senses.*

A week later, with Muirne and Edward gone home, Alisdair detected a heightened sense of restlessness in Neil. The two eldest Turner children had stayed behind to help them with farm work over the summer. Mollie and Gil had at first tried to take orders from Neil, but found he gave none. They then tried their other uncle.

"But we don't know how to do anything!" Gil lamented.

"Mark the trees to cut down?"

"No."

"Pull the plough through in even lines to mound the soil for seeding?"

"No."

"Take a sickle through the weeds between the rows of oats?"

"No."

"Well. Sounds like you need to start at the bottom, then, my little town mouse. Mairi can show you how to tend to the cows, the sheep, and the hens. That'll take a good few days."

"But that's for the women-folk to do!" whined Gil.

"And women-folk is what we seem to be short on, Gil, so that's where help is most needed! Understood?"

"Aye, Uncle."

Several days passed while the two town mice meekly learned from their country cousin the tasks to be done around the house. Mairi seemed to soak up the attention and company, no mistake. Alisdair stepped a little lighter in the field thinking of it, glad that such an exchange could do them all good. They passed a busily happy week until Alisdair rose later than usual one morning to find his brother gone.

He hurried to get his jacket on, but saw Mairi was awake, watching him with guilty eyes.

"Da's…out," said Mairi, misgiving in her wan face.

"Did he tell ye where he was going?" he asked.

Mairi looked at him with big eyes and bit her lip. "He said everything would be fine. He had to go to town."

Alisdair's own eyes grew to saucers. "What's possessed him? Leaving me here with you three and all the work——and not telling me, much less asking leave! Oh, I'll give him a piece of my mind when he returns, I will—"

When he returns… A chill swept over Alisdair. *Surely he wouldn't…desert us?*

Mairi clearly harbored similar fears. She stared at him as he uncurled his fists and took a deep breath. He beckoned to her and put his arm about her waist, swallowing to slow down his skippy breath.

"Now, I might be a bit cross at your da, but I'm sure he'll be back. Dinna fash, Mairi. He maybe won't share his business, even with us, but I'm sure he'll eventually tell us what he's planning. He wouldn't leave you, *mo nighean*."

He hugged her, and she looked a little less lost. *Right. Well. We'll just have to proceed.*

Three bloody days, Alisdair fumed. It was three days since Neil had left, and he'd sent no word. He coped with the children well enough, but the farm work was awkward and slow with one set of hands, not to mention there was no one to share the burden of authority. Mairi deferred to her cousins, who deferred to him. For the first time, Alisdair realized how Neil might have felt being in charge. *No respite.* His heart softened toward his brother's transgression until his mind cycled back to the absence without leave.

They were all at supper four days later when they heard someone tromping through the bracken, singing. Mairi's eyes lit up. They abandoned the half-burnt buns and half-cooked potatoes to run outside and face Neil. Alisdair stood stoutly, his arms crossed, while Mairi ran toward her father. Mollie and Gil looked less certain whether to welcome him.

"Singing, Neil?"

"It's good for the spirit, Alisdair. Hallo, all. How's the house?" Neil scooped up Mairi as he walked ahead. The light it sparked in Mairi's face physically pained Alisdair, and his gaze narrowed.

"Where have you been?"

"I just went to town, as I said. Did Mairi forget my message?"

Mairi shouted in his arms. "I did not! I gave it to Uncle Alisadir as soon as he woke up!"

"Well, then, nae bother, eh?"

"Ye didna say how long ye'd be gone," said Alisdair. "Or whether ye'd be back at all."

They were within six feet of each other now. Neil set Mairi down.

"I wouldna leave, Alisdair. Not me."

It was as if he had struck Alisdair, who stood, pained, as Neil swept into the cabin, cheerful as could be.

How can he? How can he rake me over the coals because the shape of my ambition is different from his? I want to support this family just as much as he does, but I want to do more. *Why isn't he able to allow me that?*

He endured it in bitter silence for the sake of the children, but a day was coming when Alisdair would throw down his gauntlet: whether this summer or next, time would tell, but he was nearing his limit of filial devotion. He wanted to honor Mam's wish for them to remain together, but he needed more.

He reaffirmed to himself the necessity of keeping his mind engaged with newspapers and literature and resolved to simply leave off trying to solve the troubles of his brother. He hoped Mam would understand.

May 1834, Luss

The Sunday before they were to depart, Sheena and Gordon joined the Marshalls for kirk and stood through a rather boring sermon. Sheena was sure she'd never heard the same sentences so many times together. Twice she peeked at the minister's face to see if he was in a trance himself, but no joy. His eyes were open, almost hidden by his eyebrows, which perched atop his brow like wintry birds' nests. She let the words flow over her and sent her gaze inward, concentrating on the inner squeezes and shiftings that showed her baby was not finding the sermon as soporific as she.

Finally, it was over, the hymn sung, and the minister processing out. She followed Gordon and the Marshalls as they waded into the general crowd of newly-woken and relaxed parishioners surging past the stone font toward the door. It was a suspiciously beautiful day as they emerged, and Sheena squinted into the broad daylight at the few wispy clouds visible. *Luss is still by a loch, so there's no telling when the rain could take up again. But I do hope it is dry for our journey tomorrow.*

They went home to a fine supper with the family. Gordon went to check the mare's legs, and Sheena tried in vain to leave some payment with Iain's wife, Skye.

Monday morning, Iain was up early to help with the saddling. Sheena sat in the kitchen of their cottage with Skye, who was nursing one of the younger children. A clatter was heard from the yard, and Skye's eyebrows shot up.

"Hope he's not having a problem with one of the horses," she said.

"Maybe it's a visitor?" Sheena rose and looked out the open doorway to the barn yard.

"Ah, the post! You're right, Mrs. Lamont. They do sometimes come early on a Monday."

"Skye, do call me Sheena. I'll be writing you, so don't go standing on ceremony now," Sheena teased.

She looked out again and saw that Iain and Gordon were conferring over something. The mare jerked her head away from Gordon. Suddenly Sheena felt cold all over her skin like she'd been dipped in the sea.

"What is it?" It was an effort to say, but evidently it did no good for they paid her no heed, even though the men stood only thirty feet away. She tried again, and it came out more as a shriek. Iain's head popped up and their eyes met. He almost-smiled, then turned back to Gordon.

Her husband had not looked up but kept staring at the paper he clutched in one hand. She went out to meet him. Iain patted Gordon's shoulder and walked the horse back toward the barn.

She walked to her husband, her hands clutching her skirts, hiding in their folds. She waited several moments, until it was apparent Gordon did not want to meet her eye. She drew breath to question him just as he finally lowered the paper and raised his gaze, not to her face but her belly. Sheena clasped her hands together.

"What is it, Gordon?"

"Stirling has sent a searing note, a cancellation of contract. Callander has written him and blackened my name, and has apparently pulled enough strings to make Stirling's hiring of me quite impossible."

"Oh, Gordon. So, none of the other——?"

"I suppose if I were to write any of the other associates of the consortium, it would be the same. Damn!"

Sheena felt at once the release of tension accompanying such a blow and the new knot forming at the uncertainty of their future. *It's not to be Barrhead after all.*

Gordon squeezed her hands with one of his, and she followed him back to the house. Skye had finished nursing the baby and held him up to her shoulder.

"Was it the post, then?" she asked.

"We've no more job to get to," Gordon said. He flung the crumpled paper onto the broad table and plunked himself on the stool by the hearth to stare at the coals. Sheena explained what the letter contained. Skye's look of dismay made her want to smile. *How does she have the energy to be so affronted?* she wondered. *I'm sure my face doesn't show my emotions so easily.*

When Iain came back in from the barn, he extended the invitation to stay longer—as long as it took to find another post.

"I'll ask down at the forge; Andy may well know a job or two needs doing."

"Thank you, Iain," said Gordon.

There was no respite in the blacksmith's news. Laborers for the summer were already engaged, the printing concern had its complement of workers, and the new architect to move into nearby Alexandria already had men for his next commission from the Smolletts.

That Monday's supper was a quiet one for the adults. Sheena retired to bed early. She sat, wondering about the timelines of finding work and having the baby, how they would intertwine. A sense of fate, of no control, somehow made her worry less this time. Gordon came in and sat heavily next to her.

"It's already May. You're due in June."

Sheena heard the tight helplessness in his tone. Was it an appeal?

"I'm sure we'll find something by then, dear," she said.

He merely shook his head, starting slowly to remove his clothing.

The next Sunday found them in the kirk again, sitting toward the back. Sheena scanned the backs of bonneted heads, searching for inspiration. Who did they know? Who did these people know? There had to be someone out of Callander's orbit; he wasn't the King, after all.

Her mind turned on Gordon's talents and what the country needed. There were the merchants and trade markets at the ports, where Alisdair was keen to start his career. There were the landowners and the agricultural improvements that many were making—but they would probably know Callander. Fishpackers, farmers, blacksmiths, clerks, shoemakers…What did they all need?

None of the netted or flowered bonnets yielded an answer. The baby was kicking and she was quite moist in the press of people on this sunny May day. The drone of the minister's voice finally ceased and people began to sing and process out. Sheena allowed room for others in front of her, not so eager to be squeezed in among the crush. Gordon stood behind her, and the Marshalls with their children stood behind him. *We need someone to direct traffic*, Sheena mused. A thought, like lightning, made her jaw drop.

She stood up straighter, turned to Gordon, saw the look of question in his face, and faced forward again with the beginnings of a smile. They made their way back to the Marshalls' home by the road, and Sheena fairly walked on tip-toes, she was so excited. When they were inside, she pleaded fatigue and went into their room, waiting until Gordon made his excuses and joined her.

"You don't seem over-tired to me, wife," he said in a low voice. "What's got into you? Holy Spirit, by Rector's words?"

Sheena flashed a smirk at him. "No," she whispered emphatically. "But I've thought of a job for you."

Gordon's eyebrows went up. "Oh, yes?"

"You know how they've only just got the coaching system sorted, with regular stages at certain times, and refreshing the horses, and making it safe at the turnpikes and all that?"

"Yes, but——"

"They're going to have to start all over, with those railways they're bringing through the towns. You know the first ones were a novelty, but they're building long stretches now to connect the important cities, and you know they'll need to put in lines to link up all the market towns. If you got in with one of those railway concerns now——"

"That's a thought, but do we know anyone in that sort of affair? I don't believe we do."

"But it's a modern trade, Gordon! Yes, the people at the top will be hobnobbing with friends, but the managers! They'll need talent. I'm telling you—all you'd need to do is present yourself for an interview. Read the latest papers about the engines and such, and you'll impress anybody."

"Oh, to be worthy of the faith of such a wife!" Gordon was smiling, and Sheena felt she'd convinced him.

"We will have to be near Glasgow. That's bound to be the center——"

"Hold on! Give me a few days to talk to some men who'd be knowledgeable on that front. Then we'll decide where we are to go." He kissed Sheena passionately and she responded, kissing her husband until she felt light-headed. *Fatigue indeed,* she thought as he pulled away and she smoothed the hair from his forehead. He left the room and she stayed for her rest, feeling a sudden confidence in the venture for no reason at all. She didn't dare question its source, but thanked the Lord for her inspiration in kirk.

It took another week for Gordon to ferret out the information he needed, but the next Tuesday they were once again saddling up the big grey mare for the trek south. Their trunk was sent ahead by rail, which made Sheena share a small smile of triumph with her husband. They would strike out for Kirkintilloch, where the blacksmith had a cousin who was friendly with the chief engineer of the Monkland & Kirkintilloch Railway.

Sheena was up most of the night before, alternately tossing and turning and getting out of bed to pace, searching for relief. *Still a month to go*, she told the finally-sleeping babe. *You had better rest while you can.* Her eyelids drooped as they rode, and she remembered to be glad that Gordon was a capable horseman and had hold of her should she drift into sleep. *And at least our trunk has been sent ahead so we don't have to drag it along.* They were on the road for an hour before seeing the summer sun bathe the soft hills to their right in golden light.

The hills south of Loch Lomond placed them in a shallow vale, where they wound their way along farm fences and occasionally saw a house set back from the road. Folk were out with the ploughs, as the plantings had to be in right soon. Sheena felt her sleepiness drop away abruptly. Farmers. Planting time. She hoped Mam was at peace and her family were coping all right. Then she uncurled her back from its hunch and turned her head slightly to kiss Gordon's chin.

"Where are we?"

"Glad you could sleep in my arms, my Sheena." He gave the top of her head a quick peck. "Kilpatrick Hills, if I make my mark. And seen nary a soul. I didn't expect the road to be so quiet."

"Besides our racket, you mean," Sheena teased. Indeed, now that she was awake, she didn't know how she could sleep through the clatter of giant hooves and creak of stiff leather.

"Yes," he admitted. "But in another few hours we shall be in a much busier part of the country, and it will be a busier part of the day, so enjoy the quiet while you can."

"Have you planned a stop for breakfast?"

"Why stop?" Gordon leaned backward, reaching in one of the leather bags slung across the horse's back. He held out a neat, paper-wrapped parcel. "You open that, and be careful not to drop any."

"Oh, how lovely of them! Their farm cheese and early apples—and a pie! What a love Skye is." Sheena unwrapped the cloth from the meat pie carefully, acutely aware again of the drop of five feet to the ground. She exposed the top half and took a bite. Bliss. She held it up for Gordon to take a bite, and the next half-mile was spent pleasantly feeding her man and herself, before they packed away the empty cloth and Gordon took a large bottle from the bag on the other side.

"Ale. Good for you."

Sheena laughed and took a few sips, letting Gordon savor most of it.

They passed more and more travelers as they turned south onto the Drymen road. The sun was high in the sky, and Sheena wished to dismount for a break from the saddle, but not with all the people about. They turned east again and the landscape changed from the green fields following a swift stream to something that felt stunted, bereft.

"We're nearing the coal belt," Gordon murmured to her, but she had already deduced that from the clacking sounds nearby and the uniform black shine the people all sported on cheeks, elbows, knees. *Can't they get themselves clean? Or do they cease to notice it? I hope I never cease to notice if I am in such a state.*

They stopped briefly at an inn. Sheena held onto the horse's rein while Gordon checked the mare's feet, gave her a bit of water, and went inside to refill their bottle and buy a bit of food for the rest of the journey.

Sheena stood in the yard. She watched the movement all around her, stretching her back covertly as she turned to watch this or that scene. It was a very busy yard; that much she could deduce. She wondered if Kirkintilloch were going to be similar. Already she'd formed an idea that it would be black, and dirty, and the people unkind, as they had been in Glasgow when she was a child.

Most of the people in the yard were laborers, the various cloth or leather aprons and peaked caps denoting their roles. The railways were mostly for coal, but they had proved so popular with passengers that Sheena knew there would be more and more demand. In the meantime, the labor force was here, next to the biggest coal seams in the country. Sheena caught the eye of one of the men walking through the yard. His face was tan, red, black, brown—filthy. But his eyes flared like chips of blue glass from underneath all the soot. He quickly looked away. Sheena hugged herself, her arms resting on her belly. *Useful you can be*, she teased the babe, who promptly turned and squirmed and made her jerk one way and hold onto a stirrup for balance.

Gordon returned, a mild smile on his face.

"We are again prepared to forge through the great unknown."

"You're a funny one. I was glad at least of the break."

He led the horse to the mounting step and she clambered up. Gordon stepped into the stirrup and slid into place behind her. With the sun beating down on them, Sheena should have got out her hat, but she'd been too fascinated watching the people. She shaded her eyes with a gloved hand instead, as they wearily made their way round the others and left the coaching inn behind.

She was not drowsy, merely uncomfortable to the point of staring intently to block out all sensation in her bum, when Gordon's arm pulled back on the reins, tightening around her.

"Sheena," he whispered.

"Mmm?"

"See that?"

He didn't point but she sharpened her senses to peer out in the long summer twilight. The sun had set but there was still plenty of hazy warmth and moisture in the air. Sheena's gaze swept the horizon but saw only shadows and the silhouette of the sky.

"No, what?"

"It's the wall the Romans left. Just there." He raised one

arm to point. Sheena just barely made out a light-colored patch in the shadow of the hill to their right.

"The Romans?"

"Emperor Antonius. Remarkable, isn't it?"

"Mmmph."

"It means we're almost to Kirkintillloch. It shall be full night when we enter the town. Let us hope that their inn is as respectable as Kilpatrick's. In the meantime—"

He drew out the parcel that contained their supper.

"Oh, water first, please," Sheena said, taking it in hand all the same.

They drank, and ate, and Sheena saw the shadowed edifice pass them by. *Not that impressive*, she thought. Sheena became aware of a strange tinge to the air. It made the back of her throat tingle and the inside of her nose itch.

It wasn't a smell, really. More like a sting of smoke or the shadow of heat. Sheena's mind grasped at explanations as she twitched her nose. They finished their second meal on the back of the horse and started talking softly, wondering who they would meet first in their new chosen town. People were few on the road again, and they hadn't seen anyone for two miles when Sheena started to see lights dancing in the sky.

"Am I lightheaded or—what is that?" She spoke sharply. There were prickles of red in the sky like she saw when she felt dizzy from standing up too quickly.

"No, it's not you," was all Gordon would say. She huffed, understanding that he wanted her to experience it, whatever the 'it' was. How did he know all this in advance, anyway?

Why was she never able to string *him* along, knowing before he did? As they kept on, the specks became moving patches, then dancing towers, then one vast flame, reflected in the dark sky.

"My god," Sheena breathed.

"It is the new hot blast furnaces," Gordon said quietly. "They need to be kept at, all day and all night, for the new type of iron. For the railway."

"It's a scene from Mr. MacManus' sermon," Sheena rasped, before realizing that Gordon had taken her advice on reading the papers to study the newest industrial developments. She squeezed his arm.

The tinge in the air felt aggressive and she put a handkerchief up to her nose to breathe in its sunny scent. By the time they dragged themselves into Kirkintilloch proper, the handkerchief was completely grey and had lost any touch of the sun-warmed afternoon when it had been dried on the line by a clear blue loch.

They found the inn, a hanging-on affair, which seemed to have been many things in its long lifetime, none of them tasteful. Sheena reminded herself she was thankful to have a roof over their heads for the night, and a privy close by. They both collapsed into bed, sinking into a sound sleep before the hubbub created by their appearance had died down.

In the morning, Sheena's nether parts and bottom were mighty sore, but at least her knees felt almost normal. She knew she should walk a little to limber up her body and got out of bed to slowly—gingerly—stretch her legs and back. A few kinked steps were all she managed before she saw Gordon watching her, his eyelids drooping, a lazy smile on his face.

"We are here," he said.

"Thought you might have noticed that last night," Sheena replied.

"Yes, well. I am happy to see you upright and in a fresh mood, after the past few days. I was prepared for much worse."

She grinned. "So I've proved you wrong. That is a nice ending to your doubting ways. Now, where will you apply today?"

"I intend to apply to the blacksmith's cousin first, get our trunk from him, then secure an interview with the engineer, Mr. Grainger. You can stay and rest, or—walk about, as you will."

His teasing smile at her early morning walk prompted Sheena to lift her eyebrows and reply in mincing tone. "Perhaps I will."

Gordon seemed to think better of it. "In truth, Sheena, it is not a likely place for a walk, in the town. Perhaps it would be better to see where we shall live and hope it has a bit more fresh air."

A bit removed from the center of town and all the iron works, he means. "But I thought this valley was all dug up in coal pits."

"It is. They're just to the south and east. Grainger tells me it's the furnaces we've got to worry about, though. Particularly bad in summer."

"Now."

"Yes."

Sheena worried about a baby being born into the worst conditions of the year, but put it out of her mind quickly. *Nothing to do about it. Hope we have a clean house and a bit of garden that sit well outside the town.*

Sheena let Gordon get on with his errands and meetings and dressed in her traveling dress again before descending the narrow, dark stairs to the ale house portion of the inn. She spied a robust teenage girl behind the bar, drying plates.

"Do you offer a cooked breakfast?"

The girl looked up. Her hair was in disarray, some of the long dark blond strands up, some down, and the apron she wore looked to have seen a thousand meals the night before.

"Oh, sorry. Ye'se early. I can knock something up for you. An egg and bread all right?"

Sheena nodded and sat at one of the few tables, as far away from the bar as possible. *Early, is it? Funny, I would have thought in a town full of miners and iron workers that there was no such thing. Just as well. I'll have my meal in peace and then return to our room.*

Ten minutes later, during which Sheena examined with her eyes every shady corner and darkened leather surface, the barmaid returned with a plate. It had a hard boiled egg, some scoops of a black, riddled substance, and two torn corners of fresh bread. She thanked the girl, who then handed her a knife and fork from behind the counter. *The napkins must be extra.*

She ate in relative silence, ignoring the clatter of plate

after dry plate as the girl finished her duties. The black, rid-dled lumps turned out to be black pudding. It was unusual, but not unfamiliar to Sheena, and she ate it, grateful for the meat and egg to keep up her strength. She still felt stronger, larger, fuller, than she ever had. *Thank goodness, or I'd never get through all this travel.* The memory of always being a hair's breadth away from scarcity clung to her, though. She hoped this would be a good situation for Gordon, and that she could let go of such desperate memories. She knew her mother never had.

June 1834, The Ridge

The adults were gone. Da and Alisdair were in the fields for the wheat sowing. Mairi's cousins stood across from her in the clearing, Mollie with fists on hips, Gil with hands folded on his head. Mairi felt dull and plain compared to her cousins.

"We've collected eggs down at our house; that's nothing different. The milking—that was fun."

"Speak for yourself," Gil protested.

"I like brushing down the cows," Mollie continued, ignoring him. "But picking their feet is a little…unsavory."

"Unsavory? Is that a plant?" Mairi asked. Gil giggled.

"No, it means…I don't like doing it."

"She thinks it's beneath her," said Gil. "But I liked it."

"What shall we do next?" Mollie asked quickly.

Mairi thought. "We can measure out the hay for the feedings later. And then there is mucking out. But not until afternoon. I usually—erm…"

"Go on, you usually what?" said Gil.

"During the summer I like to visit Mama…her grave. And now Grannie's."

"Oh," said Mollie. "Well, let's do that, then."

Her cousin gave her an encouraging smile, full of her three additional years of experience. Gil had two years on her.

Mairi led them down to the creek and showed them the fallen tree that served as bridge, warning them to step carefully. There was another crossing the adults used, of course, but it took longer. After ten minutes they reached the step of land set back under a gracefully drooping tree, Mairi's favorite part of the setting. They stood with hands folded, heads bowed for a moment, before Gil looked up.

"Aren't you going to say something? People are supposed to say something. Aren't they?" He looked to his sister for confirmation.

"Only at the funeral. I don't think it's necessary to speak out loud for visits after."

Mairi looked hesitantly at Mollie. *How does she know so much?* She knelt down and closed her eyes, speaking her prayer in her head.

Good morning, Mama. My cousins are here with me to say hello. I miss you. I wish you were here to cheer Da so he could be like he was. I hope you are happy in Heaven. And Grannie, I know you are in Heaven, too. I love you very much. I wish I could make you breakfast now—I can shake the pan for stovies all on my own now. You'd be proud.

With a sniffle, she stood back up. Mairi looked at her two cousins, who hadn't moved.

"Love to you, Grannie," Mollie whispered. Gil turned away.

They were silent as they trouped through the hanging branches of the droopy tree. Gil, in front, looked up first.

"Who are they?" He pointed upward to where the sun

showed two figures struggling up the road toward the junction that led to their cabins.

Mairi shaded her eyes and squinted, two things she'd seen Da do to see a long ways, but it didn't help much. She could just make out silhouettes with hats with the sun behind them like that.

When he got no answer, Gil made a motion toward the girls. "Well, come on, let's go see!"

They hurried toward the house, excited by such a mystery. They'd seen everyone at the funeral, hadn't they? Who could be coming now, three weeks late?

They were running a shorter track than that of the road, so they reached the cabins much sooner than the strangers. Gil stood on the step, which made him three inches taller, and picked up one of the kindling switches.

Mollie blew out her cheeks at her brother and sat on one of the stumps to wait. Mairi joined her. She tried to sit calmly, but an excited flutter in her chest made her fidget.

When the two strangers entered the clearing a few minutes later, Mairi was following Mollie's example: sitting primly on the stump, her hands in her lap, her feet close together. But she looked to see a very red man in a battered straw hat, and then—a man that was completely brown! She gaped. Was he ill? Was it mud?

She looked back to the red man and saw that he was peeling and blistered. Sunburn, then. But what had happened to this other man? He wore a dirty cap instead of straw, and walked with a stick. They both walked with sticks. Mairi looked and looked, seeing how exhausted they were by their laborious movements. They finally looked up and saw the children in front of the cabin. The sunburnt man looked nervous, but the brown man smiled. Gil's voice intruded.

"Hey! Stop right there! Who are you?"

Mairi heard the bit of wavering in his question. Gil didn't know what to do. She glanced to Mollie, who looked as if she was trying to swallow something troublesome in her throat. Mairi rose and stood beside Mollie. Her cousin stilled.

"Mairi, do you know where your father is now? Can you go get him?"

Mairi nodded. But before she left, she stepped a few paces closer to the men, who had indeed obeyed Gil's instruction, and remained twenty or so paces away.

"This is my house. Stay here while I get my da. Please."

The brown man's smile increased a little at her 'please.'

She ran behind the house, down the side path, and out to the far field, where the men were working the wheat. An ox was fitted with the plough, and the brothers stood on either side of it, as if arguing.

Mairi shouted and they both turned. She arrived, panting, and struggled to get out her message.

"Strangers…at home…two men…and one's all brown!"

She stood with her hands on her knees to catch her breath.

"Did they say where they were from?" Da asked her.

"No, they didn't say…anything…Gil yelled at them, and now he and Mollie…are waiting for you."

"What the devil…all right, Mairi. Calm yourself and walk back with your uncle. I'll see to them." Da loped away with his confident stride. Mairi had a brief glimmer of hope, seeing her father act so decisively, as he had not these past months. She turned to Alisdair.

"I'll think we'll take Carthage back with us, eh?"

Mairi agreed, and they walked back slowly with the ox's bulk between them. Twenty minutes later, Alisdair let the beast out into the paddock of the byre, tossed the harness and gear over in the milking area, and hurried up to the clearing. Mairi gazed at shock at his negligence. Apparently this was serious.

By the time Mairi and Alisdair arrived home, no one was in the yard. She followed her uncle into the main cabin and let her eyes adjust.

There he was, the brown man. And the sunburnt man, sitting next to him. They sat facing out from the table, while her da stood by the fire, facing them. Mollie and Gil stood behind him. Mairi went to join her da, while Alisdair stayed to the side, forming a triangle of crackling energy. The strangers looked toward him and back at Da.

"So who are you?" Mairi asked, when nobody spoke.

The sunburnt man looked at her and replied in Gaelic, "I'm your cousin, Mairi."

He looked like he was trying to smile without cracking the skin around his mouth.

She dismissed this and turned to the other man.

"And you?"

"I work for your cousin, missy."

"But all my cousins live in town," Mairi replied. "Or here," she said, pointing at Mollie and Gil. "You're too old to be my cousin, anyway. And where do you come from, for—"

"Mairi." Her father's warning tone made her bite her lip and merely stare, waiting. "This man says his name is Jamie MacDonald. He's come from the Carolinas, with Mr. Micah here." Da indicated the brown man, and Mairi peered closer. His skin was deeply furrowed, and he had a squashy nose, but his face otherwise reminded her of the Green Man—the spirit of the forest, wise and teasing and generous in the wooden carvings her Da had done, once. Mairi decided she liked the new men on first appearances—or rather, second.

"Your daughter has very nice manners, Neil," said Jamie.

Da glanced at her, surprised. "Thank you. Now, why don't you continue with your story."

"Aye. Well, as you can see, we were fleeing for our lives. Didn't bring no cash, didn't pack no provender, just lit out ahead of the mob, like. It's been a hard two months on the trail, with a couple of lucky breaks."

Jamie glanced toward Micah, who nodded. "Praise be," he murmured.

"We had to leave my father's settlement because there were neighbors causing trouble. We live in the state of North Carolina, as you know. In the foothills outside Charlotte, called Piedmont. My da started the settlement thirteen years ago, just before you came over, and it was wilderness then. Just like here, he says. But now there's plenty of people settled right up to the mountains, and he was worried some about the neighbors being, well, hotheads." He shrugged.

"Is Uncle Kenneth doing something they wouldna like? I thought he was doing all right with the tobacco, even if he didn't have room to give away land to all the children."

Mairi furrowed her brow at her father. Where did he get all this information? And why hadn't he shared it? She had more family she didn't even know about?

"Oh, no, Da is making a fine business of the farm and training most of us with trades for the town. Y'see, me brother Denny's a blacksmith—well, almost done with his apprentice-ship. And Charlie, he's next down from Denny, he's gone to a news-printer even farther down, in the city. It's a good plan, to earn money for the family in the town while we can still grow our own food and such."

"So where does the trouble come in then, James?" Neil asked.

James glanced at Micah, who raised his eyes for the first time from the table. "Da doesna hold with slavery. He's been up north visiting and sees that the government will eventually turn it over. Mother is one of the abolitionists ever since she set foot on these shores, and she sticks out like a sore thumb in the Piedmont. Da's tried to keep it hidden from these hothead neighbors, but there have been such rows about it— such a mess of violence and threats and malicious talk, that he had Micah here, who's a freedman working our farm, follow

Ma around to make sure she didna get any trouble."

James' accent, inherited from his father and mother even though he'd probably never spoken in Scotland—he was that young—came out stronger now, as he described the tenuous position the MacDonalds held in their Carolina mountain valley.

"So Micah had the job of being a shadow to my mother as she went about. Some of the men visiting one time—a rowdy crew 'that can only ascribe the base motives they harbor to others they see'—that's what Mam says—they got the wrong idea and thought he was following her to do her harm, when of course it was just the opposite." He paused. "No Negro there would dare harm a white woman. He'd be killed out of hand." He cleared his throat and went on. "But this crew though, they made some accusations. They wanted to find Micah's owner, get him in trouble."

"Of course—nothing bad men like better than watching others get beaten when they deserve the same," Neil murmured.

Jamie eyed his older cousin a moment. When nothing else was uttered, he continued. "Well, when they went to my father, who they thought was the owner, and that didn't grab his attention, they dispersed. But they publicized a worse slander against Micah. Unclean thoughts about my mother." Jamie cleared his throat again, working to still his contempt for whoever made up this band. Mairi wondered what slander was, and unclean thoughts.

"They were insulting both my mother and my father. They

went away that day, but it came to a near thing next day as Ma was out washing; Micah stepped in to protect her, as was his job, and injured one of those stupid mongrels. Well," he blew out air, "you can imagine how well that went over. Ma and he ran all the way back home and she shuttled him off with me to come visit you, because the Crown has different laws about it than the Americans do, and anyway, they wouldna follow us so far, and anyway, 'it's been far too long of no' seein' the family,' is how Da would ha' put it."

"Would ha'?" Da said suddenly. "Kenneth's not dead?"

"Nay! Only I didna get to see him afore I left. I know he treasures his family, reads your letters over and over. I just mean he'd've said it just so."

Da let out a breath. "Well."

There was a lapse in the conversation, the men in the room thinking over what they'd heard. Da spoke to Mr. Micah.

"We're very sorry to hear of your plight. No man should be picked on and tormented so. But we are in a rather difficult time ourselves. Can you tell me, what was your plan for when you reached here?"

Micah was very still, sitting very straight. He spoke in a low, weaving tone falling on air that seemed to hold still for him. *Is he some kind of charmer?* Mairi wondered, entranced.

"…Free hand or laborer where I was needed," he was saying. "I have no family to worry about back down South." As he said this, his face seemed to squeeze tightly and he swallowed, his Adam's apple bobbing down. "So that is what I hoped to find here: freedom from suspicion, as I'm an honest man, and useful work to do among good people. Mr. Kenneth and Mrs. Mariah are some of the best people I know, and I see their family is just as good."

"Mr. Micah," Da said. "I would like to discuss this with my brother here before deciding what we will do. Would you and James wait outside for a few minutes?"

Mairi looked to her uncle, who stood very still also, his eyes alight in a distracted daze.

Jamie responded. "Of course, cousin. Just point us to the water bucket. I need a drop and we can both clean up."

Mairi rushed to get the bucket from the back room and lugged it to where Mr. Jamie stood. He took it from her, touching her head briefly.

"Thank ye, missy."

They filed out the cabin door, Alisdair handing them clean cloths as they went. The door closed and Mairi felt Mollie clutch at her hand. But her attention was all on her father's face. What would he do for their family?

June 1834, The Ridge

Alisdair heard the door settle and looked at Neil. His glance then flickered to the three children standing behind, wide-eyed and startled into silence, for once in their young lives. He stepped closer to speak low.

"Do ye not believe them?" he asked.

"It's too fantastic a tale not to believe," Neil murmured back. "But how can we be sure? We've the young ones to keep safe, and they could be interlopers looking to take over."

Alisdair raised his eyes to Heaven, prayed for some patience toward his brother. "Neil. They're not looking to kill us and take over our claim. They're far too starved-looking for that to have been a pretense."

"Aye. We might—no. We can put them to work. After they've recovered, perhaps," he added, seeing Alisdair's eyes pop.

"Neil, if Mam were here, you know she'd welcome them with open arms. She'd also write to Uncle Kenneth to say they were here safe. What's wrong with you? Think! That will at least give us a confirmation of their story."

"But—why hasn't he written us in the meantime? Surely a letter would reach us before two months' time."

Alisdair shrugged, the impatient restlessness of his agitation making his shoulders jerk. "I don't know. It does seem strange not to receive word from him who was so close to Mam…only maybe he's just got word of her passing. Och!"

His frustration at so much unknowing, so much speculating, came out as a curse.

"Sounded like yer father there," Neil told him, a conciliatory smile lurking in his eyes. Alisdair could not understand him at all. First, distrust and inhospitality; now, yielding humor.

"Aye, well. He was probably used to encountering more impossible situations like this. But let us do what we think Mam would do. If you want, have them sleep in the other cabin. Write to Uncle Kenneth."

Neil opened his mouth then closed it. "Right. So be it. I'll write the letter now. We'll have Gil run it to the Frasers who are closer to the post road. All right, Gil?"

The boy nodded.

"And no blabbing about who we've got here, aye? We don't want tongues wagging before we know who they are for sure."

Gil shook his head.

Neil plucked the writing supplies from where Alisdair usually worked at his studies and sat down to pen the note. Alisdair blinked several times, still trying to make his mind accept that this relative he'd never known was on their doorstep, and with a freed Black to boot. He'd seen Blacks when he rode to Halifax, for the Black Loyalist settlement was outside the town, but never spoken to one. He still felt a little exhilaration from the encounter, some joy at such a discovery. that a Black man spoke, sat, and smiled much like any other. The exhilaration quickly cooled to self-reproach when he recalled that such a thing should have been self-evident. But then, it wasn't, to those of the southern States who still proclaimed slavery as their right. Alisdair's head clouded with more questions for the southerners once they could be sure of their purpose.

Then, finally, Alisdair heard Neil's phrase about putting them to work—what if their arrival was his prayer answered? Here was the labor and companionship Neil needed for the farm to continue!

He could stay until they recovered and were able to work, and Neil could trust them. Then he'd be free to leave for the city.

Everyone went to bed somewhat disquieted that night. Neil showed Jamie and Micah to the other cabin after a quick supper, the children fidgeted and whispered together in their corner, and Alisdair set up a cot by the door, to be able to hear better, just in case. He tossed and turned on his pallet, but only his thoughts were to blame. He was groggy and befuddled when he first focused on the light from the window. Past dawn, and in June…it must be near seven!

Alisdair lurched up and startled the girls, who sat at the table with their heads together.

"We didn't want to wake you, Uncle, your face looked so

terrible," Mollie said.

He waved a hand at her for the compliment.

"Where's Neil?"

"He…left again," said Mairi, looking down. "He said everything would be fine when he came back. He went to town. Again."

Alisdair strove to keep his face calm, when he wanted badly to shout and spit and hit something very hard. How could his brother leave him here, again, with the children and these new strangers? He'd never told him where he'd gone last month. Was he gone for good this time?

"That is very ill-behaved of your da, Mairi. I canna think what he may be doing, or thinking, to leave like this." He shook his head to clear it. "I'm for the privy and then we'll check on the…guests, and figure out where to start, aye?"

The girls nodded. Gil thrashed around under the blanket on the big bed, then sat bolt upright.

"What is it?" he whispered.

"Up, boy, it's past time. Follow your sister's example."

He went out. The fumes of his anger at Neil dissipated and he found himself worried. *What's Neil hiding that we don't know about? He was so ill last winter…* He ran a hand through his stiff hair and knocked on the door of the silent cabin. Alisdair mentally mapped out the field where he and Neil had been working yesterday. He'd enquire politely, of course, but he was betting Micah could work today. He'd take it slow and careful and see if the man told a different story from James, with his words or otherwise.

After a moment, Micah opened to him and invited him in. *Oh, God. I have to explain that Neil left.* A little discomfort crept into the cool facade he had decided would be best. After their greetings, he forced himself to dive right in.

"Neil had to go to town on short notice today. I'm sure it was something needful. Now, how are you gentlemen moving today after a good rest?"

He didn't miss Micah's quick look to Jamie when Alisdair broke the news about Neil, but chided himself for not thinking of the different fears it must have provoked.

"I mean, my brother didn't mention it, but I'm sure he's not going for the bounty hunter or slave-catcher or nothing. He'd never."

Would he?

Micah held his gaze a long moment.

"If you say so, Mr. Alisdair. I suppose we're at the end of the road; we gotta trust somebody."

Alisdair nodded. Jamie's lack of movement from where he sat caught Alisdair's notice.

"You moving around all right, there, Jamie?"

The young man looked up, and Alisdair saw some ugly partially-healed scabs where he'd probably had blisters pop over the summer. Finally got them cleaned, he guessed.

"Must be painful," Alisdair added, gesturing to his face. "If you want, I can get you some salve. We've still got some yarrow salve for the cows' cuts in the byre.

Jamie breathed in shallowly. "Much obliged," he said.

"What do you say, Micah? Want to come with me to see

the cows?"

The man nodded, casting a level stare back. *I bet nothing gets by that man. He seems almost to be watching over Jamie, even though his position is the more dangerous. Interesting, that.*

They walked the short distance down to the byre. The other man's eyes followed Alisdair's hands as he pointed out supplies, explained routines.

"You have the young ones helping?"

"Aye, Mairi's training her cousins on milking, sure enough."

"That's good. And you help your brother—you get all your land done between the two of you?"

Alisdair cleared his throat. "Yes, I help Neil in the summers. I was in town for most winters up until last year. School. But, Neil's wife died last spring, and with Mam going this last month, and Sheena gone back to Scotland, we're down to bare bones about the place."

The vague echo of a curse on the land stirred the hair on the back of his neck, which he dismissed as soon as felt.

Micah's eyes seemed to take it in, not staring, but wide open and appraising. He looked down then, scuffed at the dirt with his gnarled and callused big toe.

"Guess you're wondering if I back up Mr. Jamie's story," he said.

"I suppose I am. It's only natural."

"I s'pose that's right enough. Well, it's mostly true, and you'll hear all about it in the letter from Mr. Kenneth. Shoulda been here already, truth to tell. Can't imagine why it's takin' so long."

Alisdair considered the man. *Obviously in a delicate position. His life depends on Jamie, and he doesn't want to betray his trust or cast aspersion on his judgment, but he knows we need a little more to go on.*

"I respect your telling me this," Alisdair finally said. "You seem all right, but a bit of an odd pair," he said, and Micah smiled. "But we'll see about that. Now. Are you up to helping me in the field today? Jamie obviously needs a respite from the sun."

"I'm fine, as long as we take it slow. Been a working' man all my life."

Alisdair thought he might continue, but he didn't.

"All right. We'll be in the rye field today, and using the new plough Neil's got..."

Alisdair had a mostly silent partner that day. They traveled up and down rows, Alisdair showing Micah the ropes: the tension and grip and proper angles. Micah got the rhythm of the task down quickly, and they were able to do almost a quarter of the field before they heard the breakfast bell.

"That's Mairi, ready with breakfast," Alisdair said, and straightened his back with satisfaction. "Had to put the bell in after Mam died, because we'd come home and Mairi hadn't got the food ready yet, and it would waste good sunlight. This way, she tells us when she's ready. Got Mollie and Gil to help her today, too. Wonder if your Jamie hasn't come over as well.

It is a little earlier than usual."

Alisdair squinted at the sun. *Woke late, breakfast early. And Neil missing. A queer day.*

"Fine with me," said Micah. "You leave the plough here?"

"Aye. There's no rain on, and we'll be back before the hour's out."

They trooped up the hill and found Jamie, as expected, in the main cabin, already sipping something from a mug.

"Ho, the house," said Alisdair, absurdly pleased that he said it today, not Neil. *Petty of me.*

Mollie looked toward him. "Hello, Uncle."

Mairi called out from the back. "Hello! Set the dishes, Uncle!"

Alisdair grinned, happy to hear the girls cheerful and somewhat recovered. He waved at Micah to sit down and took the plates down from the rack above the sideboard. Soon they were covered with roughly triangular potato scones and boiled ramps and onions, with a couple of fried eggs alongside.

"My, you've had help today, Mairi. It's a feast!" Alisdair chuckled.

"Lots of help. We—we felt like a feast, didn't we?" said Mairi, looking sidelong at her cousin.

"Yes," said Mollie. "A celebration."

"Ah," said Alisdair. *I'm glad the children feel more comfortable with the Americans. That's good, that they've met a person of a differ-ent race and are learning a bit more of the world.* He smiled to himself about that, and felt his heart speed up at the chance these relative strangers had brought to his door. Labor! *If, that is, Neil returns.* His delight was swallowed up by doubt. He switched tacks.

"And how are you feeling this morning, Mr. James?" Alisdair used the formal address, even though they were about the same age, to keep his distance.

"Oh, much restored, thank you. I've put on the salve you mentioned, felt it doing its work for an hour or so. Came over as my stomach was rumbling—"

"Indeed. Seems to be working; your face is looking a bit better, I think."

"What happened, anyway?" asked Gil, who'd been pulling all the seats around the table. "We thought you was a red man at first."

Jamie smiled at that, then hissed, as the movement creased his face. Something began oozing again; he dabbed at it with one of the cloths from last night.

"Oh, we'll get you a new one, Mr. Jamie," said Mollie. "Just put that one in the hamper. My father says you shouldn't put a dirty cloot on an open sore."

"Cloot? Does Edward use that word, now?" Alisdair teased.

"No..." She smiled.

"Our sister Muirne married Edward, who hasn't any Gaelic. Any attempts he makes at speaking it are a source of general amusement in this house," Alisdair explained.

Micah nodded. Jamie half-smiled. "I've very little myself, you know."

"No, you were born on the boat, weren't you?"

"Just after landing in Carolina. My mother and father speak it between themselves, of course, but not so much in public. And with more and more of our hills getting to be like a village, with gossip and small-mindedness...Sorry," he said, and lapsed into silence. Micah broke it.

"Can I ask, sir, what you do with your rye?"

Alisdair was surprised. "Do? Mostly we sell it, but some we have milled into flour for our own use. Why do ye ask?"

"It's a popular grain for distilling, for some of the folks west of us," he said.

"Ah," Alisdair said.

"Uncle, what's dis-stillin?" Mollie asked.

"It means making the devil drink with our grain, instead of using it for food," Alisdair replied, with a cheeky grin. No one was a teetotaler here.

"I bet you've got barley fields for that, aye?" asked Jamie.

"Aye," said Alisdair, growing wary, but attempting not to show it. It was a normal enough question, but sounded as though the pair had worked their way around to asking it. Were they after their alcohol? Or after selling it? They didn't look desperate, sitting at the table now, but perhaps he should have heeded Neil's advice and been more skeptical.

"We make little enough, though. Just for celebrations, end of the season, Hogmanay, you know. Well, a very good meal, Sheena, I—I mean, Mairi."

Alisdair froze, then shook his head. He looked at Mairi's wee face, pale with dark hair. "What was I thinking! You do mind me of Sheena this morning, though."

Mairi preened a little, taking it as a compliment.

Good. But the feeling of being back in time and having his sister here didn't dissipate immediately. He felt the others' eyes on him.

"We should get back," he said, hurrying out. Micah followed, after thanking the cooks.

The line of questioning around the grain spirits was resolved at supper. Neil was still missing, but Alisdair tried to keep the conversation lively enough that the children wouldn't worry over it.

"My father had quite a bit of his whisky stolen after he'd sold a barrel of it down to the Old Fort," Jamie explained. "We figured some of those old boys had taken a shine to it and wanted more without paying. It is reckoned to be the best in the county. Well, was." Jamie grimaced, and Alisdair didn't ask what had happened after the neighbors' rioting.

"Anyway, if you had a secret stash, I would hope it was very secret, indeed. Theft o' that can cause a blind riot, it could."

"Indeed. Even in our mountains, you think?"

Jamie shrugged.

"I could see Mrs. MacGregor, clambering over with her stone bottle, thirsting for a dram..." Mollie giggled at that, and Gil and Mairi smiled.

"And how would you compare our farming methods with those of the MacDonalds, Mr. Micah? Up to snuff, are we?"

Micah managed a smile. "And a pinch above it, Mr. Alisdair. We grow nothing but burley tobacco, wheat, corn, and apples in our foothills, so your rye and barley will be interesting to see."

A polite answer. "Your coming here, while it may have been because of bad times back home, is really a godsend for us. A stroke of luck. I can say, while Neil's not here, that he hasn't been in good health since his wife passed. It's been a rough road but we've been scraping by. Without Mam—well."

The mood sobered. *What will we do without someone to preserve the food? Mam gone, Letty gone, Sheena abroad, and Mairi not old enough. Neil could get remarried; it's been a year.* But the thought left him hopeless; he couldn't very well find a wife for Neil himself. Alisdair cleared his throat.

"A stroke o' luck. Now, I've got some leather for new shoes..."

When the children were finally yawning, Alisdair took the Americans outside the cabin to bid them good night.

"I'll be frank; Neil's done this a couple times before. Seems to clear his head. He'll be back. And I don't like to worry Mairi."

Jamie nodded, looking down. Micah held his gaze, nodded subtly.

"I think another day of rest wouldna go amiss, eh, Jamie?"

His cousin looked up, nodded again, gratefully.

Alisdair shook their hands and returned to his cabin.

The next two days moved painfully slowly. It was high summer and the weather was fine, but Alisdair was leading both the newcomers and the young ones round the place, showing them the efficiency of the swing, how much could fit into a stook, and how to test the moisture of one before rolling it home. Micah followed his movements and easily mimicked his success. Gil did his best to wield the large tools on a smaller scale. And Mollie was quite fast at stooking by the end of the second day.

Neil returned while they were at supper, the light still bright in the cabin clearing, but their fields in the valley in shadow. First, they heard singing, then the door opened. Neil was a shadow against the light.

"Hullo, the house," he said, with a brief smile.

Everyone at table looked at each other, wondering whether he was addled with sunstroke or they were seeing things.

"And where have ye been on yer wanderings this time, Neil?" asked Alisdair.

"Here and there. Important business. Glad you've had help, Alisdair. The rye field's looking cleaned up." He glanced at Micah, who merely waited.

"Aye. And Jamie's got one more day, Mrs. MacGregor thought, before he should try the sun."

"She's been here, too? Wonderful. Glad you're healing, sir." He nodded at Jamie.

"Nothing else to say?" Alisdair asked casually, though he felt like he was being stretched on tenterhooks.

"No. No news. Not yet."

Neil was dirty from the road; he excused himself to wash

at the basin in the kitchen shed. Alisdair let the silence hang. Finally he looked at Mairi. Her face was twisted in a scowl, one that Alisdair knew was to keep from crying.

"Well. Any third helpings? No? Right, you go on and clean up, then. I'll see to the chickens tonight with you, Mairi."

Hidden expressions, covert looks. The party was broken up. He filled the water while Mairi counted heads and fastened the door to the coop. They looked up to the waxing sliver of moon before going in, Alisdair's hand on his niece's head.

His heart felt too fragile for words in that moment, but he gave her shoulder a squeeze before kissing her good night.

June 1834, Kirkintilloch

Every day was a gamble. Either she felt elated with the news from Gordon getting on with Mr. Grainger at the new office, or she lay on their humble bed in the dark shade of the house, trying not to move. Sheena could have managed either the heated closeness of the valley air or the gross enlargement of her body's borders, but both together were proving very hard going.

They had decided initially not to engage help. The cottage provided by Grainger's company was hardly big enough for another person to turn around in, but at least it was stone-built and fortified against the rains. They'd looked at a newly built wooden house that boasted an extra room, but when they'd seen the cracks under the doors, they'd thanked the man and left. The tiny stone cottage was a step backward, all right, but living in ankle-deep mud come autumn would have been worse.

After his first interview, Gordon asked around for the midwife and learned where she lived.

"At the edge of the woods to the north. Quite nice land, that bit. Still rural. Mrs. Ferris at the grocer's says she has a nice big garden there."

"How far?" Sheena asked.

"Oh, about a mile, is my guess."

They were sitting at the small table, Sheena on their trunk, Gordon on their one chair. Behind Sheena was the raised bed, without enclosures, while behind Gordon the hearth smoked and spit. Sheena was partially relieved there were no fixtures for their china, as it would seem more vulnerable on the wall. No, she preferred to keep everything not being used in the trunk. In case.

"I don't know if I'll make that distance before the baby comes. This heat swells my limbs so."

"Of course, I'll go. You should stay inside where at least the stone keeps it cool."

Sheena forebode mentioning that the same stone would make the place intolerably cold in winter.

While she couldn't walk the long distance to see the midwife, Sheena did venture out close by the next day to meet her new neighbors, yet again. Paid calls to the grocer, the laundress, the blacksmith—again. By the end of the second day, she felt more exhausted than she remembered being since Letty's funeral, and losing that child. She sat and clutched at her enormous belly. Gordon found her that way at dusk when he returned from his interview at the coal works survey office. He arrived in good spirits but quickly changed his expression when he saw Sheena's dejected posture. She smiled feebly at him.

"My limbs have stopped obeying me, husband. I am sorry about dinner. There is ale in the cupboard and potatoes cooked in the pan."

"Ah, I see." He rose to fetch plate and fork and food. Sheena hoped the tired note in his own voice didn't mean disappointment, but couldn't muster enough energy to rise to do anything about it. His next words woke her from the drowse she'd fallen into.

"I've talked to the midwife, name of Travers, Isobel Travers. She's to come by tomorrow morning. In the meantime, she gave me a list of beneficial foods for you. I found a few on my way home. I don't mind spending some extra, but it may be a bit of a squeeze, before I've been paid my first wages."

"I am an expense, am I? I would say it's your son who's the big expense."

"Well, you're the same to me, at the moment. When he comes out, we'll see how he pulls his own weight."

Sheena laughed. Felt something clutching at her nether parts. Went rigid to fight it for a moment. Gordon must have seen the fleeting expression, for his voice hushed.

"What is it, Sheena?"

"It's starting—just—slow," she said through gritted teeth, and then it stopped. She panted, and smiled in a perfunctory way. "Maybe we should have that Isobel Travers come tonight, instead."

"Of course. I'll away now and be back as quick as I can." He grabbed two of the potatoes to eat on the way. "You"ll be all right? Not hungry at the moment?"

She shook her head. "Perfectly fine at the moment."

"All right. Then I'll be back in an hour and a half or so. As quick as I can." He kissed her, drew back to look at her, and was gone.

Sheena regained some strength after a few minutes and rose to tidy up. She found a large knob of cheese in the string parcel Gordon had brought for her, and smiled, inhaling its pungency. She reached to place it in the low cupboard of cold storage and felt another clutching between her legs. It radiated in waves up the pole at the middle of her being, ringing a painful bell at the very top.

When it stopped, she was panting again, her hand gripping the table, her fingers poking brown paper into the cheese. She gulped and coughed. *They tell me these will come faster and faster, with less time between. So I had better do what I want now while it's waiting.*

And it did seem to be waiting. The baby no longer squirmed within her, but there was a great, heavy, dark feeling of pressure, as if someone inside her were jumping on the shallow basket between her two hips. Her knees nearly crumpled with it. She made her way to the bed after putting away the mottled cheese.

She put away her loose stays then took off her shoes, stockings, and outer skirts. She lay in her shift and petticoat in the wide bed, feeling both small and entirely too huge to be possible. After a few more minutes of sweating and her heart racing, she realized she couldn't wait like this for the pains to come or she would go mad. She went to the trunk again, every step a fight against fatigue and drowsiness, and opened it to retrieve one of the few books they had brought with them: Volume 16 of the *Waverley Novels*.

Clutching it to her throbbing chest, she wobbled her way back to the bed. She put her hand out for the blanket, and stood abruptly, feeling something burst and slither down her thighs. She felt dripping by her feet.

"NO!" she screamed. "No, no, no! Lord, please…" She canted forward, her knees bent, her hips at bed-height. "No," she said firmly. More wetness down her thighs. She squinted her eyes shut.

She climbed back into bed and flipped onto her back, one hand still gripping the novel. Her short, sharp breaths eventually eased into a more natural rhythm.

I don't know what is happening to me, but please let the baby be all right, she prayed.

The next hours were a wash of knotting pains, stabbing pains, radiating pains, and blissful nothingness as she lost consciousness between contractions. Sheena knew her body was still fighting, and she could only hope it was for good reason, and not a lost cause. She begged for Gordon, sometimes aloud, and sometimes screaming. Finally, she heard a rattle at the door.

It slammed open and her husband rushed to her side. A woman followed him in.

"Sheena! Are you all right?"

"I'm—"

But before she could respond the florid older woman

muscled him over.

"Is your water broke yet?" she said, in a flat voice.

"Oh," said Sheena. *Water.* She took a breath to quiet the screaming raven inside.

"I see it has," said the woman, looking down where she stood in bare feet over the cold wet floor. "Good. Now, back off here, man," and she shooed Gordon to the side of the bed. He kissed her face all over, until Sheena pushed his shoulder with her hand. She wanted a hand to hold more than a head to collide with when it started again.

"This is Isobel," said Gordon. Isobel propped first one of Sheena's legs up, then the other. Her eyes widened a moment, and Sheena's heart skipped at that.

"You're pretty far along. Good. I'd say a few hours more. But I'll still be wanting the full fee," she directed this at Gordon.

"Of course," he said. Sheena looked at him in amazement. He was so abashed, humble—afraid. That's what it was that shocked her. Never mind the woman's coarse lack of tact. Her husband was afraid. She squeezed his hand.

"I'm glad you're here, love." She saw the relief in his eyes. Some of her drowsiness flitted away, and another great moment of contraction and expelling started. She yelled and shouted and groaned and held on for dear life. When that one subsided, she looked down at Gordon's hand, expecting it to look like the mottled cheese. She felt his other hand press away the hairs that clung to her sweaty face. Her breath was quick. But the relief that it was her water broke, and not another miscarriage—yet—was giving her a renewed strength. Gordon's presence, the midwife's—those helped, too.

Dear Lord, make it a few more hours. Give me a child. Give me the child, Mam.

The hours went by like days, with Sheena feeling the giant mass in her shift and start to break through that basket between her hips. It tore. It wrenched. And then with the entire mattress soaked through, her ears numb from her own screams, and a stench of pain so thick she thought she was drowning, the woman Isobel pulled something through and out and—*there*. Sheena panted enormously, trying to see clearly through the haze of pulsing pain.

A minute later, Isobel had swathed the infant and put it aside, then set to patching up the destroyed entrance to the womb. Sheena felt pressure on her ankles as her legs were moved this way or that, and then a sort of peace settled over her. She looked up at the shadowy recesses of the thatch roof, and felt herself drifting upward. Then, a slap, and a cry. She saw the woman Isobel hand off a bundle of cloth to Gordon. Gordon's arms hung loosely down around the cloot that held the infant; he was more awestruck than she'd ever seen him. The infant's arms danced toward her and the cry increased tenfold. Sheena endeavored to feel her own arms again, and order them to move.

Gordon tilted his burden up to show Sheena. She saw the

biggest, reddest head she'd seen on a baby, capped with tendrils of dark hair.

"Good God, he's enormous," she said, as Gordon laid his weight on her chest. Her arms finally obeyed her and she cradled the baby to her. Hands came from nowhere to pull down her chemise low enough so the baby could suckle. A few minutes spent watching him struggle made Sheena nervous.

"Help me up, Gordon." She struggled to push up against the wall at her head, causing something to come unstuck between her legs. She sucked in a breath, waiting for pain but feeling almost nothing. She groaned anyway. Gordon looked back and forth between her and the midwife, unsure.

"Just get your hands under her back and pull her up," instructed Isobel. "Leave the bottom bit alone for a while." And then she went to adjust and reapply her tincture to 'the bottom bit.' Sheena was arranged to sit up finally, and managed to guide the little mouth to the right spot. The cries and fretting ceased, until he lost hold of her again, but Sheena felt something happen between the pull of the milk down into his mouth and the desperate hammering of her heart: her spirit felt raised up above the pain and sensation in the rest of her body. She stayed like that as long as she could but after a quarter of an hour, her head began to droop to the side, and Gordon took over the baby, who was somewhat sated and calmed by then. Sheena felt him tuck a bundle beside her on the bed and rub the back of her hand before she fell into the cleanest, deepest sleep of her life.

She was surprised to wake what seemed like a few minutes later, only to be told it was about noon and she'd slept two hours and a half; even Gordon had had a wee kip. The baby was crying, which had evidently woken her, and Isobel set him immediately on her breast. *What does Muirne do to feed them when she needs to be up and about?* Sheena wondered. *When am I to rise from this bed?* She smelled something strange in the house, and felt something cold at her sensitive center. Not a poultice, which is hot, but a compress. *I hope Isobel knows what she's about.*

"At least two more days in bed, ma'am. I'll come back to check on you then. Meantime, I've shown yer husband what to do to make a fresh compress each morning, nice and cold, to help the torn skin to mend."

Sheena glanced at Gordon, who looked worried and discomfited, but nodded.

"I'm going by the manse on my way home, if you've—"

"We'll bide for the present, thank you, Miss Isobel," said Gordon.

After she left, they sat and watched the boy, whose head had become less red but no less enormous, energetically suckle at first one and then the other breast.

"Bet he's going to be a tall one," Gordon said.

"Enormous."

"Your hair."

"Mm."

"She left some broth on the stove. Will you take some?"

"Aye."

Gordon fed her broth by the spoonful as the infant lay

asleep, fingers arrested in mid-curl.

"Have you thought of a name you like, wife?"

"Miracle."

"Well, that would be——"

"No. No——he's just a miracle."

"Yes. Yours. And mine."

"Kieron."

"Kieron?"

"It means Dark One."

"Kieron."

Sheena felt Gordon trying it on in his mouth, feeling it hesitantly slip off his tongue. The door rattled. A perfunctory knock made Sheena turn as best she could.

Two thin young people stood in their room. The young man wrung his hat in his hands, his homespun clothes looking wilted and dusty. The young woman twined her hands together in front of her; her dress, already ragged and dirty, fell too short to cover her bare feet. The boy spoke first.

"If you please, sir. Mr. Grainger sends his congratulations to you and his compliments to the lady——" Sheena compressed her lips not to laugh at such language when they were in a dripping, stone, one-room hut. "——And as he realizes she may be unable to perform her duties of settling into the house, he wishes you to use the services of my sister, Angela, for the cooking and cleaning. While ye get back on yer feet," he added. *A fine speech, and with his own addition at the end*, Sheena smiled tiredly to herself.

Gordon responded more formally, and correctly with the

required thanks and introductions. *Isn't that thoughtful of Grainger, Sheena thought. It is a good sign. And glad I am that Gordon will not have to be changing my bloodied compresses.*

Angela proved to be a much-needed help and a buffer between her and Gordon in the next two weeks, at the end of which Sheena was walking again but any lifting tended to lead to more tearing. Gordon was able to start work with Mr. Grainger, however, and after bringing home his first fortnight's pay, he declared they should keep Angela to help.

"But, Gordon—"

"No, I am firm on this point. You need to recover your health. You will need to devote much of your attention to the baby, and I, for one, don't want to be eating cold potatoes the rest of my life!"

Sheena smiled. "But you would, wouldn't you, to keep me?"

"If I had to, yes. Thank God I do not."

Sheena walked toward Gordon with Kieron in her arms. "My cold-potato man. What we do for love."

"Yes." And Gordon's tone was considerably softer.

July 1834, The Ridge

Alisdair looked out with pleasure into the dark. There was no moon again, which meant the Americans had been here a month. They were well into the rhythm of the farm work. Neil's attempts to assign duties had been awkwardly received, a fact which made Alisdair secretly pleased. Jamie and Micah worked with Alisdair without pausing to pass a critical eye over everything, and it made for a more efficient crew. Eventually, Neil silently acknowledged this, leaving them to the rest of the oat harvest while he took his mending kit to the far fences.

Work was feeling clean again, not mired down in resentment. The presence of his niece and nephew didn't hurt, either. Their mealtime that night had been full of cheeky questions and tall tales.

"As wide as the ocean that brought us here, I'm telling you," Jamie had said, grinning.

"There's not as much land as that," said Gil, with his seven-year-old certainty.

"There is! And all with tobacco! Which you can't even eat!"

Mairi and Mollie giggled at that.

"What about the forest? You said that's why you weren't

used to the sun," said Gil.

"That comes after the tobacco—another ocean, an ocean of trees," Jamie said with a quiet smile.

"Just like we've got here, you know," said Neil. "Like we had before we started felling trees for a house."

Mairi looked at her father, her eyes squinting in a calculating way. She must be thinking of the house that had already been here, but not wanting to contradict her da.

"Well, there was a site already, you recall," Alisdair said.

Neil flicked him a quelling glance. "Aye, but they'd cleared little enough room for crops, *you'll recall*."

He's feeling testy again. "True enough. Have the Americans heard the little ghost tale?"

"I know it! Can I tell it?"

"Aye, go on, Mollie. Let's see if yer ma's version adds up," said Neil, and the shy twinkle was back in his voice. Alisdair breathed a sigh of relief. Did Jamie and Micah feel the ebb and flow of tension? A glance at Jamie's concentrated gaze and Micah's carefully innocent face told him they did. *Ach, well. Soon enough Neil shall have to step down from his high perch to be with us mere farm-hands again. At least there are flashes of the old Neil.*

The next morning the four men and Gil were down in the fields. Neil had Gil running up and down the rows on errands with tools, which he liked much better than gleaning. Neil, Micah, and Jamie had spread out to walk the rows together. The bell sounded mid-morning and they gathered at the bottom of the drive to walk up the hill.

"I'm going to head into town for a supply and mail run today," Neil announced. He glanced around. "So if anyone would like to send a letter, best get it done at breakfast."

Jamie looked at Alisdair and shrugged. Micah kept his gaze on the ground.

"I don't think there's anything, Neil, but I've need of a couple items from Mr. Bracethwaite's. The neatsfoot oil is running low and a few more sheets of canvas for the outbuildings would be well-timed."

"Right, then."

Gil was excited to tell the girls of the birds he'd almost brought down with his stones.

"Shouldn't do that," Mollie warned her brother. "They're not hurting you."

"They might be stealing the cows' feed, though," Micah said mildly.

Mollie frowned, but didn't retort.

Manners! In the wilderness! Will wonders never cease. Alisdair smiled to himself and made a note to relate the incident to Muirne. It had been too long since he'd visited his sister in town. He suddenly felt jealous of Neil's trip to town. He squelched the feeling, wishing him fair travels, before heading back to the oat fields with Jamie and Micah. Gil opted to stay close to the house with his stones.

They managed to finish the scything that day and took a water break in the shade of mid-afternoon before starting the stacking. Alisdair asked them again about the forests of North

Carolina, intrigued by that earlier small smile of Jamie's.

"Ach, they're all after being cut down," he said. "No one has the sense to keep a community woodland. That's what my da says would be the smartest thing—otherwise we'll end up just as naked as the old country. One needs cover for game to hunt, shade for water to stay in the ground." He shook his head.

"What do you think, Micah?"

"I agree with Mr. Jamie," he said easily. "It make some sense what Mr. Kenneth say, sure."

"Perhaps. But they can do what they want with the land they own, no?"

"The Indians would say that it don't belong to them, no matter what them papers say," Micah said softly.

"That's the other thing that don't exist no more," Jamie agreed. "Damn new folk scared off the Indians that helped us. Killed a dozen in their nearest village because they didn't have it written on their map. Called it trespassing." Jamie spat.

Micah remained silent. Alisdair sensed his gaze was turned inward, and far away.

Neil returned early the next evening with the oil and the canvas, in addition to two fat letters. One was addressed to Mam, because of course Uncle Kenneth must have sent it before their letter of her death reached him. And the other was to them all, from Sheena.

Neil had opened and read them both already. He handed

the first to Alisdair as soon as he dumped his pack on the cabin floor at supper time. Alisdair read it aloud for everyone, only stumbling over the first line's sentiments:

> *My dear Sheila,*
>
> *I hope this letter finds you all well, with a new grandchild to play with on your knee. I like to think with satisfaction of the prospect that we can still find happiness even after it escapes us once. As to how things are here, this is why I write to you.*
>
> *They may have already reached you, as we had to delay writing several weeks because we were hiding in the hills without contact with anyone traveling north. If they have, I am sure your tender side has assured our youngest son James of the best care and attention, based on his family resemblance. Unfortunately, he's gotten in something of a squabble with our neighbors.*
>
> *As you know, we have a lot of them now. It is a far cry from the initial advertisement of free, open land to settlers that was put out thirty or forty years ago. We have our twenty acres, but we are surrounded by three other Scots families and two English, each on their own small patch. Most of them are from big cities, Glasgow and London, and have small experience of farming. They depend to a large degree on the slaves they buy at port, a dangerous proposition as far as I can see. I have yet kept myself on good terms, as my knowledge has been widely useful, even applied to farming in such hilly land, away from water.*

They have come from the cities, as I say, and fall easily into the American belief that slavery is a natural right, an institution of this land from time immemorial, rather than the foul practice it is. James had occasion to see the slave Micah, and his daughter, being whipped in one of the neighbor's fields. He intervened, and the neighbor, a Mr. Hennessy, didn't like it too much. Whatever the initial motive for the whipping was, James' intervention made him lose face, and Micah's fate was sealed.

Mariah was trying to reason with some of the neighbors, especially the ones we see at Kirk, about treating the slaves better and even talking them round to the cause of abolition. When James fell into this piece of trouble, it endangered Mariah as well, although of course James would never have done so if he'd known the consequences for his mother. So, we went up into the hills. It was summer and not too difficult to find food and shelter in the unclaimed backwoods, but James and Micah set off immediately. Micah's daughter was unfortunately unable to escape with him, and has had some very harsh treatment from the Hennessys, I believe. It is a family tragedy we are still reeling from, and deciding how to proceed is difficult.

Please write to me how they fare with you, and I will write to let you know when we are settled again—Mariah and me, and Caroline and her family and Iain and his wife. The rest have elected to stay near Wilmington. All my love and God's blessings on you,

Kenneth

After Alisdair finished reading, he met Neil's eye; his stare seemed to challenge him, dare him, to something. The children were silent, their wooden spoons suspended as they waited for the reaction to that word: *slave.*

Jamie cleared his throat. "You're the closest relatives we have on the continent. Da thought ye would stand by us. But without his letter, I didna know…"

"Aye," Alisdair said. "I can see you'd be afraid to put it all forward."

"But at least you know I'm your cousin, at least," Jamie added. He looked down, then peeked at Micah.

"And we know you've come for your freedom," Alisdair said to Micah. "Not unlike us."

Micah's gaze pierced his and he felt inadequate, his soul bare.

"I'm sorry to hear about your daughter," he added in a low voice, his gaze flicking down and up again. A twitch passed over Micah's dark features, then a compressed shudder. Jamie put a hand on his shoulder. The solid man seemed to collapse inward on the bench, his back curved like a tortoise shell.

"We are sorry indeed, for your loss," said Neil softly. Alisdair looked over and saw Neil watched Mairi as he said it. The air seemed heavy with water, and he wished to open the door to let in the cool night.

"Thank you," came the rumble from Micah's bowed head. He lifted it, nodded to Neil, to Alisdair. He turned to Mairi to nod as well. She looked about to cry. Micah gazed at her, and

Alisdair wished he could explain it to her in any way that wouldn't demonstrate humans' capacity for cruelty. But then, he'd received the same abrupt lesson when his father had come home from a vicious beating only to die. Neil's voice interrupted this reverie.

"The Law allows you your freedom as long as you stay in Nova Scotia?"

Micah inclined his head. Jamie elaborated.

"Or New Brunswick, or Lower or Upper Canada. Any-where in the Empire that has outlawed slavery."

"Only the place that fought for its freedom denies it to others," Alisdair said softly.

Another wet silence.

"Well, you are both welcome to be part of this household as long as you wish."

Alisdair's words came out too bright, as he attempted to dispel the fog of impossible sadness. He saw that they had lied, but he understood why. His gaze was doleful as he contem-plated Micah, whom he'd grown to trust in the field, and Jamie, whom he certainly recognized from his family stories. They'd grown comfortable with one another, working togeth-er.

"Aye, more family would be precious to us at exactly this moment," Neil agreed, a pained smile flitting across his face. "And on that subject, I've asked Mrs. Thomas down in town to marry me, and she has accepted."

Alisdair gaped at his brother. "Who?" he spluttered.

Neil seemed suddenly in motion, finished with his supper

and whisking crumbs off the table with his hand. "Mrs. Thomas. Muirne knows—of her."

"Knows *of* her? And do we?" Alisdair's face flushed. "Have you really just gone and proposed to some woman we don't even know—who hasn't even met Mairi?"

"Yes." Neil stood with his plate in hand. "But I know this family will welcome her just as openly as we have our American guests." Neil's knuckles on the plate were white.

"It's not her I'm taking issue with, it's you! Can ye not see it's plain disrespect to the rest of us?"

"Who I take to wife is not subject to your approval, Alisdair." Neil's voice was both sharp and soft.

"But whether I go to town for school is subject to yours," shouted Alisdair. He pushed back his chair and stood, leaning forward with his shoulders curling in, protecting what little hope he harbored.

"I don't want to discuss it now," said Neil. He walked to the bucket and plunked his plate into the water. "I'm bringing her up to the ridge in a week's time; you'll all meet her then."

With a false smile, he nodded toward Jamie and Micah. "I believe I'll go spruce up the smaller cabin to make it ready. You can move in here while I'm gone. Good night."

He grabbed a few cloths and a pillow and ducked out into the night. Alisdair wanted to punch the back of his head as it disappeared. He turned instead back to the table, where three of the five faces looked back at him.

"Excuse me. I shouldn't have shouted." *How I wish Mam were here.*

"Uncle Alisdair, do I have to go help Da?" Mairi's voice trembled.

"No, Mairi. Best give yer da his space at the moment."

Mollie and Gil were whispering, then buttoned their lips when he glared their way. Alisdair let out an exhausted sigh.

"Och, well. We've a week to get used to the idea. Meantime, welcome to the family, James MacDonald, and Micah—" Alisdair paused, too late realizing he didn't know Micah's surname.

Micah met his gaze. "I've had some time to think of a second name. It's Kenneth."

Jamie's head twitched in surprise; his breath gushed. Alisdair felt his lips stretch in a pained, condoling smile.

July 1834, The Ridge

When Neil had helped them finish stacking the oats, he departed. The next day, Alisdair invited the Americans down to the small burial ground after supper.

They stood under the shadows of the trees, and Alisdair took off his hat to pray silently. Jamie and Micah did the same. His thoughts turned to Neil and this engagement, and how it was moving too fast, how none of them knew the woman. He longed to hear Muirne's account of her.

A hiccup at his right surprised Alisdair, and he turned to see Jamie dabbing his face with the cloth again, his eyes full. Alisdair turned away respectfully. *He must miss his family, too.* Alisdair thought of his own father's grave down in town. He hoped Muirne kept it tidy.

When the men came back to the yard, Alisdair was surprised to see the two lanterns of a wagon bobbing in the dusky light.

"Neil?" he called. No answer.

They approached and saw the horse tied loosely around one of the stumps in the yard.

Alisdair left the wagon alone and hurried inside, followed by Jamie and Micah.

The picture that greeted him made him hesitate. Neil

stood by the table with one arm around the shoulders of a small boy, and the other across the back of a woman dressed in a plain wool dress. They faced Mairi, who Alisdair saw was curled over her knees on the floor. Mollie and Gil stood to the side, faces white as ghosts. Their eyes shifted to him and the tableau was broken.

"Hallo, the house," Alisdair said quietly.

"Alisdair! There you are. And our guests. We've had luck. Come in, come in." He let go of his two charges to shoo them all to sit at the table. Mairi on the floor he ignored for the moment. Alisdair went immediately to scoop her up.

"Are you all right?" he whispered in her ear.

She didn't answer, but burrowed her head into his shoulder and clutched at his coat lapels, something she hadn't done for a year.

They all sat, the pins and needles evident in the tentative lowering of bodies.

Neil looked at them all with a strained smile. "Mrs. Thomas, may I present my brother Alisdair."

Everyone's eyes now turned to the woman, who sat ramrod straight. She had thin dark hair under her cap and bonnet, barely visible. Ruddy, hard-baked skin with no shine to it even in the candle light. Lines from worry on her brow and lines from scowling at her mouth. Not altogether a vision of loveliness. Rather, a woman with a past. And a child.

The boy was olive-skinned with dark, straight hair. He had the same thin, straight nose as his mother, though, and greenish-brown eyes. He stared straight ahead, knowing he was being examined.

"How do you do, Mrs. Thomas," Alisdair finally said. He ignored Neil's exhale of relief at the periphery of his vision. She raised her eyes to his. A change in the shape of her eyes as she smiled politely.

"How do you do, Mr. MacLean. This is my son, Emery."

Alidair nodded at him, then turned to Jamie, but Mrs. Thomas spoke.

"The luck your brother speaks of is that he was coming to fetch us, but I had already made my way up. There was a letter for you, so I started earlier than we'd arranged. I did not know of any visitors at the time. I am sorry if we're intruding."

She spoke haltingly, so formally that Alisdair wondered if she was reading from a primer. Who was she? Where had she come from? He yearned to question Muirne, who 'knew of her.'

"No intrusion, ma'am," Neil said. "This is our cousin Jamie MacDonald, and this is—Micah."

Alisdair fidgeted, feeling about to burst but for holding Mairi in his arms.

"And these are our sister's children, Mollie and Gil," Alisdair said in an overloud voice. "And this is Neil's daughter, Mairi."

Finally, he felt Mairi sniffle and turn her head to regard the room again.

"And you are *never* going to be my mother," she said.

Mairi was in hiding, and Alisdair figured she should have some time to adjust to this sudden family. He let her hide the day after their arrival, while the new wife and child spent the entire day in the smaller cabin. Alisdair sat uneasily with Jamie and Micah and the children, observing Neil shuttle back and forth to get them food and linens. Alisdair also left his brother to his devices, not trusting himself to confront him yet. Early the next morning, he set out for the burial grove.

"There you are, Mairi," he said coaxingly. She was under the lee of the tree, just as he'd imagined, sitting with her arms wrapped around her drawn-up knees. He squatted next to her. "I've a question for you."

She turned, and he saw the misery in her face.

"What," she said in a flat voice.

"What was that you said about Mrs. Thomas being your mother? Did she say such a thing?"

The downturned mouth now hardened into a scowl. "No, Da did!"

"Did he explain?"

She looked at him accusingly at that.

"You know, my father died when I was about the same age as you."

Her face twitched, the eyebrows going from furrowed to lifted and back again. She crouched forward to lean against him.

"Did Grannie turn around and marry someone else right away?"

"No, she depended on yer da—wait, married? You're

telling me they're married and all, already?"

Mairi pulled back to watch him as she nodded.

How had he misunderstood? Neil had said the woman had accepted him, but there had been no ceremony…A big ball of anger flamed in Alisdair's chest at how Neil had done everything all wrong. Hadn't talked to his family about his intentions. Hadn't told them where he'd gone. Hadn't even told them he was getting married, and then had gone and done it without them. When? How? Why did the bloody fool feel like he needed to do everything himself?

"You all right, Uncle?"

His focus came back to the moment under the tree. Near the graves of both their mothers.

"All right. Just shocked—stunned—at what Neil has done. I'm sure he thinks it's best for you and the farm," he tried to reassure her.

The girl just shook her head sadly. "I wonder if Aunt Muirne knows."

"That's a fair question. I—" And suddenly a plan of action leapt into Alisdair's head. He could leave to see Muirne and ask her about this Mrs. Thomas. Then he could go to Halifax and see Dr. McCulloch. *He* could be the one leaving others to pick up the slack on the farm. He could escape this trap he felt closing around him.

But would it spell ruin for this little girl whom he loved so much? Was Neil really doing the right thing? He remembered their American visitors. They would take his place at the plough, and Alisdair could trust them with looking after

Mairi, until he had a job lined up. Then he would come back for a visit. Satisfied with this plan, he smiled tentatively at Mairi.

"I have a few things I'd like to ask Muirne, in fact. Maybe I'll go down to see her."

"Take me?"

"I think you are needed here."

Mairi gave him such a look that he almost gave up the idea. "So are you."

"But I need something different, lass. And you can get along without me for a while."

She shook her head and curled over her knees again.

"All right then. I'll head out this evening after I've told everyone. Camp on the way. Be back in two shakes. Or two weeks. But I'll be back."

She must not have heard him, for she stayed hunched over and didn't look in his direction.

"Goodbye, Mairi-*beag*. Be a good girl. Talk to yer da."

Without an answer, he rose and headed back with a heavy heart.

He told Jamie and Micah, who took it in stride. He encouraged them to confront Neil about the new arrangements when they were ready. Then, he bearded the lion in its den.

"Neil." He poked his head in the little cabin. "Can I talk to you outside?"

"Anything you have to say, you can say to me here," said

Neil, sitting at the table in the middle of the room. Emery the boy sat across from him, and Mrs. Thomas was scraping the last bits from a pan onto his plate. They all looked over at him. Alisdair came inside.

"I'm going to see Muirne," he said. He was on the point of telling him he was going to Halifax after, but something stilled his tongue.

"Oh? And what for?" Neil glanced up at him before spreading butter over steaming biscuits.

"That's my business."

"And a mouthy piece of baggage you're being," quipped Neil.

"*Me?* What about you? Who in their right mind goes and gets married without telling their family?"

"Muirne knew."

Alisdair's upper lip curled, twitched his nose in the pique of resentment. "Did she? When?"

"She helped make Jemima's arrangements to come up here the other day. I only went down for the license because I had to sign that in person."

"Oh, sod you and everybody! Why didn't you tell *me?*"

The woman had sat down next to Neil and put her hands together as if in prayer. The boy joined her, head bowed. His brother just looked at him, some mixture of frustration and stubbornness on his face.

"Never mind. I'm away." He went out and swung the door shut. Grinding his teeth, Alisdair went to gather his things and leave right then. If he wasn't wanted, he would go where he would.

As he threw clothes into a sack and packed tools for sleeping rough, there was a sad note in the background. Some disappointment that the relationship with his brother was so strained. But the fault was entirely on Neil's side, and Alisdair, pinched and trapped as he was feeling, could not afford to give any more. *I must seize my opportunities. And that's what I'll do.* He hugged and kissed Gil and Mollie, told them to look after their cousin. Doffed his hat at Micah, shook hands heartily with James. And left the land of his family for the city to the south.

He didn't stop to see Muirne. He felt too bitter. Perhaps his anger would cool by the time he came back this way, but right now he was angry at Neil for telling his sister rather than him. He, who would have to live side-by-side with the new woman, nay, family! He resented having to ask Muirne for money, too, so he had very little when he set out. At least he'd packed plenty dried food, enough to last him the four days into the capital.

He arrived in the evening and found accommodation at an inn. He gave the woman his shillings and pence for a week then took the light supper she provided to his sparse room. He ate the fried fish and potatoes hungrily, then lapsed into a daze, lying back on the bed.

He'd had plenty of time to work out his first few steps in the city: find shelter, find Dr. McCulloch, and start on his list of places of employment he had mentally tallied from the last trip here with Sheena. Only now he felt compelled to go by the university grounds first to see how much progress had been made. Then he could go to Mitchell & Dexter's. A year had passed, but Mr. Dexter had seemed encouraging. It would be a question of whether they still needed a clerk, or needed one again.

Perhaps I will find better news since I last heard from the Doctor in February. And if I find no such news, I will seek out the doctor himself, at the address on his card. I'll offer myself as a student in exchange for labor.

What he had tried not to think about was how everyone on the ridge would feel about his leaving. Mairi might feel betrayed, poor thing. He promised to send her a letter in the morning, something her cousins could read to her. Neil might be in a temper for a while, but it was only what he deserved, acting so high-handed. What did he expect? If only Mam were still there to give Neil that stern look and turn things around from his view so that he understood the feelings of others. He remembered Neil being so much kinder, before Mam died, before Letty died, before Letty even came over to marry him. Something had changed.

Muirne? Had she really known? He questioned Neil's statement now. Fine, then, a letter for her on the morrow as well. And Sheena. His favorite, bold, determined sister, who seemed to be running for her life last time she had written. She had pretended for them. His spirit quailed at the thought of something so insidiously evil that she had to guard her letters to family. But now, with luck, she and Gordon would be out of harm's way. And she had a baby. Was the baby born yet? He tried with little success to calculate when he had received the letter, how far along she was, and when it might reasonably be expected to come.

Alisdair sighed. Everyone seemed to be in a bit of a muddle. But at least he was acting for himself, striking out. With hopes that all could be resolved, in time.

August 1834, Kirkintilloch

Sheena was exhausted but life plodded on. Her body healed as quickly as the baby grew—by leaps and bounds. And that feeling she'd had of taking up space, of feeling fuller and stronger: that remained. Sheena was grateful.

The little stone hut inconvenienced her less than it did Gordon. She remembered the crowded cabin being built on the ridge. She remembered the boarding house in Pictou. She remembered their black house on Mull. Gordon had lived in towns all his life, and in stone-built terraced housing for most of that time. He fretted about where to put his clothes and how to keep his books and papers dry until Sheena took them from him and arranged them back in the trunk.

"They'll keep there, dear. Now, you think on your business, and forget about the house—that's my business!"

Young Angela was a great help for all the fetching and carrying out-of-doors, especially since Sheena felt glued to the bed half the day to nurse Kieron. Again, she wondered how her sister did it. She'd watched many a time when visiting New Glasgow: Muirne would be shuttling between the range and the table, stirring with the one hand, carrying a child on the other hip, then exchange the toddler for the babe, re-arrange her apron-front, and carry the babe around as she searched for more ingredients. It had all seemed so natural and efficient.

There was little news of Muirne; Alisdair had said all were well in his last letter, but most of his writing had been consumed by the incredible appearance of their cousin and the Black man who had traveled up north to escape trouble in the Carolinas. Sheena had been agog at his account, and glad to find out that their claim was just and the men seemed to be fitting into the rhythm of the ridge. She could just see Mairi's delight at having more company than her old dad. *But at least she has her cousins for the summer, too. That must be easier on Muirne as well.* Sheena marveled again at how easy her sister made child-rearing look.

From her point of view, Sheena was finding it a long, uphill slog on too little sleep. She found if she could stay awake long enough to sup with Gordon when he came home and hear the news of how the days passed with Mr. Grainger, she could fall into a good sleep for three hours before Kieron woke her up again. An hour to suckle, then perhaps another two hours' rest if she could slip back into it. Then the boy woke again, and by the time he'd fed, it was getting light out. She hoped he'd sleep more as the days got shorter.

Gordon's business was going along rapidly as well, and more often than not, he collapsed as soon as she did. For Mr. Grainger, the head engineer of the Monkland & Kirkintilloch, had almost no help managing the business end of things. There were landowners to discuss terms with, and government functionaries to explain the law—though sometimes Gordon had to educate them on its modern precedents. There was correspondence to other engineers, and subscriptions to journals that followed the latest innovations and patents, as well as feus to be granted and terms to be sought with the holders of toll-gates. Grainger had surveyors and navvies, but no secretary, and Gordon had arrived at exactly the right time to make himself indispensable.

"Today, I went down to Paisley. You may be pleased to hear that we've avoided a slump in the textile industry."

"How fortunate for us!"

"Aye, the cotton mill planned fell through and the demand for silk has gone abroad. The poor weavers are starving on six shillings a week, so I can't imagine that bleachworks being at all profitable."

"The poor families." Sheena felt the thin edge of want which had narrowly missed her this time. "I suppose we have something to thank Callander for, then—poisoning Stirling's mind against us."

"It appears so. At any rate, there are a lot of people working in those collieries and ironworks, and with the new pig-iron selling, the main men in business around here will be very interested in connecting all the producers with markets. The producers pay, the buyers pay—and we may even have regular passengers soon!"

Gordon's face lit up with excitement, then as soon subsided. "If only the things weren't so damn expensive and slow to build."

One might even compare the thing to a child, Sheena quipped to herself.

"Passengers…you mean people are being scuttled around like so many rocks?"

"They've fashioned wagons with benches. I hear there are all sorts of designs coming forward in Mr. Taylor's next publication from London."

"I should very much like to see one. Perhaps I could even ride one? It is easier than riding a horse, yes?"

Gordon laughed at the comparison. "Oh, but it's so loud —it would upset the baby. Do wait, dear. When they receive some stock that is more comfortable to ride in, you will be in the second car, right after all the shareholders."

She smiled and wondered how long that would be. She was still wondering a few days later, when Gordon was out on an overnight journey south. She knew the locomotive went by four times each day; she'd heard the whistle at the level crossing where it stopped. Sheena determined to go see for herself the ten o'clock arrival. Wrestling with the decision to take Kieron with her or leave him, she let herself be swayed by Gordon's account of the loud sounds; she asked Angela to come by early to look after him while she went on a walk.

Bundled up, she trod the quarter-mile to the crossing. The rails lay empty, but all around was activity, with laborers unloading wagon cargoes close to one side of the tracks. Black soot and red chalk swirled while the sharp tang of something bitter made Sheena thirsty. She saw coals, bricks, and lime in enormous regimented heaps. *There is something exciting about watching such efficient activity. Some sense of rightness and central, guiding authority.*

At last, some of the men began checking their watches and shading their eyes to the south. A few minutes later, the air above the rise turned black and the locomotive came into view, its full complement of metal clanging and engine puffing and spitting fitfully as it slowed. Sheena tugged the shawl higher over her shoulders and watched as the coal and brick laborers scrambled onto the wagons before they even came to a standstill.

The last two wagons had a roof and a stepping-out door, she saw. Sheena walked a few steps closer. A family of eight had climbed out of the first wagon, a governess trailing them as they went after their luggage. The second passenger wagon's door opened and out stepped a Black man in a new suit. He was followed by more, until about a dozen Black men stood by the siding.

Sheena stared. They were of varying skin tones, and dressed in a range of clothes, from the costly first new suit to what looked like sailor's castoffs. *What can they all be doing here together? This railway only goes down to Coatbridge. I suppose you can take the Monkland Canal from there to Glasgow, but—*then it hit Sheena. *From the looks of curiosity and pride the men show, it must be a pleasure outing. Now that they are free of the Tobacco Barons. They must have been upper servants in the city.* Her breath caught as she thought of Rhoda and her Mr. Wilberforce, that battle so long waged, the unfairness of the slavery compensation scheme, the oppression of the Lairds for so long—*Now, keep hold of yourself, Sheena. Don't make of yourself a spectacle.*

She didn't wait to see the loading of the train but hurried the short distance back to the stone cottage. She kept the tears at bay as she stomped down the dusty lane by honing her indignation with the whetstones of injury and vengeance. She wept over Kieron's head that night, and when Gordon returned near midnight, she asked him about it.

"What will they do here? They'll have to look for jobs just like we do, only who will hire them? They won't pay them anything near a fair rate, ye can see that right away…"

"Slow down, Sheena. I'm sure the lawmakers will have thought of that. I've heard some are actually going back to found their own country in Africa."

They stayed up late that night, trying to solve the problems of the British Empire. Sheena allowed that great minds like Wilberforce's must have been at work on the subject for a while, while Gordon agreed that Rhoda must have had quite a hot coal to warm her heart all those lonely years, if she'd been loved by him.

"I wonder where they will all go," Sheena mused the next morning while she nursed.

"America seems still to need help colonizing its vast territories," Gordon said. "The tales from the West are of a young government, a virgin land—neither logged nor cultivated."

"But America lags behind in its policy on slavery," she reminded him. "Especially the southern states. Alisdair wrote me a little of it in his last letter."

"Too true. Well, I will ask around, see what people are saying."

"Thank you, Gordon."

"But don't think this has made me forget that you went out to the railway crossing on your own."

She turned a look of surprise on him. "I didn't think you would mind, as it was the noise that—"

"The noise would be bad for Kieron, true. But being out alone in such a crowd is not advisable for you, either. I won't repeat stories of some of the navvies' behavior, but I will say they can be dangerous after drink, and—"

"My father was one of those navvies for the canal! Don't you disparage them!" Sheena's eyes gleamed in the dark of the cool cottage. Kieron started to cry.

"Sheena." Gordon's hand settled on hers as the moment and her heated gaze fizzled out. "I'm sure he was a fine man, but it is terrible work. He must have been in desperate cir-cumstances. And a man in desperate circumstances, whether starvation of his family or the craze for the drink, is dangerous. Please. Don't forget it."

"Of course. I won't. You're right."

Desperation is different for every man, Gordon. And woman. The image of Rhoda in the mill pond came floating back. She squeezed her eyes shut, insisted she look to the future. *How to be ready for what comes?* Sheena made sure to read last year's copies of Hansard's *Debates* and the *Mirror of Parliament* for news of the proceedings that summer, and otherwise kept her ears open. She had no cause to regret suggesting the railway to her husband.

August 1834, Halifax

It had been a successful week. Alisdair had met with one of
Mr. Dexter's clerks, learned there was indeed an open post,
and asked most assiduously what he should know for the job.
This man was not like the others who had laughed at him.
He'd provided him with directions to the large bookshop on
their side of town, where he would find several advantageous
almanacs and the *Lloyd's List* to study. Alisdair had gone to put
in a deposit for one of the almanacs, an enormous tome of
tables and figures, and brought it back to the inn to study.

The visit to the school site had been a small disappointment. The work was still underway, a base with the roof
almost finished. But this time, he asked one of the masons
where the main school building was, having remembered Dr.
McCulloch's remark about this being an annex. 'Down the
way,' he'd been told. With such glimmering direction, he
wandered for quite a bit before observing a very handsome
red-brick edifice in the honored position in a small square.

Carriages swooped round a fountain in the middle of the
square, and stone buildings lined the perimeter. He found Dr.
McCulloch's office on the first floor with little difficulty. It
had his name on the wall next. But no one was there. *I suppose
that is to be expected of a place not yet offering instruction.* Alisdair

tucked away his little disappointment that some miracle had not caused the legislature to give the money to make Dalhousie College operate fully.

He made his way to the doctor's home address the next morning. This time he had a card to send in. It was expensive letter paper, and written in his best hand.

"Almost as good as a printed one," Dr. McCulloch remarked, as Alisdair was shown in by his housekeeper to the study. Alisdair might have called it a sitting room, so attuned to feminine comfort it seemed to be, but as it appeared to be where the doctor had callers, it must be a study.

"I—yes. I did not have time to see to an order with a printer."

"Still impatient then, I see." His eyes twinkled. Alisdair grinned ruefully, then sobered.

"My mother has passed away, as I wrote you."

"Very sorry to hear that, Alisdair. I pray that she is happy with her Maker now."

"Thank you, sir…but there have been other, more recent complications."

"Oh?" An interested gleam.

"In confidence, sir—we have an escaped slave living with us. My mother's brother emigrated to the Carolinas, about when we came here, and he was doing all right for himself, but this summer there was an incident."

"Brought about by some of those hotheads in the South?"

"Yes, sir. In North Carolina. The slave—Micah—escaped with one of my cousins, Jamie, and journeyed to their nearest safe relations—us."

His older companion was quiet, ruminating on the legal complexities of the situation, perhaps. Before he could comment, Alisdair took a deep breath to continue. "And then, two days later, my brother Neil vanished and came back with a wife. And her son."

"His wife?"

"Yes, he's remarried without telling us anything about it. And…there's a look of the native Mi'qmak about the boy," he breathed.

His companion's eyes widened. "Well," was all he said for a few moments. His mouth worked and his fingers crawled across one another as his mind worked to see where Alisdair and his ambitions fit into this family picture.

"And so, you are here," he said finally. Alisdair nodded solemnly.

"I left a few days after Neil came back. Over a week now."

Dr. McCulloch shook his head as if ridding himself of complex calculations. "Well, that is first-rate. For a little while, you've got those burdens lifted from you, and you're here to continue as best you can. Tell me, have you money to keep yourself?"

Alisdair told him of his scant savings, as well as his chance for employment with the Mitchell & Dexter Shipping Company. Dr. McCulloch wrote him out a new reference, endorsing it and wishing Alisdair the best of luck in his interview, to come in two days when Dexter returned.

"Once you have your work-week sorted, we can go over

lessons in Greek and Advanced Latin for your Saturdays."

"Thank you very much, sir."

"Of course! I have a feeling you are going to make a very strong start, Mr. MacLean. Won't be surprised if you do abolish the Council, one of these years. After you have employment, we'll see what we can do about lodging with me, eh? It's not uncommon that I have a room or two open in this yawning edifice, now, is it?" He turned the question to his housekeeper, who had entered, and held the door open for Alisdair's exit.

It was a whirlwind. A chance to work. Possible lodgings. The compliments. The faith.

"Thank you very much, sir!"

The time for his appointment came, and Alisdair hurried to the Mitchell & Dexter building. The clerk in the chilly outer room did not acknowledge him but rose to enter the inner office. He returned a minute later and sat down again, facing him. Alisdair felt obliged to state his purpose.

"I'm here to see Mr. Dexter. I have an appointment at ten o'clock."

"To be sure," the clerk replied. "You must wait a few minutes for Mr. Dexter."

"Very well." Alisdair glanced around the space but saw nowhere to sit, and so chose to stand by the sunnier window. He'd tried to understand the table of figures enough to be able to talk intelligently about the goods that were moved out of

Halifax Harbor each year, but knew that he'd only got the broadest strokes in the few days he'd had to prepare. Still, Mr. Dexter had seemed willing enough to train up a new employee last time. Alisdair hoped this part of his predicament would resolve itself easily and settle the question of how he would pay for his studies.

A full fifteen minutes later, a gruff man with a seafaring look about him—full black beard and seaman's cap—tramped out of the inner office, looking straight ahead. He slammed both doors. *Was that standard practice, then?* Alisdair wondered. *Or is the business in some trouble?*

Blinking away the brusqueness of the seafaring gentleman, Alisdair tugged at his jacket and stood up straighter.

"You may go in now," said the clerk.

Alisdair rolled his eyes at the clerk's back and entered. Mr. Dexter sat at his large desk, a huge ledger once again in front of him, whose pages he was worrying back and forth, looking for some figure or other.

"Can I be of assistance, sir?"

The man looked up and furrowed his brow at Alisdair, kept shuffling pages, then squinted back at him again.

"Oh! Mr. MacLean. Of course. Sorry, I was a bit distracted by…never mind. Now, where were those notes…"

Alisdair waited while he found the notes, pushed aside the huge ledger, and finally indicated the chair in front of his desk. He fired off questions, first to confirm his name and place of residence, then to probe his background, not unkindly. Then there were questions about the course of study he'd pursued with his tutor, especially the degree to which he'd mastered the trigonometry and geography courses of study.

As Mr. Dexter's questions veered in the direction of subjects more related to shipping and trade and Halifax laws, Alisdair parried and defended himself as best he could, respectfully admitting when he did not yet know, but intended to study, a certain area of the business. When the inquisitor paused to temple his fingers and consider Alisdair for a moment, he pulled out the new reference from Dr. McCulloch and offered it.

"A different letter?"

"Yes, sir. A kind acquaintance I've made here in Halifax."

Mr. Dexter opened it and glanced at the signature. "McCulloch! Well. And he speaks well of you, I imagine." Not bothering to wait for an answer, he concentrated on the content of the letter. At last, he looked at Alisdair, a roguish tilt to one eyebrow.

"So you were holding this ace up your sleeve all along, MacLean. Well done. I've no qualms offering you the post. Especially with that recommendation. He thinks you'll go far, but in the meantime you've got to have a trade and you've got to get to know the big men in the city. This is a good placement. Not to mention, a good way to earn your bread."

The man grinned, and Alisdair gulped his astonishment at the quick way events were unfolding in his favor, after holding back for so interminably long. *See, I needed only to strike out, and reach out my hand. I must write of this good news!*

"Yes, sir. Thank you, sir. You won't regret it. I'll work my hardest."

"Six days a week, half day Saturday. Be here at eight, and go when Mr. Curdle says you may."

Mr. Curdle? Really.

"While you're learning, eight shillings the week—that's half-pay—paid by the cashier every two weeks. If you pass muster in two months, that'll go up to the clerk's salary of sixteen shillings per week. I suppose you have settled on lodgings already?"

"Uh, well, I'm not sure. There is the possibility—"

"Well, then, you should be out and arranging your affairs, shouldn't you?" He grinned again, and waved him off with his hand.

"Thank you, sir," Alisdair said, backing out.

"Eight o'clock tomorrow, then."

"Sir." Alisdair bobbed his head then turned around to push the door open.

"Mr. Curdle," he said gravely, feeling like he was floating past. "I shall see you tomorrow morning."

The man glanced up, annoyed. "Don't forget to register with the Institute."

"What institute?"

"Friendly society. Anyone can tell you."

"Yes, sir."

Alisdair gave a grateful salute and let himself out the second door. His heart pounded with an odd energy. He allowed himself a few breaths to calm down, and looked around him. There were more passersby than when he'd visited last year, which was a good sign for the company. It also meant he shouldn't jump in the air and let loose a wild whoop of excitement. He cleared his throat and stood for a moment beside the door, considering his options.

Friendly society? He'd heard Edward talk of the local club in New Glasgow that took care of the fishermen's families if one of the men were lost at sea. *Perhaps there is one for shipping clerks. If so, I shall be obliged to Curdle.* He asked a passerby who wore trousers and coat where the friendly society institute might be. The man grasped his chin before gesturing vaguely toward the center of town.

Alisdair walked with a keen eye for signs. A crowd of people gathered outside a shop window, blocking his path. As he tried to skirt around the drifting mass, he heard some of their murmurs.

"…can't survive on that!"

"When they don't give enough to a self-respecting…"

"…not what they was elected for!"

Alisdair backed up into the street, his curiosity piqued by the word 'elected.' Were these people agitating against the Council of Twelve? It was summer; it would be the right time to get up another candidate. They looked too shabby to be professional, though: rough homespun and dirty linen was the common line. He couldn't determine their profession.

"Excuse me, what's the matter here?" he asked the man nearest him.

"Wages are down this season," he muttered. "On account of the ship owners not having no credit left. They're leaving us out to dry."

"Is this the Friendly Society for shipwrights, then?"

"We are, but that's the office of H & A Mayer, one of the ship owners. Hold up—"

And before Alisdair realized what was happening, the mob surged forward, away from him, toward the window. A loud crash was followed by shouts and curses, then whistles. Two men came running, one in uniform, and set to bashing heads. Alisdair backed up further into the street, and heard a shout over his head before feeling something hard punch into his back. He fell forward and registered the wheels narrowly passing him by.

He stayed on his knees for a moment to catch his breath, then rose gingerly, his back smarting from the boxing of the carriage wheel hub. He took a step back toward the crowd, which had turned into a dozen bare-knuckle brawls as arms pushed there and fists flew here. Someone grabbed his elbow roughly and Alisdair turned to regard a man in suspenders as he clapped bracelets on his hands and pushed him into the fray.

Off-balance and bewildered, Alisdair stumbled into the middle of one of the fights. He careened into another man, who shoved him back: upright again. The shouting reached its peak, and more glass shattered somewhere. Alisdair grasped for a solution. *Can I make a run for it? Can I just get clear of this lot and wait to explain—*

Something like a brick hit the back of his head, and Alisdair foundered, losing himself under the waves of violence.

August 1834, The Ridge

More than a month had passed since the arrival of the men from Carolina, more than a week since the arrival of that woman and her boy, and five days since Alisdair's abrupt departure. Mairi went every morning—first thing—to the graveside, praying to her gran and mother to keep her uncle safe. She was pleased to have Jamie and Micah about the place; they made the cabin and the farm feel more social, especially with her uncle gone. But the woman.

Aunt Muirne had come up with her family after learning about Alisdair's departure. There was so much news to communicate! But she'd only stayed long enough to commiserate with them, greet the new wife, and meet the Carolina visitors. She had also come to take Mollie and Gil back to town, which made Mairi's heart burn. *Why is all this happening now? What did we do?*

Muirne took Mairi aside for a conversation the second day of her stay. They sat out by the wall of the cow byre late in the afternoon.

"I'm glad Mollie and Gil have been with you and Neil this summer, Mairi. Ye didna lack for excitement, eh?"

Mairi confined her glare to the dirt at her feet. How she wished she could howl and protest, but she knew her aunt was on her da's side and wanted her to just go along. And she wasn't supposed to show anger to her elders.

"I'm sure it's done them a world o' good to be out in the fields enjoying the weather and building up a bit of country strength, and I thank you for your help in instructing them," she continued. "But I'm taking them back with me to go to school—aye, even Mollie. There's a fine schoolmaster at the primary school these days, who can pick up where I left off"

Mairi looked up to see an encouraging smile, a cadging smile on her aunt's face. Warily, she responded. "Will I go down there, too?"

"It's possible, in a couple years, maybe. Alisdair came down to study when he was about nine? But with three men to work the farm, and a motherly presence—"

"But she's not *my* mother."

"But she may want to be *some*thing to you, Mairi. And you've got to let her try. She and Neil like each other very much, and he needs someone to—to help with managing the house and this whole place. You wouldn't want to do all that, would you, now?"

She had her trapped by canny logic. Mairi couldn't do all the work. She was too small for it, though she'd tried very hard to fill the gaps for the past year and a half. Mairi maintained a chary silence as Muirne continued.

"What I was going to say was…with the ridge well taken care of, Neil may hire a tutor to come up here and live with you. Instruct the two of you, you and Emory."

Mairi's grumpiness shifted. Emory was a queer lad. Hardly spoke. Looked down all the time. Even ran looking down, and she'd seen him fall about the place several times because of it. He didn't seem very intelligent to her. She, who could already sound out and spell so many words of English!

"I know that no one can replace your mother," her aunt said softly. "But did you know our father disappeared when we were young, too? Your da's and mine?"

Mairi blinked up at her. "I thought he died in town. Gran said—"

"That was my stepdad. He was her second husband. Y'see? People die all the time, love, and we need to give second chances."

Her fingers curved Mairi's cheek. A kiss was bestowed. *A second chance.* The new phrase gleamed in her mind: uncertain, dangerous. Mairi huffed a sigh and scuffed at dirt with the toe of her shoe.

"If Mrs. Thomas is Da's second chance, and she makes him happy, I'll give her a second chance, too. And…and Emory."

"Good girl."

Mairi stood now at the top of the bluff that overlooked the oat fields. She could spy Da and Jamie working on either side of the Scots plough they pulled along. She knew Micah was off visiting the Black Loyalist settlement in Windsor. Da had never explained why they called it that, but Mairi imagined all the best and most loyal Black People went there to find friends and live together. Mrs. Thomas was behind the cabin that used to be Mairi's home, flapping about a great sheet. *And Emory is probably in the yard, scratching in the dirt.* He was older than she was but so…skittish.

Mairi thought of her aunt's challenge to be kind to them and sighed, turning back to the cabins. As she walked toward them, she saw a figure coming up the road beyond. Micah! She quickened to a trot and matched paces with him as he came into the yard.

"So you've been to Windsor? Was it nice? Will you take me with you next time?"

"Missy Mairi, that is entirely up to your father! But yes, I've been, and yes, it was nice." He beamed a little more than was warranted by this bland statement and Mairi wondered what, or whom, he had found to light him up so.

"I'm very glad for you," she said.

"And I've also got two letters from the postman, since he didn't want to climb all up your dusty road."

"Oh, let's see! Is one from Uncle Kenneth?"

"No, no Carolina postmarks or nothin' here. One from Halifax and one from…can you guess?"

Mairi racked her brain for other people she knew. "Mrs. Conaghey?"

"No."

"Alisdair?"

"No." At this, Micah sounded sad; he must know how she wanted her uncle to come back.

"Oh, it must be Aunt Sheena! In Scotland!"

"I think you must be right. Scotland, it is."

He handed the two envelopes over and Mairi took them and peered at them. The heavier one looked more beaten up.

That one must have come from her aunt, the farther distance.

"Oh, must we wait 'til supper and everyone is home?" Mairi wanted to read it now, without her stepmother and stepbrother hearing it at the same time.

"I'd say we should. Only a couple hours to wait. I'm sure you can make yourself useful before then," Micah said, throwing her an admonishing sort of look.

"I'm sure I could," Mairi agreed. She took the letters and dutifully set them on the table, then turned around to pull off beet greens from the vegetable garden. She washed them and set the pile next to the pot of water to be boiled, then returned to the garden to take out the dead growth of weeds that had shriveled in the powerful sun.

She'd worked her way across most of one side when she heard the men coming back up the hill. A door creaked open and she got up from her knees to see Jamie go in to the main cabin while her da stopped to embrace Mrs. Thomas in the doorway of their own cabin. Mairi turned away. She plopped down among the cabbages and beets and let herself cry quietly. *Not against Aunt Muirne's rules. I shall try to be kind, even though watching her is like a stab in my belly.*

Pretty soon, Mrs. Thomas was calling to Emory, and they walked into the main cabin to start supper for everybody. Her da didn't turn around to look for her, even though she was just a half-turn away in the vegetables. The quiet cry turned into a grimace of pain and stifled sobs at his dismissal. He hadn't even looked for her.

She didn't intend to stay there in the garden. She was just

realizing that everything was going to change, and the weight
of it, the unstoppability of it, seemed to press her in place on
the ground. Her tears dried as the light failed. It was maybe
half an hour later, when the main cabin's door was thrown
open. She snapped her head to stare: Da's face was white in
the dark, searching. She got up and hurried over.

"Here, Da. Just in—"

"Mairi," he said, in the gravelly tone he used with her
since Mam died. His eyes were bleak as they turned to her. He
crouched down and held his arms out; she walked into his
arms and felt his chin fit over her head. He hugged her hard,
and she was flooded with fear down to her toes. Why? What
had happened to make her Da change so?

"It's yer uncle, Mairi. We've just had terrible—" Neil
stopped to wipe his sleeve across his face, then pulled her
away from him to look her in the face again. "I don't know if I
can—there's just no way—"

Mairi couldn't take the level of despair oozing off of him
without some answers. She strained against his arms to be
taller. "What happened? Is he dead?"

"No," but his voice was defeated. *He might as well be*, it
said. "He's being transported, by the courtesy of the King."

"What's that mean?"

"He's going to be away for a very long time, and there's
nothing we can do about it."

The door squeaked and Mrs. Thomas appeared. "What's
this about, Neil?"

He cleared his throat and withdrew a little from Mairi's

person. She took the chance to grab the paper he clutched. Her eyes scanned it quickly, but only inconsequential words jumped out: at, on, the, he. She looked for the larger letters: A, for Alisdair, yes. C, that one she didn't know. A, another one she didn't know. "Auss-tra-lii-a?"

"Australia." Neil said it, dropped his hands from her, and proceeded to crouch on the ground, hammering the dry grass with his fists. A keening sound struggled free of his throat. Mairi remembered that awful sound from her mother's funeral. Her uncle was as good as dead then? Her stepmother stood against the cabin wall, with Emory in the doorway. The boy looked on with inscrutable detachment, while his mother looked flustered, her clean hands clasping, crossing, fidgeting.

Mairi went to her father's side. "Just when he got his hopes up," he was muttering. She put a hand on his back as he shook. He stopped after a moment, opening his arms to her again. She was his world again, and she was glad. But she wondered what this place was—Australia—that was not death, but as good as.

August 1834, Kirkintilloch

"The time is right for a christening now," Sheena said. "Miss Isobel says he is making good progress. It's the fastest she's ever seen a baby focus his eyes like that!"

Gordon was home after a long three days of travel. He had washed his face and hands upon entering the cottage but still wore the dusty leather boots and ripe-smelling shirt and breeches from his ride. Sheena could smell him three feet away. Instead of commenting, she occasionally buried her nose in Kieron's neck as he lay in the sling round her shoulder. She appeared to have retained a sharper sense of smell than before the pregnancy.

"Will you want to search out a Dissenter kirk?" Gordon asked.

"The nearest one will do," she said. "I wish Mam could have seen him."

Gordon's lower lip compressed in a wistful smile. "She would have been delighted."

"I will send a letter to my family. With the christening date. Alisdair's reply to my last one was so beautifully done. Do you recall?"

"I do. He is very clever with words, your brother."

Sheena sighed. "I hope he got on well with that Dr. Mc-

Culloch. A new start will be good for him."

Angela came in the back door with two buckets, struggling to carry them and get in without the wind closing the flimsy door on her. Gordon rose to hold the door.

"Ah, Angela! Right on time. Go ahead, the cauldron is already in the fire." The girl trudged over to empty the buckets in the cauldron, then headed out again.

"Is it very blustery out?" Sheena asked.

"No, just our very special wind that likes to press the door closed."

"That's good. It takes three trips to fill the tub enough to really wash. Which you no doubt need to do."

Gordon closed his eyes and smiled. Sheena sipped more of her broth and dipped her head, grinning into her soup.

"The journey was a success," Gordon said. "We've got our next landowner signed on, and only two more to go before Mr. Grainger's plans are approved by the Company and we can begin the works out by Blairhill."

"Who did you meet with, this time?"

"Oh, Baird, he holds the land up against that great mill and down the other side of the river. It's that we'll probably have to do the most work on, to get the rails level and all."

"And is he a Lord, or—"

"Oh yes, he's got a seat in the Lords. But much more hospitable than you'd think. Seems like he's trying to advance his methods of agriculture. We had a most interesting discussion…"

Sheena felt Gordon's confidence coming back, smoothing

the way with others, making her feel secure again. By this time next year, they would have a garden, she predicted. And the year after that, perhaps her husband would stand to represent the district in London. If he had the ear of important men, why not?

The letter arrived the next day, before she had talked with the rector at the tiny parish church of Kirkintilloch. She had dispatched Angela to the stream with the laundry and walked around their wee cottage several times, singing Kieron to sleep in the sling. She was having a hard time getting him to sleep longer even with the light failing earlier. *So much for that idea.* A wagon rolled to a slow stop before their door, and the driver leaned down with a letter. Sheena thanked him and leaned against the door to read it in the ample sunshine.

Kieron felt the change in his soft cocoon and stirred at her hammering heart. When Sheena's breath came in gasps he set to bleating like an upset lamb. And her one escaped scream of frustration close by his head set him to wailing. Sheena took him inside where it was dark and cool. She set him in the bed of blankets, where he gradually quieted.

Sheena stared down at him, her fists shaking. The letter— where was it? The sharp point of the enveloped peeked out at her from the clump of cloth that was the unwound sling, thrown onto the cottage floor when she came in. She picked it up with two fingers. A knock came on the door, and Angela entered.

"Are you all right, missus? Janie ran for me because there was a shout..." Sheena could feel the girl's gaze slide to the bed, where Kieron lay kicking his heels about slowly.

"He went to Halifax to meet with someone about work, and got taken up in a mob riot about laborers' wages. In jail one night, then sentenced the next day for rioting. No one to speak for him. They've sent him to—somewhere called New South Wales. Where on earth is that?"

She turned glistening eyes to Angela but the girl just looked back: sympathetic, terrified.

"Of course it's a terrible mistake. Neil must be trying to put it to rights even now. But Alisdair!"

Angela watched, mute, for several moments as Sheena composed herself. She apologized for worrying her, took her hand, said she was all right.

"It is some bad news from home, but I hope to hear something of a change in the next letter, I'm sure I do," she explained.

When Gordon came home, he was in an expansive mood. Sheena tried to smile, but he immediately perceived she had been crying.

"Oh, it is bad news from home--Alisdair has been taken up in some riot." She handed the letter to him to read. "Neil says he's been sent to South Wales or something, but he will be writing to press for his return, and we know a solicitor, from when—"

"South Wales, Sheena? Or New South Wales?" Gordon looked shocked.

"New? I don't know it. Do you know it? Is it a jail in Lower Canada?"

The shock gave way to a stricken expression. "Oh, my Sheena. I'm sorry. It is round on the other side of the world, and the opposite hemisphere. By the South Pole." He tried to gather her into his arms, but she went rigid, her crossed arms becoming bands of iron that she threw up in the air.

"My family continues to tear itself apart, with no apparent choice in the matter! The South *Pole?* Will we ever see him again?" She flung the letter up and away from her and covered her face with her hands to sob unabashedly.

All she could do was imagine Alisdair's night in jail, his terrible aloneness at such a trial, and the terrible people who would surround him on his months-long journey to the end of the earth. She bit back the sobs, slowed her breathing.

"I'm sorry, love. Alisdair's a smart one. I'm sure he'll figure something out."

Sheena's eyes darted away, calculating. Yes, Alisdair was a smart one, but being branded a criminal was not the new start he'd been planning for so tenaciously.

"Why was the trial so hasty? Why didn't they notify the family? How can they take a man—clear round the world— on no evidence? It's—it's—barbaric!"

Kieron started whimpering again on the mattress. Gordon sighed. "It is, Sheena. But try to be calm. There is nothing we can do at this distance, at this remove of time and authority. Calm down; you're upsetting the boy."

Sheena closed her eyes, the better to imagine her heart as cold and hard as ice. She recalled the globe at the old New Glasgow school. There was she, in Scotland; there were they,

Neil and Muirne, in Nova Scotia. And Alisdair, he who dreamed of being the radical to make the rotten politicians listen, was now on the other side of the world, in chains, locked up with murderers. *Ice. Ice.*

The secretary of state for the colonies. She'd read his name in Hansard's *Debates. Goderich, wasn't it?* He would oversee both Nova Scotian courts and the colonies in the South Seas. If Mam were alive, she wouldn't rest until she'd appealed to the top of the chain, just like when she'd appealed to the Laird for their croft. Sheena would do no less.

"Forget the minister. I need to talk to a solicitor."

Gordon crinkled his brow, not following her thoughts.

"It will take some time to get the details of his arrest and deportation, but I will write to Neil for them and take them to the secretary of state. They will not get away with this."

"The—the War Secretary in London? Sheena." Gordon sought to bring down her expectations, to throw cold water onto her furiously burning flame.

"Nothing shall keep me from it. I *will* fight for my brother's future. You must allow it. My mother—" She paused. "We owe it to him. He was at home so long, supporting the others, and now he is alone—it is not right. He is innocent."

She picked Kieron up from the bed and bounced him gently, making shushing sounds and running her lower lip back and forth on his forehead before unbuttoning her apron-front. Gordon watched, conflicted.

"We have found this position and to this position we will cling. It is good work, is it not? I will write to Neil and tell him my intentions, and he will do all that is necessary there. He and Muirne can collect character references. And then I will make them listen to me, with all the authority I can bring as a respectable wife of a professional man—I will! He is one man—why would they want to pay for his keep? I will make them send him back to us. And we will pray his spirit survives the interval. It is right."

Something shifted in Gordon's stance; he stood straighter, his cheeks lifted a little when his sad frown became more of a watery smile.

"I have a feeling you will become the Member of the Assembly your brother meant to be, in order to get him back!" He placed his fingertips at the sides of her throat and leaned close.

Sheena's heart raced with fear, but her head just registered the remark. The Assembly? No! But… "Anything to keep that dream of his going—of justice."

"Indomitable woman."

Epilogue

Years later, as he prepared to send his first grandchild to boarding school in England, Alisdair MacLean considered the expanse of glittering water poured out before him, Sydney Cove. It had been a long, rough road, but he was master of himself now. Not only that, he'd learned a respected trade from a senior draftsman, who'd then introduced him into the Legislative Assembly. He had a home, a devoted wife, three grown children, and four grandchildren. Life had hurried him along just as he supposed it had done his sister, Sheena.

They had not seen each other for thirty years, but kept up a faithful correspondence, and she knew his whole heart. How he had despaired for a time, until she reminded him of what Mam would have wanted. New South Wales was still a huckster's arena, and he had to fight hard against the egregious greed he saw in the gold-rush millionaires' eyes, but then again, the chaos of that arena was what had allowed a reformed convict like him to rise up as he had.

He thanked his luck that he had such a sister, who would not rest until she found him in the rolls and watched his progress in indenture, making sure every master knew she was watching from her perch as a wealthy railway baron's wife back in Scotland. Though it was not justice, he had not ended up like his father.

He was proud of his children, aye, but the tears had

threatened to choke him when he read of his niece Mairi's decision to strike out for the Oregon Territory with her husband. She carried the best of all their courage west with her, and her grannie's fiery spirit. He was not at all surprised to receive a letter in her own hand about the newspaper they had started in Salem. Alisdair contemplated the ocean below his window, and thanked it for touching also upon her shores.

Did you enjoy this book?
Please post a review.

Reviews like yours help this book find its way into the hands of new, grateful readers. This helps self-published authors gain readers online and through word of mouth.

Reviews are much appreciated at Amazon.com, Goodreads.com, or any other review sites. Or spread the news through your own networks on Facebook and Twitter!

You are welcome to visit my author website for blog posts, events, news, and giveaways:

www.margaretpinard.com

Good books should be shared!

-Margaret Pinard

Acknowledgements

I grow as an author with each book I write. Thank you to all those who helped water and fertilize my process for the past three years! To my parents, who have always given me a sweet deal and a leg up. To my editor Susan DeFreitas, who challenged me to make the characters grow as much as I. To my proofreader Alison Cross Buttafuoco and her crack team of botany researchers.

To the crew at Another Read Through, together 'til the end! To my compatriots in Scots Gaelic language study, for going after what they love. To the coaches at One Free Planet who served as base coaches, helping me round third. To the courageous ladies of Spiral Leadership who helped me see past the box I'd made for my publishing career, especially Jilly Hindman. To the Moon Circle for helping me feel the meaning of my own words. To the Sacred Healing Path herbalists who have helped ground me in the form of spiritualism I can translate to the page.

To the Portland writing community, especially Steve Arndt, that fluffer-up of writers' souls. To Ko-Fi contributor and community enthusiast Marcus Kaneshiro, who isn't afraid to show up and speak out. To Marshall Anderson, who helped finance the writing schedule *de la maniere la plus agréable*. To Elizabeth Beechwood doubly, for organizing the writing retreat of 2019 at Colonyhouse, and for being the first pre-order!

To Elizabeth Mitchell triply, for pre-ordering, being a goddess of the faith-in-yourself mantra, and being queen of the writer dates. She knows what it's like to GSD!

To my sisters for their faithful support and bolstering

pre-orders, as well as Yosemite humor till the horses make it back to the barn.

To my tenacious Californian, Turkish, and SAIS friends who follow from around the globe. To the many wonderful British friends made on research trips, including Laura at South Craighall B&B, Jon of the St. Ives Guest House, Rosemary and Donald of Persabus Farm, Lynn of Dunchraigaig House B&B, the dauntless ladies of Sgioba Luaidh Inbhirchluaidh at Auchindrain one rainy September day, and the Robert Fergusons of Dalgarven Mill Museum.

About the Author

MARGARET PINARD is a writer, bookseller, singer, language-lover, and tea-drinker living in Portland, Oregon. Her first documented inspiration for writing fiction was *Newsies*. After a doomed attempt to pass as normal, she was inspired again to write for her very survival by the *Outlander* novels. She now leads a madcap existence pursuing what she loves.

You can connect with Margaret on her website, Facebook, and Twitter:

www.margaretpinard.com

www.facebook.com/wetastelifetwice

www.twitter.com/tastelifetwice

www.ingramcontent.com/pod-product-compliance
Lightning Source LLC
Chambersburg PA
CBHW032208180726
48284CB00001B/240